saving it

saving it

MONICA MURPHY

Entangled Publishing, LLC
2614 South Timberline Road
Suite 109
Fort Collins, CO 80525
Visit our website at www.entangledpublishing.com.

Crush is an imprint of Entangled Publishing, LLC.

Edited by Stacy Abrams & Alexa May
Cover design by April Martinez
Cover art from ThinkStock Photos

Manufactured in the United States of America

First Edition November 2017

Chapter One

EDEN

"Can I ask you something?"

I glance up from my notebook I'm doodling on to see that one of my best friends, my only real male friend, a guy I've known for what feels like forever, Josh Evans is studying me with this intense look on his face. As in, he's being serious.

And one thing Josh rarely is, is serious.

"Sure." It's the Friday afternoon before Thanksgiving break, and we're in study hall, which is a total waste of time. There's nothing to study for. There are no tests, no homework assignments, no nothing. So we're all just talking and hanging out. Messing around on our phones. Making plans for the weekend and for the next week, when we're off from school.

I'm stuck at home with my boring family, since we don't go on glamorous vacations or even regular visiting-grandma-type road trips. We're hosting Thanksgiving dinner this year. Everyone's coming to our house, which means Mom will put me to work, and if I'm not at home, then I'll actually *be* at work. And that…

Sucks.

But there are only a few more months until I'm free. I'll go away to college. Be a new person, do new things, learn new things, meet new people.

Like new boys. Excuse me, I mean *men.*

I can't freaking wait.

"This is serious," he says.

No duh, I want to tell Josh. He leans forward, that intense expression still on his face. He's not smiling. He's not laughing. It's weird. "You can't tell anyone else what I'm about to ask you."

"I won't."

"Not even Molly."

Crap. Molly is my other best friend. The one who knows all my secrets—and Josh's, too, even if he doesn't know it.

All. Of. Them.

I roll my eyes. Sigh heavily. Make a dorky face and cross my eyes in the hopes he'll laugh.

Josh doesn't even crack a smile. I swear, I think he might even be—sweating?

"Fine," I say on a sigh, acting put out. "I won't tell Molly."

"Promise?"

"Promise."

"Pinky swear?" He holds his hand out toward me, his pinky finger extended.

I hook my pinky around his and tug, just like he does. "Pinky swear."

"Okay." He blows out a harsh breath. Scoots his desk closer to mine. Mr. Ward, the P.E. teacher who supervises our study hall period, doesn't even lift his head from the book he's reading. And usually he yells at everyone for one lame reason or another. "This isn't easy to say."

Oh boy. Have I mentioned how…dramatic Josh can be

sometimes? And sensitive? Not that he's weak or anything like that. He's very athletic, as in he plays every sport out there. He's smart. He's driven to the point of being annoying.

"Go ahead, Josh. Say it." I scoot my desk closer to his, too, because I think he might be nervous. And he probably doesn't want anyone else to hear what he's about to confess, so it must be major.

"Okay. Here goes," he mutters under his breath before he turns to look at me. "I really need your help, Edes."

Oh. He needs my help? I can do that. "Of course. You know I'll always help you," I say in pure, solemn friend mode. "Whatever you need."

"Cool. Cool." He runs a hand through his golden-brown hair, messing it up. He does the cute boy with messy hair look well. "*Ineedyoutohelpmelosemyvirginity.*"

My mouth drops open, but no sound comes out. Um...

"What did you just say?"

"You heard me." He doesn't even blink. I'm starting to think he doesn't look serious after all—more like he's terrified.

"No. I don't think I heard you correctly." There is absolutely no way he said what I thought. "Repeat yourself."

"You heard right," he says firmly. "That's exactly what I need your help with."

"But..." My voice drifts, and I think of all the girls. All the many, *many* girls he's dated since middle school. Though I know he wasn't trying to sex up any girls until hmm...ninth grade? Tenth?

"So Leila Montes?" His first serious girlfriend—and when I say serious, I mean the first girl I caught him groping at a party. At my eighth grade graduation pool party, as a matter of fact.

He shakes his head, makes a face. "She was a terrible kisser."

That's right. She was. He told me. Too much tongue, I think the problem was.

"Tati Rodriguez?" She's beautiful. She graduated last year. They went out when we were juniors and she was a senior. Josh strutted around school like he was the king of all studs, bragging about his older girlfriend who taught him so *many* things.

Ugh. I didn't want to hear about those many, *many* things she supposedly taught Josh, but he told me anyway.

So. Gross.

"She blew me off." His cheeks actually turn ruddy, and I realize there's more to that story, but I'll ask those questions another time.

I'm saving the big one for last. The one girl he keeps going back to over and over.

"What about Kaylie?" My other best friend—fine, yes, I have a lot of best friends—who has gone out officially with Josh off and on since we were in the sixth grade.

The *sixth* grade.

It makes sense that they'd finally do it together, just to do it, you know? So they're each other's firsts.

He slowly shakes his head. "Never with Kaylie."

"Not even close?" I'm shocked.

Josh shrugs. "Sort of close. We got as far as her letting me—"

I hold my hand up. "Please. I don't want to know any details."

He shrugs, his cheeks still pink. "You're the one who asked."

"Well, I take back my question." God, now my cheeks are going hot. This is an embarrassing conversation, and I can't believe he's asking me this in the middle of study hall. Like we're supposed to casually discuss our sexual status with each other while surrounded by friends. No thanks. "So. Do you want to talk about your—*plan* later?" Honestly? I so do not want to talk about this plan later.

More like never.

"Maybe. I just need to know first. Are you in? Will you help me?"

"Um." This sounds like a very bad idea.

"Come on, Edes." The nickname is from eighth grade. When we got super close and he became one of my best friends despite everyone telling us it was a bad idea. Girls and guys can't be friends, they said. It won't work. It never works.

Josh and I proved them wrong. We're friends, and that's it. I have zero interest in him. Thinking of kissing him...

A shiver moves through me.

Ew. It's too weird to comprehend.

"Josh..."

"Just say yes."

No way can I agree to this. That he'd even suggest something so outrageous fills me with wariness. The fact that he wants me to readily agree, too, is also wary-making. Josh is crazy. He's always been a little crazy, but that's what I like about him. He pushes my limits. He makes things fun.

Life's a lot more interesting with Josh Evans in it.

"Wait a minute." I sigh and shake my head. "You need to tell me exactly how you want me to help. Then I'll make my decision."

• • •

JOSH

I knew she'd ask me that. Eden has to know the how's and why's of everything. It's why she's so frustrating sometimes.

There are lots of other ways she's frustrating, too, but that's definitely one of them.

"I want you to help me..." I swallow, still having to force

the words out. Doesn't matter how much I practiced saying these exact words to her, it's still difficult. "…lose it."

"Lose your…" Her voice drops to the barest whisper, and I lean in so I can hear her better. I catch her scent, something light and flowery and familiar. "…virginity?"

Nodding, I remain quiet.

"Are you saying what I think you're saying?" she squeaks.

"Well, yeah." I know, I know. She's shocked. So am I, if you want me to be honest. I thought I would've gotten rid of this a long time ago, but yeah, I'm a seventeen-year-old virgin. Not without trying though, you know what I mean? Every one of those girls she just mentioned, I thought something would happen with them. That we'd finally do the deed or whatever.

But I failed. Miserably.

My virgin status sucks. It sucks bad. None of my guy friends are virgins. No one on the varsity basketball team is a virgin—they've all done it, except me. I need to get rid of my V-card before the end of my senior year. I can't be a virgin college freshman. The humiliation is too much for me to even comprehend.

I'm going to be eighteen in January. I'd love to get rid of it by then, but I don't think I can work that fast.

Well, maybe with Eden's help…

"So you want us to…" She wags her index finger between us, like she's implying that I want to lose my virginity with *her*.

"No. *No*. It's not what you think, Edes." She's my best friend. How awkward would that be? *Oh hey, Eden, let's do it once and then go back to being friends because I want to lose my virginity and I bet you do too because you're still a virgin, right?*

Right?

I frown. Is she still a virgin? I don't know. She would've

told me if something happened. We share everything. I mean, *everything*. I've told her things I would never tell anyone else. Stuff my guy friends wouldn't understand because...they're guys. They're jerks. And they take nothing seriously.

Eden actually listens to me and offers good advice. Advice I can use. She listens to me, and she cares, and that...

Matters.

If we ever got involved—like boyfriend/girlfriend involved—it would ruin *everything*. I need Eden as my friend. I like having her in my life.

We take it in a different direction? Forget it. A relationship wouldn't work between us. Even if it could, it would eventually end, because it always ends. Then I'd lose her forever.

I can't risk it.

"So you don't want to lose it with me." She blows out a harsh breath. "Thank God."

The relief in her voice is obvious. I'm vaguely offended. "Have you done it yet?"

"Maybe." She's not quite looking me in the eyes.

I give her a look. She's so full of shit. "You can't answer maybe. It's a yes or no question."

"Maybe I'm going for mysterious." She tilts her nose into the air, swinging her long, dark brown hair over her shoulder.

"That's dumb. I know everything there is to know about you, Sumner." It's true. I know she dated Cole Browning both in the eighth grade and then again for most of our junior year, and only let him get as far as second base. Poor guy had the biggest case of blue balls known to man. I sometimes tease her about it.

Cole also happens to be one of my closest friends, so I give him shit about it, too.

I also like to call her by her last name every once in a while because she hates it. And sometimes it's my job to drive her crazy.

It's a super easy job.

Eden's irritated voice snaps me out of my thoughts.

"You don't know all my secrets, Josh."

"I know a lot of them."

"Not the most secret of the secrets," she replies, her eyebrows up, lips pursed, like she's challenging me.

Another one of her irritating traits. She's always challenging me. Makes me nuts. Can't she just be agreeable? I like agreeable. Agreeable is pleasant.

Until it gets boring.

I shove the niggling thought out of my mind.

"Don't forget. We made a pact," I remind her, because it suddenly hits me. We *did* make a pact. One I should hold her to.

She frowns, little wrinkles forming between her eyebrows. It's kind of cute. Listen, I'm not dead. I can admit Eden is really cute. Beautiful, even.

Yeah. Okay. She's beautiful. But she's just a friend. Doing anything with her would be like doing it with my sister.

And that's freaking weird.

"What pact?" Her nose wrinkles.

"You don't remember?" I try my best to sound extra offended, because yes, now I really am offended. "Come on, Edes."

"I have no idea what you're talking about."

"Freshman year, our first school dance. I was bummed out. You were bummed out. Kaylie had just dissed me. That one kid you were hot for laughed when you asked him to dance." I remember every detail of that crappy night, yet there is no recognition happening. I can tell from the blank look on Eden's face. I can't believe she doesn't remember.

Then realization dawns, and the frown disappears, replaced quickly by shock. And the slightest hint of panic.

"You didn't take that pact seriously. Did you?"

"I did." Not really, not at the time. But hey, it seems like a good idea to bring it up now.

"We were joking!"

"I wasn't."

"We were frustrated." She's whining. Eden's not a whiner.

"Hell yeah, we were. That's why I took it so seriously." First dance our freshman year and already we were both disappointed in high school in general. Eden had big plans, and she'd convinced me our lives were gonna get so much better when we got into high school.

Didn't happen. Not immediately, at least.

"You just said a few minutes ago you didn't mean your, uh, *request* that way," she points out.

"I didn't. I still don't. It's just—a backup plan. And I knew if I brought the pact up, you'd freak out." Which is true. Eden loves a good freak-out. But I don't want to lose it with Eden.

I want her to help me find someone to lose it with.

"I would not." She sounds defensive. A little snotty. We've had these types of arguments before. This is usually when I kick in and really start giving her a hard time.

"You would, too." I lean in close, our heads practically touching, silently daring her to look away. And she doesn't. She stares at me, her lips parted, her brows scrunched together...

"The foreplay act between you two is getting way old," shouts my best friend Abraham Chen. I don't even look at him, because if we make eye contact, he'll just get worse. "Just do her already and get it over with, Evans!"

Eden's cheeks go pink. My heart rate picks up.

Because fine. You want to know the truth? Well, guess what? I'm a guy. And I've thought about...doing Eden. Who wouldn't, especially if you're me? I've spent a lot of time with this girl. Hanging out with her in class or at lunch, going over to her house on the weekends, texting her, Snapchatting her, whatever. We talk all the time. People think we're a couple. We do act like an old married couple. Even my mom says so.

It's not like that, though. My friendship with Eden means too much to me to screw it up by…screwing her. We're just friends and that's it.

"Shut up, Abe." Eden glares at him before turning that glare on me. "We were idiots back then. We've changed. You can't hold me to a pact we agreed on three years ago."

My smile is smug. "Watch me."

"What are you saying? If I don't help you find someone you can have sex with for the first time, then you're going to force me to be the one who pops your cherry?" She starts laughing when I scowl.

"Yeah, exactly that. Though I wouldn't force you, Edes. I'm not a rapist." I'm only making this worse, so I need to shut the hell up. "Come on, I need your help. You in?"

"Yeah, right." Eden laughs and shakes her head. "I don't think so, Josh."

Chapter Two

"Can I come over after school?"

I shut my locker door with extra force, savoring the loud clang it makes as it slams into home. I keep my back to Josh, because I'm still thinking about what he asked earlier. Like, it's all I can focus on.

Finally, I turn to face him. "Why do you want to come over?"

"So I can convince you to help me?" The hopeful look on his face is cute; I can admit that.

But it's going to take more than cute looks and puppy dog eyes from Josh to convince me that I need to help him find a girl to lose his virginity with.

"Like I have time to help you with your weird plan."

"Fine." He's frowning—those cute puppy dog eyes are long gone. "Maybe you could just help me with my list."

"List?" I play dumb, taking him in, trying to see something different, but I don't. He's just...Josh. Tall, lanky with good shoulders, thick-haired, blue-eyed Josh. Wearing his usual outfit of dark gray Nike sweatshirt and black shorts, even though it's November and like, fifty degrees outside. "What list are you talking about?"

"I dunno." He shrugs those good shoulders, and my gaze goes to them. I've cried on those shoulders more than a few times. So have plenty of other girls, including the ones he's dumped. "I was hoping you could help me make a list."

I start walking fast, because school is done for the next nine days, and I don't want to waste a single second being here when I don't have to. "A list of what? Girls you want to do?"

He catches up with me, a scowl on his face. "Geez, Eden. Keep your voice down."

"Oh, sorry. Forgot you don't want everyone to know, considering you asked me in the middle of study hall." My sarcasm is heavy this afternoon, but seriously. He *did* ask me in the middle of study hall, surrounded by all sorts of people we know. Or people who like to eavesdrop.

"No one heard me."

"Abe could've." Abe is Josh's best male friend and so freaking obnoxious he makes me crazy. Plus, he has a big mouth. That also makes me crazy.

Fine. Abe makes me crazy in all the ways.

"He didn't. Like I can tell him anything anyway. He'd blab to everyone." At least Josh knows his friend's weak points.

I stop short just before we reach the double doors that lead to the senior parking lot. "You really want to make a list?"

I love making lists. Josh knows this. I love planning. Organizing. My favorite store is Paper Source. Or Office Depot. My favorite time of year is back to school, which is weird, I know, I know. But all the notebooks, fancy pens, highlighters, and folders make my organized heart sing.

"Isn't that the best way to start this project?" He lifts his brows, his gaze locked on mine.

Ugh. He just said one of my favorite words.

Project.

"Oh, we're calling it a project now?" I push the door open and walk out into the crisp midafternoon. I can feel the excitement in the air—everyone's ready for Thanksgiving break, including me.

"I don't know what else to call it." We both stop at the front of the parking lot. "You need a ride?" he asks.

Molly's nowhere to be found, so yes, I do need one. Dang it. Now I'm stuck talking about Josh's so-called project the rest of the drive home. Do I really want to help him? What he wants is crazy. But then again, Josh is a little crazy, so I shouldn't be surprised.

I can't answer so quick, though—can I? I'd rather take some time and mull it over first. Helping my friend find someone to have sex with for the first time is a big deal. Like a major deal, if I'm being honest. This is epic, making memories type of shit.

"Edes? You need a ride or what?"

I blink up at him. "You don't mind?"

"For you?" He makes a noise. "Never. Come on."

I follow him through the parking lot toward his car, really paying attention to the people we pass. Usually I'm running my mouth and not giving a crap who is saying what to Josh.

But now—now I pay attention. I see the way the girls look at him, with the exception of Kaylie who offers a friendly hi to me as we walk by each other, yet she doesn't say a word to Josh. She doesn't even bother looking in his direction.

That relationship didn't end well. At all.

There are plenty of other girls at school. Josh didn't choose his words lightly. He said list because he knows I'm a total list maker and that would appeal to my organizational side. This is an example of when it's bad that your friends know you so well. They use your personality traits to their advantage.

"You really want to come over?" I ask once we're both in his dad's old Toyota Tacoma and he's backing out of the parking space.

Josh sends me a quick look before putting the truck into gear. "You really want to help me?"

Not really. "I don't know. Maybe." I shrug, then open up the notes section in my phone, staring at the blank page. "Are you thinking of anyone in particular?"

Did I really just say that? I'm agreeing to help him without actually saying yes. What is wrong with me?

He remains quiet as we pull out of the parking lot and hit the main road. I live about ten minutes from school. Josh lives in the same neighborhood. This is how we became such good friends. We rode the bus to middle school together, and at first, we totally ignored each other. Because that's what you do when you're twelve, right? Boys had cooties, and they were disgusting and said stupid things and always talked about sports and boners and R-rated movies and the raunchy lyrics in their favorite rap songs.

At least, that's what the boys in my class used to talk about.

In the seventh grade, Josh and I had a couple of classes with each other. We paired up for a history project and discovered we actually worked well together. In eighth grade, we shared four classes, and of course, still rode the same bus. We eventually started to sit together in the morning. Then in the afternoon, we did, too. His friends gave him endless grief, saying we were hot for each other, but he denied it. So did I. We were friends. We *are* friends. That's it.

We still have classes together. Lots of mutual friends, as

in we hang in the same social circle. We talk every single day. Sometimes it feels like I'm closer to him than I am to anyone else, and that includes Molly.

"Josh," I say when he still hasn't spoken, "is there someone you're thinking of? Like, do you have a crush on someone?"

He always has a crush on someone. It's amazing how quickly he gets over a girl, even Kaylie, though he always circles back to her. If he wants to get back together with her yet again, I don't know how I feel about that.

"I think I'm going to leave it up to you," he finally says when we stop at a red light. "I've been making bad choices, so—"

I snort laugh under my breath, cutting him off. "I'll say."

"Hey," he sends me an irritated look, but he's smiling, "I can't help it if I fall for a pretty face."

Gag.

"There's nothing wrong with falling for a pretty face," I say hesitantly. I don't want to insult him, so I'm walking a fine line here. "But you have to make sure she has some substance, too."

He's quiet for a moment as he drives, and I stare out the window, worrying over what I said. Yeah, I probably offended him. I'm being serious, though. The girls he chooses aren't always the best match for him.

And I like doing that. Playing matchmaker. Can I admit something? My favorite reality show back in the day was *The Millionaire Matchmaker.* I even told my mom I wanted to own a matchmaking service, like Patti Stanger. Mom just laughed and told me, "We'll see."

Which is Mom code for, "That's never going to happen."

Maybe it can, though. Maybe for Josh, I can be his matchmaker. Find the perfect girl for him, so he'll fall madly in love, have sex with her, and be with her forever…

"So you're telling me the girls I've gone out with lack substance," he finally says, his voice flat.

I wince. When he says it out loud, the words sound worse. "Sort of."

"Like your friend Kaylie. She lacks substance?"

"She wasn't the right choice for you."

"Tell me about it," he mutters.

A thought occurs to me, and I turn to look at him. Like *really* look at him. "You're not still into her, are you?"

"Kaylie? Hell no." He looks straight ahead, his jaw tight.

Crap. I know all of his tells. This is what happens when you're friends with someone for years. And his tells are telling me he still likes her. I can't freakin' believe it. "You want to lose it to her?"

"Lose what?" He glances at me before returning his attention to the road.

"Oh my God." I roll my eyes when our gazes meet. "Your *virginity,* Joshua. You want to lose it with Kaylie?"

"There's no *with* when it comes to Kaylie," he says mysteriously. He's being royally confusing.

"What do you mean?"

"Because she's already lost it to someone else."

Okay, this is news to me. "Who?"

• • •

JOSH

"I don't know his name." That's the truth. Kaylie admitted it was some college dude she hooked up with last summer. She was working at an ice cream shop downtown and met the guy there. He was a tourist on vacation with his family, they hung out together for a few days at the beach, and they did it in a sand dune under a full moon. She told me it was very romantic, and I just stood there nodding the whole time, not saying a word.

Her so-called romantic story made me want to puke.

"So it was a random stranger hookup? Seriously?" Eden shakes her head. "And you fell for that?

"What are you talking about?" I sound defensive because I feel defensive. I don't know what Eden's trying to say, but I don't like it. "I didn't fall for anything."

"Kaylie is totally lying to you." She says it so assuredly it's kind of blowing my mind.

"How the hell do you know?"

"Because everyone has that random sexual experience with a stranger story. It happened with someone they don't know, who's there and gone within a matter of days. And it's the most magical experience of their lives," she explains, like she knows what she's talking about. "Don't you have one of those stories?"

"No." If I did, that would make me a liar, and I hate liars. My father was a liar, and now he's gone. He was the one who chose to leave and break up my parents' marriage. Half the time I think his leaving made me want a long-term relationship. I didn't want to be the bad guy. I didn't want to leave.

But now I'm wondering if that was a mistake. Maybe I should have a quick hookup, a meaningless relationship full of fun and...

Sex.

"Oh." Her eyes go wide, and at that exact moment, I stop for the red light. Which is great because I can look right at her now. "I, um, I have one."

"Seriously?" My voice breaks, and I clear my throat. "Tell me."

"Josh..."

"Edes, I deserve to know." My voice is solemn. She always caves when I pull something like this. "This will bond us forever."

Eden pauses, and I know I've got her. She always wants me to reaffirm that we're going to be a part of each other's lives until the end of time. Guess we both like knowing that no matter what, I'll be there for Eden, and she'll be there for me.

"We've been bonded since the eighth grade," she reminds me.

"True, but this will make our bond even stronger." Now I'm dying to know her fake story. "Have you told me this story before and I just—forgot?"

Doubtful. I know pretty much all of Eden's stories. I don't forget them, especially when I've heard a lot of them multiple times.

"No." Her cheeks are pink, like she's embarrassed. "I've only told a couple of people."

"Like..."

"Um, Cole. I told him." She looks away, almost like she's embarrassed.

For some weird reason I'm offended. No, I'm hurt. Hurt that I don't know this story, that I had no input in helping her come up with it. We've done a lot of crazy things together over the years, and this sounds like something I would've loved to help her with.

I mean, I'm not a fan of liars, but if she wants to come up with some crazy story for someone else, I'm down. Only if she tells me what's going on, though.

"You going to come clean?" I ask.

"I'm not dating you, am I?" Eden smirks.

Right. We're not dating, so I guess I'm not worthy. Whatever. "I guess you're not."

"We should definitely come up with a list."

Her abrupt change of subject is very Eden-like, so I go along with her. I'll get her to tell me the magical hookup story another time.

"Maybe we should go to your house to put it together."

"No one's home," I remind her. Mom is working. And it's just her and me now. My older sister and brother are already gone. My brother is married and working in an actual career like an adult, and my sister is in her final year of college. They rarely come home. I think Mom misses them a lot.

Me? I like having the house all to myself. Mostly. Mom either works all the time, or she's out with her boyfriend.

"That's perfect, because everyone's home where I live." Eden has a younger brother—Travis—and her parents both work from home. "It'll be easier if it's just the two of us working on the list and not having to worry about Travis butting in with his opinion."

Huh. The problem is I actually value Travis's opinion most of the time, while Eden is always telling him to get the hell away from her—and that's me using restraint. She says way worse things to her brother, and I always feel sorry for the dude. He takes a lot of abuse from Eden.

I should probably defend him more, but then Eden would get pissed, and that would cause a lot more trouble than I want to deal with.

"Let's go to my house then," I say, and within minutes, I'm pulling into the driveway, hitting the button on the remote so the garage door slides open.

We walk into the house together, and I wonder how many times we've done this. Hundreds of times? Gone to either her house or mine after school to hang out, do homework, watch movies, sneak booze from her parents' cabinet, play video games with Travis—she really hates it when I do that, but Travis is a video-game master. We have all the movie channels, so Eden would hang out and watch them with me.

Our parents swore we'd end up together. Eden's mom admitted she predicted our relationship when we were in fifth grade and that Eden freaked out. Said she thought I was gross and no way would she ever date me.

I didn't even know she existed until seventh grade, so there's that.

Eden's moving around my kitchen like she lives there, and I check out what's in the fridge while she grabs snacks out of the pantry. We settle in at the counter, Cokes and potato chips our chosen snacks, and Eden's pulled a notebook out of her backpack, already writing in it.

I watch her write for a while until I finally have to say something. "Aren't you going to ask for my input?"

"Absolutely not." She studies the paper in front of her, tapping her pen against the edge of the notebook before she writes something. "You're lucky I'm helping you with this at all. When we left campus, I told myself I wouldn't do it."

"What changed your mind?" I ask, curious.

"I have a thing for matchmaking reality shows."

"Like *The Bachelor*?" I'm starting to sweat. Why am I starting to sweat?

"No." She shakes her head. "Like *The Millionaire Matchmaker*."

I'm frowning. "Never heard of it."

"Doesn't matter." She waves a hand. "Now. I think it's best if I come up with the list first, and you tell me which ones you want to get with."

"Wait a minute—which *ones?* As in multiple girls?"

She sends me a total *duh* look. "Well, yeah. That's why we're making a *list*. You can't just narrow this down to one girl and hope she'll be the one."

"Why not?" That had been my plan from the get-go. Not that I had a real plan. Or had anyone particular in mind. This is why I asked for Eden's help. She knows everyone, like all sorts of girls, even freshmen. Everyone likes Eden because she's chill. Like for real. There's no drama with Eden. What you see is what you get.

"That's not how it works, Josh. You need plenty of options." She focuses on the paper, scribbles what I assume are a couple more names, and then lifts her gaze to mine. "I've got ten so far."

"Ten?" I shove a bunch of chips in my mouth and start chewing. Ten girls? I can't come up with the names of ten hot girls at our school. I mean, I know there are more than ten hot girls on campus, but I don't know their actual names. "That's an awful lot," I say after I swallow.

"Not really." She shrugs. "I can add a few more if you want me to."

"No way." I wag my fingers at her in a gimme motion. "Pass it over. Let me see the list."

"Wipe your hands first. They're greasy with chip crumbs." She wrinkles her nose, and I grab a napkin, wiping each individual finger over and over again until she starts laughing. "Okay, here you go."

I take the paper from her and check out the list, frowning as I see each name. "Whitney Gregory?" I glance up to find Eden's watching me.

"What's wrong with Whit?"

"She's a sophomore."

"Very mature for her age."

"I'm not having sex for the first time with a fifteen-year-old." I swallow hard the moment the words leave my mouth. It's embarrassing, talking about this, even with Eden. And Eden knows everything about me.

"She's almost seventeen."

"What? How?"

"She was held back. She should be a junior; she'll turn seventeen in March."

Huh. Whitney Gregory is hot. She's a cheerleader. Nice body. Pretty face. I sound like a dick, but I can't help it. Eden would tell me I'm a pig.

She's probably right.

"Is she nice?" I ask.

"Whit is lots of fun."

"Is she smart?" I like smart girls. I've realized this over the years. I like a girl I can hold a real conversation with.

"Um."

I frown.

"Well…"

"Don't lie to me, Edes."

"She's not the smartest girl, but she's not totally stupid, either." Eden makes a face. "Sometimes I think she puts on an act. Like she pretends she's dumb, but she's really not."

Pass. "Cross her off." I drop the paper onto the counter and push it toward her.

Eden crosses Whitney Gregory off the list and adds another name to the bottom before passing the paper back to me.

"You have names on reserve in your brain or what?"

She smiles before grabbing a couple of chips out of the bag. "Maybe."

I read the list again, hating that she added Kaylie as the optional name. "I'm not going back to her."

"Oh, come on, Josh. You can admit you still want to be with Kaylie." Funny, how Eden knew exactly who I was talking about.

"But I don't." Not really. Well, sort of. I don't know. Maybe? Not that I want to admit that to Eden. She'll give me endless shit, and what's worse, I deserve it. How many times have Kaylie and I circled around each other, gotten together, only to fizzle out fast? Too many times to mention.

It's embarrassing. My friends are over the two of us together. So is Eden. Hell, so is my mom.

"Whatever." She sounds irritated, but she's smiling. And

that annoys me. I definitely don't want to go back to Kaylie. I don't want to be with any girl that's my usual type. It's pointless, right? Because we'll go nowhere, fast.

"Pick them out for me." I shove the paper toward her. "Pick a couple of names."

"Really?" Her eyes are sparkling, and I can tell she wants to bounce in her seat. "Are you sure you don't want to choose?"

"I'll choose wrong, remember? I don't pick right. They all lack substance." I'm smirking, and I know I just made her feel bad.

Good. That was my goal.

"Not all of them lack substance…" she starts but I shake my head.

"Pick them out. Tell me which ones you want me to talk to." I frown. "And how exactly do you want me to talk to them, anyway?"

"You need to text them."

I frown. "I rarely text anyone but my mom or my sister."

"Text them in Snapchat. Or send them a message on Instagram."

My frown forms into a smile. "You want me to slide into their DMs?"

"Yes, that's exactly what I want you to do." Eden's smiling, too. "Get to know them by talking first."

"You want me to talk to *all* the girls you choose?" I mean, I talk to lots of girls on a daily basis. No one can ever call me shy. But when I find one I'm interested in, I focus only on her.

"There's no law against talking to girls," Eden points out, sounding frustratingly logical. "But the minute you get serious about one, you need to dump the rest. Nicely."

"How am I dumping them if we were never together?"

"Good point." Her gaze drops to my shorts, then drifts up, lingering on my chest. Holy hell, I think she's checking me out. I've never caught her doing that before. "You need new clothes."

My ego deflates just like that. "What's wrong with what I'm wearing?"

"You're wearing shorts and a hoodie."

"Yeah, so?"

"You wear shorts and a hoodie, like, every single day."

"At least it's not the same shorts and a hoodie, right?" I laugh, but Eden doesn't, which makes me shut up. "Fine, I'll get new clothes. I'm due anyway. My mom was just trying to get me to go shopping, but I told her no."

"I'll go shopping with you." Her gaze settles on my head, which is weird. "You need a haircut, too."

Oh. That explains it. "I'll get a haircut. With you."

She's smiling. "Perfect. Let's go Monday. I work this weekend."

"I'm free Monday."

"Great." Eden reaches into the chip bag and pulls out a handful. "Now let's watch a movie."

Chapter Three

EDEN

"What do you think of Tana Martin?"

Molly is sprawled across my bed, lying on her stomach, elbows propped on the mattress as she scrolls through Instagram. "I don't really think much of her at all. Why?"

"What do you mean by that?" I'm sitting on the floor, wrapped in my favorite PINK fleece blanket Mom got me for Christmas last year. It's Saturday night, and since both Molly and I are boyfriend-less, we're hanging out together.

We've done this far too much lately. All those plans we made when we were juniors about our amazing senior year with the hottest boyfriends ever hasn't happened so far.

I'm afraid it might never happen.

"I asked you why first." Molly glances over her shoulder, her shrewd hazel eyes meeting mine. "As in, why are you asking me about Tana Martin?"

"Why do you sound so defensive?"

An irritated growl escapes my best friend, and she

resumes scrolling through Instagram. "Tana Martin gave my brother a blowjob after a school dance out behind the gymnasium."

I gasp. "What? When?"

Molly turns so she's sitting on my bed, facing me. "He only just told me a few days ago. It happened during homecoming."

"Homecoming? That was almost a month ago." I can barely wrap my head around someone getting a blowjob behind the school gymnasium, let alone it being Molly's younger brother.

"I know. But it's not like my brother and I talk about blowjobs on a regular basis, you know?" Molly mock shivers.

Ugh. Yeah. I don't want my little brother Travis coming to me saying stuff like that. He's sixteen. He's had a regular girlfriend since the seventh grade—and not the same girl, either. He's a total player compared to me, which makes no sense, because, ew, he's my annoying little brother. Though I'm sure he's had plenty of blowjobs—

Brain bleach. I can't even begin to think about this.

"Tana's a junior," I say to take my mind off my brother.

"Yeah, so?" Molly frowns.

"Michael is a sophomore."

"He's also a total man whore." Molly rolls her eyes. She's quiet and sweet and has freckles across her cheeks. She's tiny, and everyone called her Mouse when we were in elementary school. She's the good girl. Her brother is the bad boy, which is hilarious to me because I remember when he used to eat his boogers. And when he was in kindergarten he wet his pants for, like, two weeks straight because he was afraid to use the bathroom.

Seriously.

"What about Marin Herzig?" I ask Molly, keeping my voice casual. She's going to get suspicious about my questions.

She always does.

"What about her?"

"Do you think she's cool?" I sit up straight, snapping my fingers. "And what about Taylyr Howard? She's nice, and cute. Though she's super competitive." Taylyr plays volleyball, basketball, and softball. To call her super competitive is probably an understatement.

Molly frowns. "Why are you asking me about these girls?"

I press my lips together, thinking of my promise to Josh. I'm not supposed to tell anyone I'm helping him find someone to lose his virginity to. Not even Molly. "I don't know. I've been thinking about them lately."

"And the reason you've been thinking about them is…"

"No reason." I shrug. "I just was."

Molly peers at me, like she's trying to see inside my mind, my soul, whatever. She does that a lot. Sometimes I wonder if I make zero sense to her. She's logical and methodical and all of those "cal" words where I'm not. I'm not dumb, not by a long shot, but sometimes I can be flighty and impulsive, which is a total contradiction considering my love for all things related to organization. "Are you trying to tell me something, Eden?"

I'm frowning. "What do you mean?"

"Are you interested in these girls? Like *interested* interested?"

"What? No. Not at all." Not that there's anything wrong with that, but I'm not into girls. You'd think Molly would know this by now, considering how long we've been friends. "Fine, I'm trying to help Josh."

Molly makes a face. She and Josh are friends, but not as close as Josh and I. And there has been…jealousy between the three of us over the years. Molly's jealous of Josh. Josh is jealous of Molly. It's understandable yet annoying. "Help

Josh with what?"

I can't tell her the truth. If he found out that Molly knew, he'd never trust me again. "Find a new girlfriend."

"Oh, whatever." Molly waves a hand, dismissing my words. "Tell him to go back to Kaylie. He always does eventually."

Ugh. No way. "I'm not telling him that. He needs to find someone new."

"He doesn't need any help. He always manages to convince a girl to go out with him. How I'm not sure," Molly mumbles, making me shake my head. She must be feeling extra anti-Josh tonight. "Hey, I have a good idea. Why don't you help *me* find a boyfriend?"

Uh-oh. Molly is notoriously picky. And known for keeping the boys she's interested in a big fat secret, including from me. "Like you'd let me."

"I'd let you help me now." Molly's face brightens. "I need a date to winter formal."

"So do I," I mutter. Why did I think I'd have an amazingly hot boyfriend my senior year again? I was being totally unrealistic. There are no amazingly hot boys in my class.

Well, that's a lie. There are some. They're just all taken. Or they're one of my best friends. Because yes, I can admit it: Josh is hot. He has a nice body. He played football. He's currently playing basketball. He's super competitive like Taylyr Howard, which means they might make a perfect couple…

"We can help each other out, Eden. Surely between the two of us, we could each come up with a decent date," Molly continues.

This isn't a bad idea, even though I have my hands full with Josh and the list. Now I'm going to have to find someone for Molly, too? And for myself?

I wanted to play matchmaker but not turn it into a full-time job.

"Are you crushing on anyone in particular?" I ask.

"Please. We don't crush on boys anymore. We're too old for that." Molly likes to act like she's extremely mature and above it all. I think this is why she has a hard time finding a boyfriend. She expects too much out of them when really, boys are pretty simple—and the majority of them are still immature. At least the ones I know. I like Josh and all his friends, but most of the time they act like they're twelve years old when they get together.

That is so not Molly's style.

"Okay, let me rephrase." I clear my throat. "Are you liking anyone lately, Molly, my darling?"

Molly laughs. "Not anyone in particular. Not really."

See what I mean? Even if she does like someone, she won't tell me until she makes it really obvious and usually by then, it's too late. Molly's biggest problem? She plays it as if she doesn't like a boy, even when she really does. And he might even like her, too—this has happened more than once—yet she acts like they're just friends or she makes fun of him or whatever, and then he moves on. Because he doesn't believe he has a chance with Molly.

It's almost like she's subconsciously sabotaging herself.

"Really? So you like no one?"

"How about you?" She's a master at changing the subject, as am I when I want to avoid a particular topic.

I shrug. "I've known them all too long, I think. I'm over it."

"Fiona's going to a frat party Monday night." Molly's eyes sparkle. Fiona is Molly's older sister. She's a sophomore at the local university, and on very rare occasions, she's taken us to a college party. And when I say rare, I mean super rare. As in, she's taken us to one party.

Yeah. One.

"She won't take us."

"She doesn't have to. We can just go. I know which frat is having the party."

"Are you sure this isn't bogus?" I ask. "We're all on Thanksgiving break."

"It's some annual party they have for the students who stay on campus during the break, and for the locals. I remember Fi going last year." Molly bounces on the bed, making the box spring squeak. "Come on, Eden. Let's go. It'll be fun."

"I don't know." I sort of love the idea of meeting college guys. Someone different, someone I don't know, someone older and gorgeous and not some boy I went to school with for twelve years straight. "I have plans on Monday. And I work tomorrow—the closing shift."

We live in a small coastal town that thrives on tourism. As in, the tourists are out in force right now for Thanksgiving break. I work at a tiny gift shop downtown, right by the pier, which means it's extra busy with people from out of town soaking up the salt air while buying ugly sweatshirts and overpriced trinkets. It's a fun job, but I worked today, and it was exhausting. Tomorrow will be more of the same.

"You work tomorrow, Eden, not Monday. Geez, you sound like an old lady. Who do you have plans with?"

"Josh." Should I suggest he come to the party with us? Nah, Molly will hate that. "I'm helping him shop for new clothes."

Molly makes a face. "That'll take, what? A couple of hours in the afternoon with you holding Joshy's hand while he picks out more hoodies and basketball shorts? Big deal." Now she's smiling. "We're so going."

"What if Fiona doesn't want us to come with her?"

"Screw Fiona." Molly stands on my bed and starts jumping. The box spring is really squeaking now. "We'll crash the party, like anyone cares."

Her enthusiasm is catching. I stand and join her on the bed, grabbing hold of her hands before I start jumping, too. If my dad caught us, he'd be furious. "Let's get dressed up."

"And curl our hair."

"I'll do a cat eye on you." I've watched a lot of makeup tutorials on YouTube over the years. I can do an excellent cat eye. Adele would be jealous.

"I'll bust out the contouring kit." Molly has watched a lot of makeup tutorials, too.

"We're gonna look hot," I say just before I drop butt-first on the mattress. I bounce so hard I practically fall off. I start giggling and so does Molly and the next thing I know, we're both on the floor laughing hysterically.

Guess I'll focus on finding Josh a girl tomorrow.

Or Monday. Yeah, Monday.

• • •

JOSH

"Why am I over here this early again?"

I toss the basketball in Abraham's direction, and he catches it with ease before aiming for the basket. He misses. Ha. "Because we need to work on our shots."

Obviously.

"It's Sunday morning." Abraham dribbles the ball. We're playing in my driveway. Dad put up a basketball hoop above the garage door for my older brother, when I was just a baby. I've used it a lot growing up. It's like the only thing I still have that reminds me of him.

"Yeah, so?"

"The Sunday before Thanksgiving, and we have no school all week." Abraham makes a face.

"We still have practice," I point out. Coach is fanatical about practice, even on holidays. Can't blame him. We're both on the varsity basketball team, and we have the potential for a great season. Our first game is next week, and he wants us fully prepped.

Abraham takes the shot again, and this time he's successful. "It's ten o'clock in the morning. I should still be in bed."

"I didn't force you to come over." I take the ball from him and make my own shot. I'm taller, and I'm better at completing three pointers. Abraham is only a couple of inches shorter than me, but he's fast and can steal a ball like nobody else.

"True." To prove my point, he steals the ball from my hands and throws another shot. "I wanted to talk to you anyway."

"What about?" I grab the ball and throw it against the garage door, the metal clanging. Mom spent the night at her boyfriend's house so there's no one around to tell me to stop. And for some reason, I like the noise the door makes every time the ball hits it. It's loud and annoying yet also... satisfying.

"Personal shit," Abraham says right before I pass him the ball, and he throws it against the garage door, too, then turns his grin on me. "Remember how pissed your mom used to get when we did that?"

"She's not here to get pissed, so let's keep doing it." Moments like these, it feels like Abe and I are still thirteen and annoying as hell.

We bounce the ball off the garage door for a few minutes, enjoying that satisfying rattling sound, until we both get bored. I grab the ball and hold it, my gaze meeting Abraham's. "What sort of personal shit did you want to talk about?"

"This is awkward." Abraham runs a hand through his spiky black hair, looking away. "I want your opinion on... someone."

"Someone?"

"Yeah. A someone you know very well, who you're close to."

Unease slips down my spine. "Who exactly are you talking about?"

"Freaking Eden." He sighs and runs both hands through his hair now, tugging on the ends. "I think I like her."

"What? No way." They don't really like each other. Abraham is my closest friend beyond Eden. Their relationship is sort of like mine and Molly's. We tolerate each other. Sometimes, we get along great. But most of the time, we snap at each other or sling insults. I would never admit it out loud, but I get jealous of all the time Molly spends with Eden. And I think Abraham feels the same way about Eden stealing me away from him, too.

Or so I thought.

"Way." Abraham nods, looking miserable. "I've liked her for months. Since school started."

"I'm having a hard time believing this." When he sends me a confused look, I continue. "You two hate each other."

"Hate is a really strong word, my friend."

"Fine, you despise each other. Strongly dislike each other. Whatever."

"I did. I used to. But then she started to grow on me. And something happened over the summer, because now I can't stop thinking about her," Abraham admits, kicking at a stray piece of bark and sending it back into the nearby flower bed.

"You've been thinking about her since the summer?" Like, I am seriously having a difficult time wrapping my head around this. Eden and…Abraham? If I told her he liked her, she'd laugh. I know she would.

Huh. I frown. Would she? And would I be okay with that? My frown deepens. Probably not.

Abraham nods. "Since August, at least. She's cute, Josh.

Actually, Eden's more than cute. She's freaking hot. Have you looked at her lately? She has a great rack and a tiny waist and..." He stops talking when he notices how I'm glaring at him. "Aw, come on. Don't be a protective asshole."

"She's my best friend, and you're talking about her like she's just any other girl." And she's not. Abraham knows this.

"Are you telling me I'm not allowed to notice that she's gorgeous? Like she's off-limits since she's your best friend? Because that's not fair, bro." Abraham is the one glaring now, and I take a step back, rubbing my hand against my suddenly tight chest.

Abraham called Eden gorgeous. He likes her. He thinks she has a great rack and a tiny waist. I shake my head. I feel like I'm in some weird world where everything just flipped upside down. Seriously, what the hell is happening?

My stomach twists, and I swallow hard. I can't imagine them together, but what if it happens? I'd hate it. But why?

Face it. You're jealous.

Uh, hell no.

"I never said that," I finally murmur, keeping my gaze fixed on the ground. "If you like her, I can't stop you from pursuing her. Though I gotta admit, it's kind of weird."

"I know, right?" I can hear the relief in Abraham's voice. "There's just something about her. When she's not insulting me or making me feel dumb, she's really funny. Hell, she's really funny even when she *is* insulting me or making me feel dumb."

True. Abraham brings out the sarcasm in Eden. But I can't imagine them together. Ever. "You two are total opposites."

"Not really. We have a lot in common. Like you."

"So you're gonna go out with her and talk about...me?" I grimace and toss the ball at him. He catches it with a grunt. "That's just weird, bro."

"We won't talk about you. God, you're such an arrogant asshole." Abraham backs up and tosses the ball, making the shot. "You need to talk me up."

"Talk you up?"

"To Eden. Tell her what a great guy I am."

"You two have been friends throughout high school. Doesn't she already know what a great guy you are?"

"We haven't been that close. Only in the last year has she started tolerating me. But I want more than that. I want to get to know her better." Abraham drops the ball and lets it roll into the nearby grass. He turns to look at me, his expression dead serious. "I need your help."

"I'll put in a good word on your behalf."

"Find out if she has a date to winter formal."

"You want to take her to winter formal?"

"Yeah, totally." He nods vigorously. "Where is she right now? Is she at home?"

I feel sort of sick to my stomach. Why is he pushing this so hard? "She's working."

Abraham smiles. "Let's go visit her at work."

"It'll probably be busy down there." I'm making excuses. Why am I making excuses? I go visit Eden at work all the time. I've brought her lunch. I've brought her iced coffees. Hell, one time I brought her a box of tampons because she started her period and she couldn't get a hold of her mom or Molly, and holy hell, I actually went into the local Walgreens and bought a box of freaking tampons like it was no big deal.

I'm a damn good friend. I'd do anything for Eden. I'd do anything for Abraham. But hook the two of them up together?

Uhhhh...

I think of our stupid sex pact. If I were to call her out on it, now would be the time. I'd do it with my best friend than have her hook up with Abraham. And I know that makes me sound like a terrible, selfish person, but I can't help it.

I don't want the two of them to get together.

"I'll buy a magnet. She can't refuse my business, right?" Abraham slaps me on the back, so hard I take a stumbling step forward. "Come on, man. Help me out here. It's only a few weeks until winter formal. I want Eden as my date."

"I need a date, too," I admit.

Abraham chuckles and claps me on the back again, but this time I'm prepared. I stand my ground. "You've been keeping secrets or what? Who are you hot for?"

If he only knew I really have been keeping secrets. I know Abraham has done the deed. He confessed all near the end of ninth grade, when he hooked up with some older chick on the track team. He gave up the girl and the track team by the beginning of our sophomore year. "No one in particular," I say, which is the truth. "But I sort of want a girlfriend."

"You know you can hook up without all the strings, right?" Abraham starts laughing. He's always given me grief for my commitment issues. As in, I love to commit. But it's true. I'm not a hookup kind of guy. I like having a girlfriend. Yet I haven't had one in a while. Haven't really felt the need.

Until now.

"Maybe I like strings," I say defensively. But do I? Maybe I should take Abraham's advice and go for a chick with no commitment. Get laid and get it over with.

Huh. That's not a bad idea. In fact, that's a great idea.

"You're the only guy I know who does. Come on. Feed me and then let's go see Eden."

"Maybe I'll take your advice," I tell him as I lead him back into my house.

Abraham frowns. "What do you mean?"

We enter the kitchen, and I grab a bag of bagels out of the pantry. "Forget the strings. I need to find a hot girl to hook up with."

Abraham grins as he opens the fridge and pulls out the orange juice. "Now we're talking. Have anyone in mind?"

"Not really." I shrug and carefully tear the bagel in half, drop it into the toaster, and then grab a paper plate while Abraham pours himself a giant glass of orange juice with ice. When he's not paying attention I sneak a text to Eden, making sure she's cool with us coming to her work.

Mind if Abraham and I stop by?

Yeah come by. It's not very busy. Though leave Abraham at home. LOL

Huh. This might not go so well.

He wants to say hi.

Please. He just wants to give me crap.

We'll be there in about an hour.

I'm not getting out of this am I.

Nope. Neither am I. :|

See you in an hour then! :)

Chapter Four

JOSH

I feel like I'm walking into a war zone, and I don't know why. I have Abraham with me, who's jabbering on and on like he's hopped up on caffeine, which he sort of is because we stopped at the Java Hutt and picked Eden up an iced vanilla latte. He's nervous, too, which he never is. He's got a big mouth and loves to show off, but he's also funny and a loyal friend. He's always been there for me, and so has Cole, Eden's ex-boyfriend.

Yeah, we live in a small community, so we all have these overlapping relationships that can sometimes make things weird, but we're used to it, I guess.

Anyway, we park down the street from the gift shop Eden works at and push our way through the crowds of tourists filling the sidewalk. The weather is perfect—a clear, sunny day with a predicted high of about seventy. The breeze is coming off the ocean, and the seagulls are calling as they fly overhead. I usually avoid this area because of all the tourists.

The only time I come down here is to see Eden or go to that one restaurant that has the best clam chowder in a bread bowl.

"Let me give her the vanilla latte," Abraham says as he takes it from my hand.

"I bought it," I protest, not wanting to give up the glory of bringing Eden her favorite drink.

"I'll pay you back. Thanks." Abraham grins, nodding his head to the music pouring out of the store we just passed. "This will score me some points. I know how much that girl values her caffeine."

He's right. She does value her caffeine.

We finally come upon Moonstones, the store Eden works at. Some old hippie chick named Matilda owns it, and she's a little strange, but Eden loves working for her. The store is small and packed full of trinkets and T-shirts and sweatshirts. There are already a bunch of customers milling around, and Abraham charges right inside, holding up the drink when he spots Eden behind the register ringing up a customer.

"Look what I brought you, E." He sounds triumphant, like he just killed for her or something. "Your favorite coffee."

She smiles at the customer as she hands over the change and then the bag. "Hope you enjoy," she murmurs before turning her attention to us. "Hey, Abraham."

"Eden." He sets the plastic cup on the counter in front of her and even bows. Sometimes, he's ridiculous. "An iced vanilla latte just for you."

She eyes it warily before lifting her gaze to his. "Um, thanks?" Her gaze flicks to mine, and I remain standing behind Abraham, shrugging like I have no idea what's going on. "What are you two doing today?"

"Not much. Thought we'd come see you." Abraham has taken over the entire conversation, like I'm not even here when I'm usually the one who does all the talking with Eden.

Plus, he's trying to turn on the charm. I've seen him do this countless times, but I think he's only confusing her.

"That's...great." She smiles and grabs the drink, examining it. "You didn't put poison in this, did you?"

Abraham laughs, but it's overly loud and kind of fake sounding. "I wouldn't try to poison you, E. I like you too much to want to kill you."

Eden's eyes go wide, and she sends me a look. One that says, *what the hell is going on?*

I shrug again because what can I say? I can't tell her the truth in front of Abraham. He'd kill me.

"There's a customer up front. I'll be right back." She dashes off before we can say anything, and the moment she's out of earshot, Abraham turns to me, his expression nervous.

"You think I'm doing okay?"

"Yeah, I do."

"She doesn't seem into me."

"Dude. You can't expect her to do a 180 and be into you all of a sudden. Not after the two of you have fought all these years," I remind him just as my phone buzzes. I glance at the screen to see I have a notification.

Snapchat from Eden

Turning away from Abraham, I open it to find a text from her.

What the hell is up with Abraham and why is he acting so weird?

I answer her immediately.

I thought you had a customer.

I lied. I'm hiding behind a rack of discounted T-shirts texting you. Tell me what's up.

Nothing's up.

You're lying.

No I'm not.

Why'd he give me the coffee?

I don't know. He wanted to do something nice for you for once?

Please. There's something going on and you're not telling me everything.

Glancing up from my phone, I watch Abraham, but he's staring at his phone, too. My phone buzzes again.

What's his motive? What does Abraham want from me?

Nothing. Can't a guy just give you coffee?

Not Abraham. You know what's going on so tell me!!!

This girl knows me better than anyone else, and it freaking sucks.

"Where's Eden?" Abraham starts heading toward the front of the store. I send her a quick warning.

Better move quick cos here he comes.

Her head pops up, and she starts straightening the folded sweatshirts on a table. He approaches her from behind, and I can hear him chatting her up, though I have no idea what he's saying. I hang back because that's what friends do, right? I can be his wingman, but I don't want to ruin his game.

And right now, Abraham is running his game on Eden.

Irritation flares as I watch them. The two of them…they don't make sense. They would never make sense. I didn't even think they liked each other that much, so I don't understand what's going on. It's…

Weird.

He laughs. Then she joins in, but it sounds fake. I know her fake laugh. For some reason, relief seizes hold of me, and I can't take it any longer. I'm gonna break this party up.

"You ready to go?" I ask Abraham as I approach them.

"I guess." Abraham turns so he's facing me and standing beside Eden. "We should probably let you get back to work."

"Yeah." Eden doesn't fight our leaving, and usually she's begging me to stay because she's bored or wants the company. Matilda doesn't mind if I hang out here. She usually just puts me to work. One time she had me reorganize her stock room and bought me lunch plus paid me fifty bucks for my trouble. "Thanks again for the coffee."

"Anytime," Abraham says, grabbing hold of her hand and pulling her in for a quick hug. "See you soon?"

When he lets her go, she stumbles a little bit, like she might pitch over from shock. In all the years they've known each other, I don't think I've ever seen them hug. Ever. "Um, sure." Her gaze meets mine, and the look she sends me is murderous. "Talk to you later, Joshua."

She only says my full name when she's annoyed with me, so great. I hustle out of the store, and Abraham follows after me, launching into a rambling speech the moment we're outside.

"I think that was the right move, buying her coffee. She looked happy I brought her one, right? Don't you think? I need to score points, and I think that got me some major points from Eden. She smiled at me. And she hugged me." He's full on grinning now. "That's a positive sign, don't you think?"

He's the one who hugged her, but I don't point that out. "Sure," I say easily, smiling at a pretty girl as we walk by. She smiles back, flipping her long, dark blond hair over her shoulder as she passes. Tourist. She's wearing a California T-shirt. No one from here actually wears a shirt that says California across it. We know where we're from.

"I'm glad we stopped by and saw her. Now you need to take me to breakfast." Abraham flicks his chin.

"I just fed you breakfast," I remind him.

"Yeah, but I'm hungry again. Let's grab doughnuts." He points at the nearby bakery across the street. "Or maybe cinnamon rolls. They have the best cinnamon rolls ever. When does Eden work again? Should I bring her a coffee and a cinnamon roll next time?"

He keeps repeating himself. And if he brought her one of those giant cinnamon rolls the bakery is famous for, she might get pissed because she'll think he's trying to fatten her up.

"You really think there'll be a next time with Eden?" I ask with a wince.

And that was the wrong thing to say.

"Hey." Abraham comes to a stop, and I do too, the both of us ignoring the people as they push past us. "I told you I like her, and you seemed cool with it, but I don't know. Do you have a problem with me and Eden, or what? Because if you do, you need to tell me now."

My best friend is challenging me right here in the middle of the sidewalk. I can't freaking believe it. "I don't have a problem with it. You can date whoever you want."

"Including Eden?" His voice rises like he's ready to fight.

"Including Eden." My voice, on the other hand, cracks when I say her name. Like I actually might have a problem with the two of them...together.

I don't know how to feel about that.

• • •

EDEN

"Okay, spill." I curl up in bed, pulling the covers tight around me, my phone propped against a pillow. Josh FaceTimed me a few minutes ago to talk about our plans tomorrow, and since his earlier visit at the store with Abraham has been bugging me all day, I decide to get right to the point. "Why did Abraham want to come with you to see me this morning?"

"Did you like your vanilla latte?" Josh's expression is pure innocence.

I'm not falling for it.

"Yes, I did. Thank you for getting that for me."

"I didn't get—"

"Don't bother lying. I know you're the one who ordered it, paid for it, and brought it to me. So thanks." Josh knows my favorite coffee place—and it's not Starbucks. He knows how I like to order my vanilla lattes at the Java Hutt—skinny and with an extra shot of espresso. That drink tasted like perfection, which means Josh had a hand in ordering it, not Abraham.

"He said he'd pay me back."

"Well, good for Abraham." I make an irritated noise. "What's going on with him, anyway?"

Josh sighs and runs a hand through his hair, destroying it completely. "I'm not allowed to tell you."

Unbelievable. I'm loyal to Josh to a fault. I tell him everything. "If Molly was crushing on you, I'd tell you." Abraham acted so weird I'm almost afraid that's what Josh is going to tell me.

His jaw falls open. "Molly has a crush on me?"

"No, you egomaniac. I said *if* Molly had a crush on you, I'd tell you." I pause for effect, hoping he'll cave, but he remains quiet. The jerk. "Please don't say Abraham likes me."

"Okay then. Abraham doesn't like you."

He's lying. For some weird reason Abraham does like me. I don't understand why the sudden change. "He's always hated me."

"More like you've always hated him."

"The feeling was mutual and you know it. Ugh." I roll my face into the pillow and contemplate screaming. But it's kind of late, and even though the sound would be muffled, the walls are thin in my house and my parents might hear me. I shift away from the pillow so I can stare at my phone's screen. "I find this really hard to believe."

"What, that he likes you? Do you really have that big of a problem with Abraham? He's pretty chill. He's smart, he's funny, he's athletic." The look on his face almost tells me it pains him to talk about Abraham like this.

So why is he?

"Sounds like you're the one with a crush on him." I immediately regret what I said. I sound like a bratty four-year-old.

"Sadly, he's not my type. Though speaking of my type…" Josh grins and rubs his hands together. I know where he's going with this. "Did you pick out the girls on the list for me yet?"

I'm thankful for the change of subject. It feels weird to talk about Josh's best friend liking me…his other best friend. That is all sorts of awkward, and while I'm flattered, I have never once imagined what it would be like to be with Abraham. We are complete opposites.

"Edes?" Josh's questioning voice snaps me out of my thoughts.

"I did pick out a few girls." Well. I sort of did. Meaning I picked two, but I really wanted to have three names for him. I decide to wing it, which probably isn't the best approach when we're talking about Josh's future sex life, but whatever. Sometimes winging it leads to the right decision. "Are you ready?"

"Yeah." He runs a hand through his hair again, then leans his head from side to side. "Shit, I'm nervous."

"Aw, that's cute." I sit up and grab the list off my bedside table and clear my throat. "So…I think you should talk to Marin Herzig, Taylyr Howard, and…Whitney Gregory."

Josh is silent for a handful of seconds, which makes *me* nervous.

"I asked you to take Whitney off the list."

"Give her a shot. She's sweet. I think you might like her."

"Who the hell is Marin Herzig?"

"Go look her up on social media. She has an awesome IG

account. Very artsy. She's a great photographer."

"I know Taylyr Howard." He puts me on pause, and I know he's going through his phone, probably on Instagram looking up Marin's profile. "Marin's cute."

"She is. She's really nice." I don't know this for sure, for sure, but I've heard she's nice. And I adore her Instagram. I think I've liked every photo she's ever posted. They're always so artistic.

"Taylyr Howard is into every sport there is."

"Right, and so are you, which means you two would be a great match." His face reappears on my phone screen again, and I smile at him. "Go hit them up."

He's not smiling, though. He's frowning. "You want me to go hit them up? Like how?"

"Josh." I sigh and grab the phone so my face fills the screen. "Don't play dumb. You know how to chat up a girl, flirt, whatever. You've had a lot of steady girlfriends over the years."

"Yeah, so?"

"Well, now you're acting like some sort of noob who has no idea what he's doing. Get some confidence back and act like the stud that you are."

"You think I'm a stud?" He sounds surprised, but I know what he's doing. Fishing for compliments. How many times have we had this conversation?

Too many to mention.

"Yes, you're a total stud with such big muscles and a great smile and all the ladies loooove youuuu." I say it robotically, which makes him laugh.

Huh. He does have a nice laugh. But I won't tell him that. It feels too…real to say it.

"I gotta go. Got some girls' DMs I need to slide into," he says, still laughing.

"Have fun. Keep me posted." I'm about to end the call

when he starts yelling.

"Edes, Edes, Edes, wait, wait, wait."

"What?"

"Tomorrow. What time do you want to meet?"

"Oh." I remember what Molly said about the frat party we're going to crash tomorrow night. "Let's go early."

Josh winces. "How early is early?"

"I don't know, around ten? Pick me up."

"Okay. See you in the morning." He ends the call before I do, and I lean back against my pile of pillows, staring up at the ceiling. Abraham really likes me? That's sort of weird. And when did this happen? He's never seemed into me before. Most of the time, I thought he found me annoying. Or he liked to give Josh and me endless crap about being friends. Like he seriously thought we were secretly banging or whatever.

Which is so not the case. Wouldn't Abraham die if he knew I was helping Josh *find* a girl to bang? Though when you really thought about it, it's kind of weird. Why am I trying so hard to help Josh find a girl to have sex with? Better that it's someone else versus me, right? No way can we go through with that dumb sex pact we made when we were fourteen and lame.

But wait. I'm pushing girls on him, and that's kind of weird. Does this mean I'm a pimp?

I grab my phone and send Josh a quick text.

Tell me I'm not a pimp.

He responds immediately.

You're not a pimp.

But I feel like one. It's kind of freaking me out.

Because of you helping me?

Yeah.

He goes silent for a moment, and I start to panic. This is messed up. What we're doing. It's dumb. It's crazy. This is not sweet matchmaking. It's me helping Josh find a girl to have sex with. Though I'm hoping he strikes up a serious relationship with his chosen one, which he most likely will since that's how he operates.

What if these girls found out I had a hand in all of this? They'll hate me for pimping them out, though that's not my intention. That was never my intention.

Oh my gosh, I so shouldn't have agreed to his insane plan. Did I ever really agree? It's more like I fell into it. Maybe I need to fall right back out of it.

Josh finally answers.

You're not a pimp. Think of it like that reality show The Bachelor. You're the producer of the show, finding girls that could be the potential match for the Bachelor. And I'm the Bachelor.

I'm frowning so hard my forehead hurts.

How the hell do you know about The Bachelor?

Come on it's been on for like a million years. Plus my mom watches it.

Oh. Okay.

I pause, staring at my phone. I like Josh's idea. Yeah, I'm not a pimp. I'm like the girl in charge of *The Bachelor*. Instead of a rose, he'll hand over his virgin status as the main prize.

The giggles threaten, and I press my face into the pillow. I've seriously lost my mind. And I blame Josh for it.

Chapter Five

JOSH

I'm a hardcore fan of *The Bachelor*.

There. I said it. It's my secret shame. No one knows about my love for *The Bachelor*. It's true, my mother really does watch it. But we watch it together. It's our weekly bonding moment. We bag on the crazy girls, we bag on the Bachelor or Bachelorette, we bag on everyone. We root for the ones we really like, and we enjoy the hell out of all the drama, especially the tell-all specials near the end of the season.

None of my friends know I'm a *Bachelor* fan. Not even Eden, and she'd probably give me the least amount of shit out of all of them.

Maybe.

I show up at Eden's house about two minutes after ten, and the moment I put my truck into park, Eden's practically running out the front door. She hops into my car so fast, I barely have time to process it.

"Hey." She smiles at me, and I smile back, shifting the

truck into drive. "I had to get out of there. Dad was lecturing us on the importance of keeping our bathroom clean."

"That's very important," I tell her as I pull away from the curb. My voice is serious—I'm trying my best to copy her dad.

"Whatever. I'm not the bathroom slob. Travis is." She grimaces. "He's so gross."

I don't want to talk about Travis and the gross bathroom. I have better news to share. "So I talked to them."

Eden frowns at me. "Talked to who?"

"To *them*. Last night. All three of them." She's still frowning, so I explain myself. "The girls. Taylyr, Marin, and Whit."

"Wait a minute. You talked to all three of them?" She sounds incredulous.

"Well, yeah. Isn't that what you told me to do?"

"I didn't figure you'd go for it that fast. Though I should've known." She's slowly shaking her head. "How did it go?"

"It went pretty great. Right now I'm connecting the best with Whitney." Weird, because she's the one I was the least interested in, and it turns out talking to her is the easiest. She didn't act suspicious when I slid into her DMs on Instagram last night. We followed each other on Snapchat immediately and talked for at least an hour about miscellaneous stuff, and she was very flirty. Plus, she sent me a cute photo of her that I wanted to screenshot so I could show Eden, but I didn't want to look like a creeper so I didn't.

Maybe I should stalk her Instagram and take a few screenshots. Though that's weird. Eden would definitely tell me that's weird.

"Whit, huh?" Eden shoves my shoulder, making me lean away from her. "I told you that you two would be a good match."

"She's a big flirt."

"You like big flirts."

True. "Marin had no idea who I was."

"Aw, was the pretty boy's ego crushed?" Eden singsongs in a weird baby voice. And did she really just call me *pretty boy*?

"Shut up." I shake my head. "We talked for a little bit, but she was reluctant. I could tell."

"Maybe she thinks you're some freak trying to get in her pants." Eden snaps her fingers like she's had a realization. "Oh wait, you *are* some freak trying to get in her pants."

"Yeah, and you're the pimp helping me out. You have no room to talk." I say that just to get under her skin.

And it works.

"Don't call me a pimp. You're going to give me a complex." She starts chewing on her lower lip in that nervous way she does. "I'm a matchmaker, okay? That sounds a lot nicer."

"You're right. Matchmaker does sound nicer. And I agree, you're not a pimp." I reach over and squeeze her knee, checking her out from the corner of my eye. She's wearing black leggings and an oversize sweatshirt, her hair swept up into a sloppy bun and not a lick of makeup on her face. I'd guess she got out of the shower not even fifteen minutes ago. Not that I expect her to dress up for me. Not at all.

It's not like that between us.

"What about Taylyr?" she asks. When I send her a blank look—on purpose—she sighs irritably. "You know, the girl with the dumb spelled name."

Right. Taylyr. "Dumb spelled name?"

"Who spells Taylyr with two y's? It looks ridiculous. It should be T-a-y-l-o-r, don't you think?"

Only Eden would pick on that, though she does have a point. "I guess."

"Well, whatever. Do you like her?"

"We probably have the most in common, but I don't

know."

"What do you mean, you don't know?"

"She's kind of…"

"Scary?"

"Not exactly."

"Intimidating?"

"Yeah. Intimidating. Forceful. Like, she was pushing for us to see each other over break almost immediately."

Eden grins, and her blue eyes light up. She has really nice eyes. I've always noticed that about her. "But that's great! It means she must like you, right?"

"She wants to get together so we can shoot some hoops." I shrug. "I think she wants to kick my ass out on the court."

Eden's smile fades, and she points her finger at me. "Don't be a jerk just because she plays sports. She's really good."

"Yeah, but what if she *does* kick my ass out on the court? That's embarrassing."

"Aw, poor baby Joshy, his ego is going to get bruised." There she goes, talking in that weird baby voice again.

"Stop with the baby talk. It sucks," I mutter.

"Whatever." She laughs. "You're being ridiculous."

"Maybe I should stop talking to Marin since she doesn't seem that in to it. In to me."

"No, don't stop talking to any of them yet. You need to keep this going at least for a little while."

Seriously? "How long is a little while?"

"A couple of weeks, maybe?" She starts wiggling in her seat, which is normal for her. It's like sometimes her energy can't be contained. "Turn right at the next light. I want to go to that one store we like."

I know exactly which store she's talking about. "A couple of weeks is a long time to talk to three girls at once." Talking to three different girls at the same time sort of makes me feel like a douche. Am I a douche?

"I think you can handle it," Eden says with confidence.

"But maybe I've already made my choice."

She sends me a look. "Joshua. You can't move too fast. That's your biggest problem, I think."

"What is?"

"Your impatience. Once you set your mind on something, you're ready to chase after it and make it happen immediately. Sometimes you need to slow down and really assess the situation," she explains. "Like picking the right girl you want to have sex with."

When she puts it like that, I get uncomfortable, which is stupid. But I can't help it. This entire situation is crazy, yet Eden is the only one I can trust who'll help me and not make fun of me beyond the occasional weird baby talk comment. I can handle that.

What I can't handle is someone making me feel like an idiot because I haven't gotten laid yet. Locker room talk makes me feel stupid because I feel like I can't fully contribute. All this pressure to lose my virginity I'm putting on myself, and I'm starting to wonder if I'm handling it right. As in, I should just find a girl and do her, you know?

Yeah, those are the thoughts of a complete and total douche.

"Abraham texted me last night," Eden says out of nowhere.

"What? He did?" I turn right at the light like Eden requested and pull into the shopping center parking lot. It's packed, so I head toward the farthest end, not wanting to fight the traffic. "What did he say?"

"Nothing much. We made small talk. We also talked about you." She sends me a knowing smile as I pull into an empty parking spot.

I cut off the engine to my truck and turn to face her.

"What about me?"

"Oh, just how you're such a great friend to us both." Her voice has this mysterious tone to it, making me wonder if she's hiding something.

"Really?" I wonder if she's covering. Maybe they talked shit about me, I don't know. Though I doubt it.

"Well, yeah." She turns to look at me, her expression serious. "I don't know what else to talk to Abraham about. So we naturally started talking about you. It's the one thing we have in common."

"You didn't tell him about..." My voice drifts, and I swallow hard. I will lose it if she told Abraham about what we're doing.

"Of course not! I promised you that was our secret, right?" She smiles sweetly, and the sharp pain that formed in my chest slowly eases. "Come on, let's go to Wavelengths and pick out some clothes."

She hops out of my truck, and I follow after her, my gaze skimming her from the top of her head to the black Nikes on her feet. I sort of forgot how great her butt is. And it's like...really great, especially in those black leggings. They're kind of thin. I swear if I squint I can see her underwear through them. Yeah, in fact I can see there's writing across her backside.

"Edes."

She glances at me over her shoulder. "Hmm?"

"Does your underwear say 'Go elf yourself' on the butt?" I am barely containing my laughter, and when her cheeks turn bright pink and she yanks her sweatshirt down so it's covering her ass, I let loose.

I am laughing hysterically.

"You're such an asshole," she tells me as she starts increasing her speed. Like she wants to get away from me. "You and your stupid dirty laugh. I hate it."

My dirty laugh? I didn't know my laugh sounded dirty. I chase after her, and since she's so short and doesn't run very fast, I catch up with her easily. "Come on, I'm just teasing. You're being too sensitive."

"I forgot these leggings are so see-through." She tugs on the sweatshirt hem again, her expression in full-on irritation mode. "I wonder if anyone else heard you say that."

"There was no one around, I promise." She's still walking fast, and I grab her arm to stop her. "Come on, Edes. It's funny. Your underwear says go elf yourself. That's hilarious. Merry Christmas."

She turns to face me, her eyes narrowed, her mouth a straight line. "It's totally embarrassing, especially when you yell it as loud as possible."

"I did not."

Eden tries to jerk out of my hold. "You did."

"Edes." I'm grabbing both of her arms now, staring into her eyes. They really are pretty, even when she's not wearing makeup. Though maybe she is? On her eyelashes? Mascara? Yeah, I think she's wearing mascara. Why am I noticing this again? "I'm sorry. I didn't mean to embarrass you." I hate it when she's mad at me. I really do.

Her expression softens, and the tension leaves her body. "Fine. It's okay. I'm just feeling stupid, I guess. And confused."

"Confused about what?"

"I don't know. Everything that's happening lately, especially with Abraham. I don't get it."

Abraham. I let go of Eden and take a step back. "Do you like him?"

"Not like that." She shakes her head. "I've never even thought of him like that before."

"Maybe you should give him a chance." I can't believe those words just came out of my mouth.

Do I really want Eden going out with Abraham? My best friend besides Eden? I don't know.

I don't think so.

But shit, why do I have a problem with it? Why would that bother me? I should be happy for them. My two best friends, together. If they got married, that would be awesome.

Yeah. No, it wouldn't be awesome if they got together. I'd lose Eden. I know I would. And I can't stand the thought.

"Oh my God, I can't deal with this right now." She waves a hand and starts walking once more. I fall into step beside her. "Forget Abraham. Let's concentrate on the Joshua Evans makeover. You'll have all three of those girls panting after you in no time, I promise."

"All because you're making me buy pants?" When she sends me a dirty look, I start laughing all over again.

•••

EDEN

Josh is so annoying sometimes, yet I can't ever stay mad at him for too long. He knows just what to say to make me feel better, or make me laugh. If the moment gets too serious, I can always count on Josh to lighten things up.

We wander through Wavelengths, Josh checking out the shoe section while I dig through the pants. I find him a pair of dark rinse jeans and some twill dark khaki pants. When we meet up again a few minutes later, he's grabbed a few T-shirts and—of course—at least three hoodies. I grab the hangers out of his hand with a shake of my head.

"No more hoodies."

"I love hoodies." He gestures toward my sweatshirt. "So do you."

"How many do you own?"

"How many do *you* own?" he throws back at me.

"This isn't about me. It's about you." I start putting the three sweatshirts away on the store racks, Josh trailing after me. "Don't you want to look good? Don't you want to impress these girls?"

"Is that all I have to do to get laid?" The amusement in his tone is obvious. "Dress to impress?"

I stop and whirl on him, standing so close our chests bump. "If you don't want my help, just say so."

He holds his hands up in the air, his eyes gone wide. "Geez. Settle, Edes. No need to be hostile."

Ignoring his comments, I head over to a circular rack full of long-sleeve button down shirts. I grab a couple in his size and thrust them toward him. "Try these on."

"I don't wear shirts like this," he says with the faintest sneer.

"Exactly. This is why you need to change it up." When he sends me a confused look, I roll my eyes. "You're a senior, Josh. This is your last year of high school. You've filled out college applications. Soon you'll be eighteen—a legal adult. I think it's time for you to start dressing like one."

Without a word, he takes the shirts from me and heads for the dressing rooms. I follow after him, making sure he takes the pants and jeans, too, before he goes into the first dressing room on the right, jerking the curtain closed with a loud yank.

Yeah. I made him mad, but I sort of don't care. He's being ridiculous, asking for my help, yet when I give it to him, he acts like what I'm doing is nothing but a big joke.

I plop down on the bench near the dressing room area and check my phone. I have two notifications from Snapchat—one from Molly and one from Abraham. I open Molly's first. It's a photo of her making a kissy face along with a caption.

Can't wait until tonight!!!!!!

I smile. Right. The frat party. She tried talking to her

older sister about it, but Fiona was like no way. So we're going by ourselves.

I take a selfie and add a caption before I send it.

Me too! SO EXCITED.

Then I check Abraham's Snapchat. He sent me a selfie, too, one where he's like…trying to give me full-on smolder. His expression is serious, he's freaking shirtless, and his black hair is damp, like he just got out of the shower. There's also a caption. Of course.

Whatcha doin' sexy?

I smother the laugh that wants to escape. Seriously? Sexy? I don't even understand what's happening right now. Life is so weird.

Holding my phone up, I make a strange face, forcing my chin down so I have like three of them, and I take a photo. I look hideous.

Perfect.

Nothing much hot stuff. What are you up to?

I add a few laughing emojis to counterbalance the hot stuff comment and send it to him before I overthink myself.

Josh pulls the dressing room curtain back and walks out, holding his arms out at his sides. He's wearing a black button down shirt and the dark khaki pants and um…

He looks.

So.

Hot.

"I'm totally overdressed."

"No, you look…" I shake my head, at a loss for words. Which is stupid. It's just Josh.

It's.

Just.

Josh.

"I look what? Bad?" He's frowning, staring down at his chest, running his fingers over the shirt buttons.

"You definitely don't look bad." My voice is firm. My thoughts are going haywire. I think about the pact we made, how crazy I thought he was for bringing it up.

But hey. Maybe there's something to this "let's lose our virginity to each other" deal.

Nah. That's crazy talk.

He lifts his head, his gaze meeting mine. "So I look… good?"

"You look great." Understatement. He looks hot like fire. But I can't tell him that. "You need a haircut." I say this to break the tension, because there is so much freaking tension right now. Am I the only one who's experiencing it? Or does he feel it, too?

"Yeah. I know I do." He runs a hand through his hair, messing it up so it's a riotous mass on top of his head. My gaze lingers, and I'm tempted to run my fingers through his thick hair and straighten it out.

Oh. My. God. Stop thinking like this!

"Go try on something else," I tell him, waving my hands and shooing him away. He needs to go. Get behind that curtain and hide for a few minutes so I can gather my thoughts. "Try on one of the flannel shirts and the jeans."

"Okay." He sends me a questioning look before he slips back into the dressing room.

I breathe out a sigh of relief, my shoulders slumping. What just happened? I don't like feeling this way toward Josh. Thinking he's hot, being attracted to him. It makes me…uncomfortable?

Well, it *should* make me uncomfortable.

"Your boyfriend is cute."

Glancing over my shoulder, I watch the sales associate who greeted us when we first walked into the store approach. She's super cute with a bohemian vibe. Long wavy golden hair almost to her butt, a black choker around her neck, she's wearing a flower print, flowing dress that swirls around her ankles when she walks.

"He's not my boyfriend," I tell her.

Her eyebrows go up. "You could've fooled me."

I'm scowling. "What do you mean?"

"You two looked totally into each other."

"Yeah." I laugh, but it feels forced. "No. We're just friends."

"Uh huh." The knowing smile she sends my way tells me she doesn't believe a word I'm saying. Whatever. "Let me know if you need any new sizes or whatever, okay?"

I watch her walk away then check my phone. And again, I see Molly and Abraham have sent me Snapchats. Molly asks where I am, and I remind her I'm shopping with Josh.

Abraham's I open with trepidation, wincing before I actually see what he said.

It's another photo of him working the smolder, his lips slightly pursed, his eyebrows up. He doesn't look half bad. Abraham's a good-looking guy, I can't lie, but he's... Abraham. I used to call this dude my archnemesis for the love of all that's holy.

Shaking my head, I read the caption.

You really think I'm hot?

Okay. I think I've gotten in too deep with this, and I've barely started.

"I like this shirt," Josh says as he exits the dressing room, smoothing the front of the blue and green plaid flannel he's wearing. He's got it buttoned up practically to his chin, which looks kind of dorky, but the color is totally good on him. "My mom always said I look good in blue."

I'm sure she did. It really brings out the blue of his eyes.

Like I have no control of myself, I stand and go to him, reaching for the button at the base of his neck. "Undo this. You look like a nerd." I touch him, slipping the button out of the hole, then I undo the next one, too, my fingers actually brushing his bare chest. My fingertips tingle, and I drop my hands quickly, smiling nervously at him. "There. That looks way better."

He laughs, tugging at his collar uncomfortably. "You like the shirt?"

"You look good. The jeans are good, too." Play it neutral. Act like this is no big deal. It's Josh. Joshua. Joshua Evans. Your best friend. The guy who used to hold you down and fart on you. The boy who complains to you when he's constipated. The boy who used to go into graphic detail when he described make-out sessions with his now ex-girlfriends.

Yeah. That guy. The one who's just your friend.

"Thanks. I like the other flannel, too, even though it's red and black. Think I should wear red? Or will I just look stupid?" His questioning gaze meets mine, and I stare into his blue eyes, getting a little lost for a moment. I shake myself, offering him a quick smile.

"You definitely won't look stupid." I glance at my phone, checking the time. "Maybe we should go ahead and buy this stuff, and then get you that haircut? I need to go over to Molly's soon."

His face falls, like I just disappointed him. "Wait, seriously? I thought you were mine all day."

I thought you were mine all day.

That's an interesting way for him to put it. "Um, no. Molly and I are hanging out tonight."

"Doing what?"

Do I want to tell him what we're doing?

No. No, you don't.

"Going to a party." The words fall from my lips like I can't stop them.

Josh is frowning now. "Where at? And why wasn't I invited to this party?"

"Because it's not anyone we know from school." I step closer to him, not wanting anyone else to overhear. "It's at the university. At a frat."

"Wait, what? You and Molly are going *alone* to a frat party?" He looks...furious. And he keeps shaking his head. "No way."

I back away from him, irritated. "What are you, my dad? We're going."

"Not without me you're not," he says, sounding extremely possessive, which is just...weird.

"Dude, you're going to ruin everything if you go with us."

"What are you talking about? I'm an excellent wingman." He actually looks offended.

"No, you're not. Whenever we're together at a party or whatever, people think *we're* a couple." It's true. He's a terrible wingman—at least for me.

"So? That'll keep the college dudes away, then."

"That's the whole point of us going to this party, Josh. Maybe we don't want to keep the college dudes away."

He crosses his arms in front of his broad chest, glowering at me. Usually this look only makes me furious, but right now, he's giving off—ultra sexy and protective vibes. Vibes I should not find attractive. *Ugh.* "Abraham and I will go to the frat party with you."

"Oh, hell no," I groan, shaking my head. "I don't want Abraham with us!"

"Why not?"

"He's acting like he's totally into me, and it's kind of weird. Seriously, he just called me sexy a few minutes ago in a Snap."

"What? He said you were *sexy?*" Josh starts laughing, and I can't help it. I start laughing, too.

"It is weird, right?"

"Yeah, I mean come on. You're not sexy." Now he's full

on laughing.

And in an instant, I'm not. I'm so not.

Instead, I turn and start running through the store, storming out of Wavelength's front door without looking back once. Josh is calling my name, but I don't reply.

I'm too flipping mad.

"Edes! Come on! Wait a minute." Then he's outside, too, right behind me and with the bohemian girl chasing after him.

"Hey, you can't leave! You haven't paid for that stuff yet," she's yelling, but we both ignore her.

I turn to face him, seething with anger. I know I'm not what anyone would consider sexy, okay? But I don't need him to remind me of that fact. Talk about adding insult to injury or however that saying goes. It's pretty accurate for what I'm feeling at the moment.

"I'm sorry," he says, his expression forlorn. He's hurt my feelings, and he knows it. "I didn't mean it."

I raise a brow but don't say a word.

"Hey," the salesgirl says, her earlier easygoing demeanor disappearing in a flash. "You need to come inside right now and either take those clothes off or pay for them before I call the cops."

"I'm going to buy all of it, okay? Just give me a minute," Josh snaps, making the girl rear back.

She mutters a few choice curse words under her breath as she walks back into the store, though I catch her lingering by the door, spying on us. Not that I can blame her.

"Edes." He slowly comes toward me and touches my arm, his fingers gentle as he tugs on my sleeve. "Come on, you know I was just shocked Abraham said that about you, only because it's so hard for me to imagine the two of you actually together."

Right. I do know what he means. But his words are the

hard, cold dose of reality I need to put me back in my place. The place where I look at Josh as just a friend, and not some hot boy who cleans up really nice. A hot, sexy boy who's out to find an equally hot, sexy girl so the two of them can boink like bunnies all night long and rid themselves of their pesky virgin status.

Well, Josh wants to get rid of his virgin status. I don't think he cares if he's ridding it with a fellow virgin or not.

"Forgive me, okay? I'm sorry." His voice is soft, and when I look up at him, his eyes are soft, too. He looks sad. Contrite. And like the sucker I am, I heave a big sigh and offer him the words he wants to hear.

"Fine. You're forgiven."

He exhales loudly and pulls me into his arms for a quick hug. I don't even bother savoring it. What's the point? He'd never go for me like that. We don't feel that way about each other. We're not each other's type. He likes beautiful, tall, athletic girls, and I'm a short, sort of cute, hates any kind of exercise girl.

I need to find a boy who actually wants to hug me because he thinks I'm gorgeous and funny and smart. A boy who wants to kiss me because he thinks I'm…kissable.

Maybe I'll find one at the party tonight. Anything's better than hanging around Josh and feeling less than.

Chapter Six

"Can I be honest?" Molly asks.

We're standing at her bathroom counter, curling our hair and staring at our reflections in the mirror. We're looking pretty good, both of us wearing short flower print dresses that show off lots of leg. Though with me, there's not much to show.

Our gazes meet and I nod. "Go for it."

"I'm glad Abraham and Josh are going with us tonight." Molly clamps her lips shut and slowly pulls the curling iron from her hair, creating a perfect curl. Molly has great hair, dark blond and thick, that falls just past her shoulders and always looks perfect.

Mine? Yeah, I'm curling it and I'll add plenty of hairspray when I finish, but these currently fabulous curls will fall out within the hour, if not sooner. I don't know why I'm wasting my time, but I always do.

"Why are you glad?" I'm shocked she'd say that. She's not the biggest fan of Josh or Abraham.

"I was kind of nervous about going to the party alone. With a bunch of college guys." She sends me a look, one that clearly says *you can't trust college guys.*

Molly has a point. I didn't even think of that, which probably makes me too stupid to live.

"They could drug our drinks or whatever and next thing we know we're waking up in a guy's bed, naked and with our heads pounding. Oh, and of course, we can't remember a thing," Molly says.

"You've been watching too many Lifetime movies," I mumble as I start curling another section of hair. "So dramatic."

"Better safe than sorry." She sets her curling iron on the counter and unplugs it, then winds the cord around the base. "What time are they showing up?"

"Around eight." It's already past seven-thirty and honestly? I'm nervous. Is it because I have to deal with the suddenly attentive Abraham? Or is it because of what happened between Josh and me earlier today?

Though nothing necessarily *happened* between Josh and me. I'm starting to think it was all in my imagination. He seemed perfectly normal the rest of the time we spent together. He bought all those clothes from the pissed-off bohemian girl at Wavelengths, and then we grabbed lunch at a nearby sandwich shop. I went with him when he got his haircut and made sure the hairstylist didn't cut it too short on the sides or on the top.

He dropped me off at my house around two with a cheerful good-bye, and I immediately went to my room, where I collapsed on my bed and stared at the ceiling for a solid hour, going over everything that's happened between Josh and me over the years.

Okay, not everything because cramming almost five years of memories into one hour is difficult. But I hit all the highlights and eventually came to one solid conclusion.

Josh and I are just friends. We've always been just friends. I can't have more than friendly thoughts about Josh. That's just playing with fire.

And I'm not in the mood to get burned. Not by my best friend.

"We're going straight to the party after they pick us up?" I ask Molly.

"If you want. Or we could kill some time and go somewhere else with the boys," Molly says.

"Maybe." The boys. Okay, I'm definitely wary of hanging out with Abraham tonight. I need to tell Molly about it, too. "So. Guess who likes me."

"What?" Molly practically shrieks, making me jump. "Who, who? Tell me!"

"Calm down, it's kind of an awkward situation." I lower my voice. "It's Abraham."

Molly's face falls, like I just told her that her dog died. And she loves Waffles the silly little mutt way too much. "Abraham likes you? Really? Wow. Um. That's great."

Wait. That's not the reaction I expected from Molly. Though really her mouth is saying one thing while her face is saying another. "You think it's *great* that Abraham likes me?"

"Well, sure." Molly shrugs and busies herself by cleaning up the bathroom counter. She opens a drawer and sweeps all the makeup she'd just been using inside before slamming it shut. "He's cute and smart, and he's so funny. You two would make a great pair."

Say what? Hmmm. "It almost sounds like *you* like him."

"No way. I do *not* like Abraham." Molly says those words too quickly and with too much force. That tells me she's totally digging freaking Abraham.

I can't believe it.

"Molly." I whine a little. I want her to know I'm onto her

game.

"Eden." She whines back at me, and we both smile at each other at our reflections. "I don't like him."

I raise a brow.

"I don't."

Both brows shoot up.

"Seriously, Eden. I have no interest in Abraham Chen. None at all."

I still remain quiet. I'm trying to get her to crack. And finally she does.

"Fine, I think he's cute. But that's it." She hangs her head, like she can't look at me anymore.

I'm still silent, and she lifts her head, blowing out an infuriated breath as she glares at me through narrowed eyes. "I'm totally into him, okay? And that's the honest to God truth. I've liked him since the beginning of the school year."

"Oh my God, are you serious?" I'm the one squealing now. Like how cute is this? My best friend and Josh's best friend could be possibly falling for each other? So adorable.

"Stop, it's nothing. Totally wasted feelings considering he likes you," Molly says miserably.

Oh right.

Guilt swarms me, and I sigh heavily. Why did Abraham have to think he likes me? He's messing everything up. "But I don't like him at all. Not like that."

"You should. He's the total package."

I send her a look. "What do you mean?"

"I don't know." Molly shrugs. "My mom says that all the time. She'll meet guys and say they're the total package. Like they have everything a woman could ever want or whatever."

"Your mom also always says that she's single and ready to mingle," I remind her. Molly's parents divorced a few years ago, and while it was an amicable breakup and there were no hard feelings, Molly's mom has been on the prowl for a new husband ever since. Molly finds her mom's behavior incredibly humiliating most of the time.

I think it's kind of funny. Molly's mom is cool. She's having a good time, proving that you can still have a great dating—and sex—life, no matter what your age.

Molly groans. "Why'd you remind me?"

We both start laughing. While I love Molly's mom, she also says and does embarrassing stuff sometimes.

"Well listen, we're both single and ready to mingle at this party, so forget Abraham and everyone else," I say as I turn to Molly and grab hold of her by the shoulders. "Let's focus on nabbing some hot college guys tonight."

Molly frowns. "And by nabbing you mean…"

"Flirting it up, getting a phone number, or a Snapchat add or whatever, maybe even sneak a kiss."

Molly's mouth pops open. "Sneak a kiss? You don't even know this guy."

"Exactly, and you're already freaking out over this *fictional* guy. Stop." I shake her by the shoulders. "Don't take things so seriously. Let's have fun tonight. Hey, I know. Let's give the boys we meet fake names."

"Fake names? Why would we do that?" Molly's frowning, her delicate brows furrowed, and I let her go. "What if I really like the guy and feel a connection?"

Molly's biggest problem is she's always ready to really like a guy and feel a connection. I get it, I really do, but sometimes I think she takes all of this too seriously. It's not always about connections, right?

It's about talking to cute guys and flirting. I've been looking for a new relationship since Cole and I broke up last year, and I can't find one. Maybe that's a sign from the universe I need to stop trying so hard.

The doorbell rings, and we both look at each other, our eyes wide. Molly's expression slides straight into panic, and she starts fluttering around the bathroom, waving her hands in front of her like she doesn't know what to do.

"Want me to get the door?" I ask calmly. I'm going for cool and collected, but deep down I'm a jumble of nerves—which makes me even more nervous because I never feel this way around Josh or Abraham.

Until this very moment.

"Yes." Molly sucks in a shaky breath. "Give me a couple of minutes and then I'll be out."

Vaguely irritated, I head for the living room. Molly does this every single time we go anywhere. She's always running behind when I'm ready to go. It's kind of annoying. At least her mom's out on a date tonight so we don't have to deal with her. Like I said, I love her, but she gets frantic like Molly, and the two of them together are like hyped-up Chihuahuas running in endless circles.

No thanks.

I exhale my own shaky breath before opening Molly's front door. Josh and Abraham are standing there, the both of them immediately scanning me up and down, making my skin go warm.

Me? I've only got eyes for Josh.

Ugh. Stop.

But it's like my brain is telling me can't stop, won't stop. Josh is wearing the black shirt and dark khaki pants he tried on earlier at Wavelengths, and he looks damn good, plus with the freshly cut hair, that faint smile curling his lips, and his hands shoved into his front pockets, I'd call him top notch swoon material.

Freaking ridiculous, right? Seriously, what is wrong with me?

"Looking extra sexy tonight, Sumner," Abraham says with a low whistle, interrupting my Josh-fueled thoughts.

I'm tempted to roll my eyes. Bad enough he called me

sexy, but then he calls me by my last name, too, and that makes his comment even less flattering.

"Hey. You guys look good, too." I open the door wider. "Come in. Molly's almost ready to go."

"Running late as usual, huh?" Josh asks as he walks past me.

I catch a whiff of his cologne or aftershave or whatever he's got on, and I inhale deeply, savoring it. Since when did he start smelling so good? Molly and I call it hot boy smell, and Josh has it tonight, that's for sure. "Yeah, you know how she is."

"What? Does she always run late?" Abraham looks from me to Josh as I close the door.

For someone who hangs out with us all the time, he sure is clueless about Molly's behavior. That's what I like about Josh. He pays attention. He knows what's up. He's not only focusing on himself. Most of the time, he actually cares.

"Not always, but a lot of the time, yeah," I tell Abraham. Josh sends me a knowing look, and I smile in return. Abraham's oblivious to our secret silent exchange, and I like that we can share this tiny moment, Josh and me. After all the years we've spent together, we have a lot of private jokes.

"Nice dress." Josh stands next to me, and when I look over at him, he's totally checking out my legs. Um, okay. "Trying to pick up college dudes with that short skirt?"

"Yep, that was the plan." I nudge him in the ribs with my elbow, and he pushes back. Somehow we collide. He's warm and solid, and he has muscular arms and holy crap, I need to stop thinking like this. He doesn't want me like that. He's wants to find some other girl he can get with. Not me.

Not.

Me.

It's not that I don't think I'm good enough for him…or do I? He's never noticed me like that before. Oh, he may check me out and make the occasional lewd yet somehow complimentary comment, but otherwise, we are friends only. Hands off. He sees me as one of his bros.

"Hey, guys!" Molly sweeps into the room, all smiles and her perfectly curled hair bouncing around her shoulders. "Ready to go?"

"Let's do this," Josh says with a smile, taking a few steps away from me like he needs the space.

"Molly, you are smoking hot tonight," Abraham says with a shake of his head, his gaze locked on all the leg she has on display. And she has better legs than me. She's taller and more slender. We took dance together for years when we were younger, and she was the one with the perfect, graceful dancer's body. I was the one with short legs who just liked to shake her ass up on stage.

Hey, at least I can admit it.

"Thanks, A," Molly says, her cheeks pink. "You look pretty smokin' yourself."

Josh sends me another one of those secret looks, though this time his brows are furrowed, like he's confused. I just shrug and smile in return.

• • •

JOSH

After about five minutes of arguing, I give in and let Eden drive. She's got her mom's Honda Accord, which is more practical than my truck—*yes Eden, I actually agree with you for once*—and besides, most of the time Eden drives like an old grandma, which is probably best considering we're going to a frat party and some of us might want to drink.

"I'm ready to get hammered tonight," Abraham says as he slides in the backseat with me. Because not only does Eden drive like a grandma, but we're riding together like a bunch of senior citizens, with the girls sitting together in the front and us old dudes in the back.

"Yeah, if we can even get in this party," I mutter with a slight shake of my head.

I can't stop thinking about how freaking sexy Eden looks tonight. The dress she's wearing is giving me dirty thoughts thanks to that short skirt, which isn't normal. I mean yeah, I've had dirty thoughts about Eden before—hell, I've had dirty thoughts about Molly, which doesn't happen often, but they're there. I'm a guy after all.

But something happened with Eden and me today. Some weird shift in our friendly universe. And now there's this weird vibe between us that I can't quite put my finger on. We got into that minor argument in front of Wavelengths, and I know I made her mad when I told her she wasn't sexy, which is a fucking lie.

She's extra gorgeous tonight, too. Like she's trying to prove a point that she is sexy as hell, thank you very much.

"Don't be such a downer, Evans," Abraham says, knocking me from my Eden-is-so-sexy thoughts. "We'll get into this party. Not like they have a bouncer at the door."

"We'll get in," Molly says firmly, turning in the passenger seat so she can look at us. "My sister has gone to a lot of parties at this frat, and she said they're cool, especially to the girls."

"I don't know about you, Evans, but I'm definitely not a girl." Abraham grabs his crotch to—what?—prove that point, making Molly blush and turn away.

I glance up to catch Eden watching me in the rearview mirror, a little smirk curling her lips. I roll my eyes. Her smile grows, and my heart starts to race.

What the hell?

"Ready to pick up on some fine ass college tail tonight?" Abraham asks me, his voice low like he doesn't want to be heard. Not that the girls are paying us any attention. They're too busy talking.

"Fine ass college tail?" I repeat back to him. "You sound like you're in some weird teen movie from the nineties."

Abraham frowns. "What are you talking about?"

"No one talks like that, dude. If they ever even did. But yeah, I'm all for going to this party and meeting new people," I say.

Abraham shoves my shoulder, making an irritated noise. "Whatever. You sound like an old man."

"Right, and you sound like every sexed-up teen cliché come to life." Abraham starts to laugh when I scowl at him. He rarely stays pissed at me for long, if ever. It's just not part of his makeup. He's an easygoing guy—a pain in the ass sometimes and totally ridiculous most of the time, but pretty easygoing.

"What the hell ever, man," Abraham says as he starts scrolling through his phone.

I do the same, opening Snapchat. I have a bunch of Snaps, but I only check the ones from Taylyr and Whitney. Whitney's is a cute selfie that looks like she sent it out to a bunch of people. I take a quick photo of myself and hit send.

The one from Taylyr is actually to me. It's a photo of the sunset with a caption.

What are you up to tomorrow?

Huh. This girl is pushy. But maybe I should go for pushy. Whitney's flirty, but she might be flirty with all sorts of guys, I don't know. Taylyr has zeroed in on me and while at first I was thrown by it, I have to admit it's flattering.

I take a photo of the streetlights we pass by and add my own caption.

Nothing much. How about you?

Taylyr doesn't bother sending me another photo. She goes straight to chat.

Want to get together?

I raise a brow, staring at the words until they start to blur. Do I want to get together? If Eden were sitting next to me, she'd encourage me to say yes.

Sure. Want to grab lunch?

Yes. :) That sounds fun.

Give me your address and I'll come pick you up around noon tomorrow?

Taylyr wastes no time and sends me her address. We chat a little more, and the next thing I know, we're at the party. Eden parks a few blocks down from the frat house. We get out of the car, and we can hear the music and the dull roar of a lot of people talking from this far.

"Sounds busy," Molly says apprehensively.

"It'll be fun, Mol." Abraham slings an arm around her neck and rubs the top of her head with his knuckles, making her yelp. "Come on, loosen up."

Eden and I fall into step behind them as we head toward the house. She says nothing, and at first neither do I, but that just feels weird. Why isn't she talking? I thought she'd be excited about going to the party and full of nonstop chatter like usual.

But she's not. She's quiet. Does that mean she's thinking about Abraham? Maybe she does like him. Maybe she's upset because he talks about fine ass college tail and now he's flirting with Molly.

Then again, she's walking with me.

"I talked to Taylyr just now," I say to break the weird tension between us.

"Oh?"

"Yeah. We're getting together tomorrow. I'm gonna take her to lunch."

"That's nice." I glance down at her to see she's looking up at me. "So I guess you don't mind that she's so pushy after all?"

"She's the one who asked if I wanted to get together." I

shrug. "I figured you'd tell me to go for it, so I did."

"Good. I'm glad you took my advice." I can hear the amusement in her tone, and I chuckle.

"You would've told me that, and you know it."

"You're right. I would've. I'm glad you went for it. She might be a good match for you."

Is it me or is there something in the way she just said that Taylyr and I might be a good match, that she maybe sounded...disappointed? Nah. "Yeah, I'm thinking so, too."

"Even if she spells her name in the dumbest way possible. Though I guess I shouldn't hold that against her. It's her parents' fault," Eden says with a little laugh, making me laugh, too. The tension eases, just like that.

I like it when Eden laughs. It's one of my favorite sounds.

"So you think it's a good idea? Me and Taylyr?" I sound serious, because I am serious. I might be moving too fast, but isn't that the point? I'm on the fast track to sex, which sounds kind of awful if I'm being honest, but hey, if I'm down and Taylyr's down, then what's the harm in it?

I'm trying to be like Abraham. No more strings. No more relationships. I need to be free and single when I go to college. Free and single and rid of my virgin status once and for all.

"If you like her, Josh, then I say go for it." Eden's answer is way too vague.

"Yeah, I don't know. I guess tomorrow will tell me if I like her or not, you know?"

"You can't base your decision on one date."

"Are you being serious?" I'm surprised. "I firmly believe if there's no connection from the start, then there never really will be."

"But is that what you're looking for? A connection? Or are you just looking to get laid?"

Huh. She does have a point, not that I want to admit it. "I don't know."

Chapter Seven

The minute we got to this dumb party, the girls ditched us. I knew that would happen, but I'm still a little butthurt over it. And while there are hot girls crawling all over this house, most of them aren't interested in a high school boy, even if I am a senior.

Not that I told them I was in high school, but I swear I must give off some sort of vibe that screams *he's only seventeen*. Maybe it's because of Abraham acting like an immature asswipe, but whatever. I'm drinking foamy beer and checking out hot girls and thinking about Taylyr.

And Eden. Where's Eden?

"You wouldn't believe who I just ran into." Abraham is standing in front of me, his expression anxious.

"Who?"

"That chick from the track team. The first girl I ever had sex with." Abraham shakes his head. "I never thought I'd see her again. It's weird, man. She goes here. She's in a sorority, and I swear to God, she somehow got even hotter."

This doesn't surprise me. "Is she still into you?" He went on and on about this girl for a while, and then one day, he was over her. It was kind of odd, and he never did tell any of us what happened between them to end whatever it was they had. I don't even remember her name.

"I don't know. She was being super cool just now." He glances over his shoulder, and his expression brightens, the smile on his face downright blinding. "Oh hey, Nicole."

Nicole sidles up next to him, resting her hand on his arm. Abraham's right. She's hot. With long, bleached blond hair and dark brown eyes, her full lips covered in shiny gloss. She's wearing tight jeans and a cropped black sweater that reveals a flat stomach. Plus, it shows off her big boobs. No wonder Abraham's all wound up. "Hey." Her gaze locks with mine, and she smiles. "Who's this, Abe?"

No one really calls Abraham Abe, but I guess he doesn't mind when it's a gorgeous girl like Nicole. "This is my best friend, Josh."

"Hi." I smile at her.

"You're adorable," she tells me before she rises on tiptoe and whispers something in Abraham's ear. He turns about fifty shades of red, and when his gaze meets mine, he looks almost embarrassed.

"You care if we go upstairs for a few minutes?" he asks me.

"Go for it." I flick my chin at him.

"Nice meeting you, Josh," Nicole tells me before she curls her arms around Abraham's and leads him away.

At least someone is getting some action tonight. Not that I'm jealous.

Okay, fine. Maybe I am. That was so freaking easy for Abraham. Why can't I find one of my exes at a party and just do it with her?

Problem is, I don't think I want to have sex with any of the girls I used to date. Not anymore at least.

I start searching for Eden and Molly. I want to make sure they're okay, and I haven't seen them in at least a half hour, maybe longer. I push my way through the crowd, finally spotting Molly in the kitchen talking to some guy who towers over her. His cheeks are flushed like he's had a few too many to drink, and he's got a thick gold chain around his neck. He's kind of cheesy.

So I decide to approach them and make sure she's okay.

"Hey, Molly."

She glances in my direction and smiles. "Josh! Where've you been?"

"I should ask you the same question." The guy is glaring at me like I'm trying to take his property.

"I've been talking to Kirk." She waves a hand toward the gold chain guy, who scowls at me in return.

"Nice." I nod in his direction before I ask Molly, "You okay?"

"Oh yeah." She nods, her smile wide. Kirk is still glaring at me.

"Cool. Have you seen Eden?"

"She was out in the backyard a few minutes ago."

"I'll go look for her, make sure she's all right." I wave. "See ya."

"Bye!" Molly dismisses me in an instant, focusing on whatever Kirk of the gold chain is saying.

He doesn't look like her usual type, but whatever.

I head outside to find the backyard packed with all kinds of people. I send Eden a quick text, asking where she is, but she doesn't reply.

And I'm kind of starting to freak.

I search the backyard, checking the clusters of people that are drinking, smoking, and talking, but no Eden. My phone buzzes and I check it, but it's just a snap from Whitney. Another sexy selfie that I again sense is sent out to a bunch of us versus just me.

Ignoring it, I pocket my phone and go around the side of the house to see if Eden is over there. There's a small group of people circling one of those metal fire pits, and I spot her, standing on the far side of the fire, near the fence. There's a guy next to her, and it looks like he's talking to her.

It also looks like she's trying to ignore him.

My protective instincts rising, I watch them, my fingers curling into fists when the guy leans in even closer to her, causing their shoulders to brush. She steps away from him, sending him an irritated look. Clearly she doesn't want this dude talking to her, and he's not getting the hint.

It's when he tries to touch her arm and she jerks out of his hold that I spring into action. Without thought I head toward the fire pit until I'm right beside them, interrupting their conversation.

"Keep your hands off her," I say, glowering at the guy. He's shorter than me, but he's bulkier, got more muscle. I bet I could take him.

"Who the hell are you?" The guy's eyes are bloodshot, and he's slurring his words. I'd guess he was drunk, which means I could totally take him no problem.

"Josh. What are you doing?" Eden asks, her voice rising.

I turn to look at her and gesture toward the drunk guy. "Is he bothering you, Eden?"

"Um…"

"Hey, asshole, get out of here," the drunk guy tells me, grabbing hold of Eden's arm yet again. "I saw her first."

I grab her hand and pull her toward me so the guy has no choice but to let her go. "Yeah, well she came with me, so fuck off," I tell him in my fiercest voice as I tug on her hand and we start to walk away.

The guy calls me a few choice names, but I ignore him. I'm not looking for a fight, though my blood is pumping hot and fast in my veins.

"What was that all about?" she asks, but I don't answer her. I'm too worked up, adrenaline coursing through me, anger making it hard to speak. I hated seeing how that guy touched her like he owned her. I hate worse the fact that she's questioning me like she doesn't understand why I just defended her.

When I still haven't said anything, she starts talking again. "Seriously, Josh. You're freaking me out. Why are you acting like such a Neanderthal? You totally went caveman on me back there."

"I did not," I mutter. She wants to see caveman? I could go balls out if she really wants me to. "He's the one who claimed he saw you first." A total asshole remark, too.

"He *was* kind of a jerk."

"Right." I turn to look at her, and we stop walking. "I was trying to save you."

"I know." She sighs and shakes her head. "You don't always have to run to my rescue. I could've taken care of myself."

"He was touching you, and you didn't like it," I point out.

Her brows go up. "How do you know?"

"I could tell just by the look on your face. I know you pretty well, Eden," I remind her.

She looks away, toward the fire pit, a wistful expression on her face. "I'm failing miserably at this college party thing."

"Why do you say that?"

"Instead of flirting with a cute college guy like I should be, I'm standing here talking to you."

I shove my hands in my pockets. That almost felt like an insult, though I don't think she meant it that way. "Right back at you. I should be talking to some hot sorority sister, and instead I'm rescuing you."

Eden turns so our gazes meet. "Where's Molly?"

"Talking to some jackass." I'm thankful for the change of subject. I don't want to fight with her. "Big burly dude with a thick gold chain around his neck."

She barely contains her smile. "And Abraham?"

"Upstairs with the first girl he ever had sex with." Eden's eyes practically bug out of her head, so I explain myself further. "Her name is Nicole, she's a freshman here, and he seemed pretty excited to reunite with her."

"Oh. Well. I guess that's a good thing." She breathes out a sigh of relief. "Maybe that means he'll leave me alone for a while."

"If you're lucky," I tease her. The relief that floods me at her words is surprising. I didn't want her liking Abraham. I've never cared about her boyfriends in the past, so why am I suddenly worried she might end up with my other best friend?

"Whatever," she says with a sigh. We start walking again toward the opposite end of the backyard, until we come across a giant lounge chair that could fit two people easily. "Want to sit with me?" she asks.

"What about Abraham and Molly?"

"They'll be occupied for a while, don't you think?" She sinks onto the lounger, tugging her dress down so it covers most of her thighs. "I'll text Molly and let her know where we are. And check in on her."

"She was in the kitchen a few minutes ago."

"She's probably still there." I settle on the lounger beside her, trying to ignore that she's so close and I can smell her familiar floral scent. Our shoulders brush, and when I move my leg, I kick her ankle. "Sorry."

"Remember when you were shorter?" she asks with a mischievous smile.

"I was never shorter than you, though."

Eden pushes my shoulder. "The beginning of eighth grade you were kind of short."

"I wasn't by the end of eighth grade."

"True." She tilts her head back to stare up at the sky. "Lots of stars out."

I tip my head back to study the sky, too. "Yeah. It's a beautiful night."

"A little cold."

"You cold?" I hold my arm out so she can snuggle in. We've done this before in the most platonic way possible, so the gesture means nothing.

Nothing.

Our gazes meet, and I can see the hesitation in her eyes. Why is she hesitating? What did I do to suddenly alter our relationship? Nothing, that's what.

So why is she being so weird?

Eden gives in and slides toward me, resting her head on my chest. I let my arm drop around her shoulders and squeeze her close, trying to get her warmer, that's all. Definitely not trying to cop a feel.

Or so I tell myself.

All the girls I've ever dated have been tall. I'm attracted to tall, sporty blond girls; I always have been. That's why Taylyr Howard would be my perfect pick. Yeah, she's a little intense, but so am I sometimes. She goes after what she wants, and I tend to do that all the time.

Eden's short, five-foot-two, tops. She barely reaches the middle of my chest when she stands next to me. She was in dance for years and was a cheerleader our freshman and sophomore years, but she doesn't really have what I consider a lean, athletic body. Not like the girls I've been attracted to in the past.

In fact, Eden's the total opposite of who I'm usually attracted to.

So why am I having all of these weird feelings about her now?

• • •

EDEN

Josh and I are literally cuddling together on this giant lounger. Sure, we've done stuff like this before over the years. Most of the time it only lasts for a few minutes before we break apart. It's this sort of behavior that makes people question if we're a couple, and we always protest that we're not. We don't feel that way about each other, is what we say. We're just really good friends. That's it.

But everything feels so different. Maybe it's the idea of him so hot to find a girl to have sex with. Why not me? Why hasn't he tried to collect on that pact we made when we were fourteen and dumb ? Weren't we supposed to make it happen by senior year if we were still virgins? So what's the problem? Is there something wrong with me? Maybe I don't measure up. Maybe I've never measured up in Josh's eyes.

I'm just friend material. That's how he sees me. And that's how I've seen him until…what? I'm not even sure what changed. It's probably all the talk of him looking to have sex with someone else. I never imagined having sex with Josh before. Not really.

Well, maybe. Just out of curiosity. Because he's cute. He's more than cute. And he's sweet and funny and he frustrates me and makes me laugh and challenges me and makes me think and yeah.

Oh God, maybe I *like him* like him.

What am I supposed to do about that?

All I know is at this very moment, I don't want to let go of him. I want to lay like this forever, Josh's strong, muscular arms wrapped around me, my head on his chest so I can hear his heartbeat, our bodies pressed close…

"So you're going out with Taylyr tomorrow," I say to break the tension and remind myself that my thoughts are made of crazy.

Let's be real. Josh and I getting together would ruin everything. A few days ago I would've made a gagging noise at the thought of even *kissing* Josh.

Yet look at me now.

"Yeah. For lunch." He shifts and presses his body even closer to mine. "Hope it goes well."

"I'm sure it will." Why wouldn't it? Those two are practically made for each other. Taylyr is his type. He'd be blind not to see it.

"You have plans after lunch with her, too?"

"I wanted to see how it went first."

"Smart." I'm silent for a moment and wish I could play with the button placket on his shirt. But that would be taking it way too far. "Have you talked to Whitney or Marin?"

"Marin hasn't even opened the snap I sent her this morning, so I'm thinking that might be a no-go. Whitney and I have been talking, but I think she's talking to a lot of guys."

"Whit's always been a big flirt."

"Yeah, I can tell."

We go silent for a while again, and I can hear people talking and laughing in the near distance. My phone buzzes in my hand, and I check to find it's Molly sending me a text letting me know she's okay.

"So, Eden," he says when I'm done checking my phone.

"So, Josh."

"I've been thinking. I'm going to ask you an important question, and I want you to be honest."

My heart starts to race. "Okay."

"Have you had sex yet?" He only allows me about ten seconds to answer before he starts talking again. "I know you said maybe and I didn't really believe you, but then I started thinking about it, and maybe you and Cole did actually do the deed. Or maybe you hooked up with someone else, I don't know. I always tell you everything about my love life and most of the time, you don't tell me shit."

"I tell you stuff all the time," I say, feeling defensive. And I'm also trying to change the subject.

"Not really. I mean, I knew you and Cole were dating for a long time, but you never gave me any dirty details."

"I'm not as open as you are about the dirty details," I tell him, sounding like a puritan.

"So. Have you done it?"

I sigh and stare up at the sky, my stomach twisting into knots. "No."

His entire body goes tense. "Really?"

"Really."

"Not even with Cole."

"Nope."

"And not even with some fake rando dude."

"Oh. Well, yes, I have had fake sex with a fake rando dude, but that's…fake." I start to laugh, and Josh joins in.

"You and Cole messed around though, right?" he asks once the laughter dies down.

"Yeah." I swallow hard. How much do I want to admit to him? Not much, even though he's never had any problem telling me what he's done, right down to the very last detail.

"Like…what have you done?"

I rise up on my elbow, digging it right into his chest and making him wince. "Joshua. Why do you want to know all the details about my mostly nonexistent sex life?"

"I don't know. I'm curious. I'm like an open book with you, and you're pretty tight-lipped."

"Some things are personal," I say primly.

His gaze meets mine, his blue eyes so serious. "You don't

think I can keep a secret? Is that it?"

I know he can. I've told him lots of secretive stuff over the years, and he's never blabbed once. More like, it's totally awkward to talk about sex stuff with Josh. He's a boy, I'm a girl, and it always felt weird. Though he never seemed to have that problem.

Without a word I resume my position with my head on his chest. He tightens his arm around my shoulders, holding me closer. "Are you warm enough?" he asks in a low, sexy murmur.

Ugh, I need to put all thoughts of low, sexy murmurs out of my head.

"Definitely," I tell him. Josh has always run hotter than me, but right now I feel like I'm burning up.

"Considering you're not gonna spill about your sexual experiences, I'm going to change the subject," Josh says. Oh, thank God. "Have you ever watched porn?"

My cheeks go hot, and I'm not even looking at him. What a way to change the subject. "Well, yeah." Who hasn't? It's so readily available on the web.

"Anything good you can recommend?"

I slap his chest. "Stop."

He's laughing, the jerk. "What did you think of it? The porn you watched?"

This conversation is insane. "It wasn't that good."

"Why not?"

"I don't know. It felt really fake. The girl had huge breast implants, and her hair was bleached white, and there was all of this makeup on her face. The guy was older, and he wasn't even that good looking. There was nothing real about it. Lots of phony moans and groans, and everything was super exaggerated and over the top."

"So you prefer romantic porn," Josh teases.

"Seriously, you're the worst." I hit his chest again, and

he flinches a little. "There's no way real sex can be like that."

"What do you think it's like then? I mean, I have my suspicions, but what are yours?"

I'm not even sure why we're talking about this. But since we don't have to face each other, it *is* easier to say what I want and not feel too embarrassed. "Basing it on the other stuff I've done, I'd say it's pretty exciting."

"That's it?" He sounds incredulous. "That's all you have to say? Pretty exciting?"

"You want me to say it'll be magical and that one special moment will transcend all space and time?" Now it's my turn to laugh. "I'm just trying to be real here."

He's quiet for a moment, like he's absorbing my words. "So be real," he finally says. "Tell me how you *really* feel about sex. What it's going to be like. How you think it'll make you feel."

We've had deep conversations like this before. I can always count on Josh to push me. And I can trust that he'll keep my thoughts between us. Though it is sort of embarrassing, what we're talking about. But hey, if I can't be honest and real with my best friend, then there must be a problem. "It's probably going to be sweaty and awkward and kind of weird. For me, it might hurt, though I don't like to dwell on that part. But I know it will also be special."

"You really think so?" He sounds doubtful.

"Well, for me, I hope it will be, as corny as that sounds. I want the first time I have sex to be with the right person, you know? A guy who I really care about, and he cares about me."

"So not some quick and easy lay, like what I'm trying to make happen?" He doesn't sound angry or insulted. Just curious.

"If that works for you, then that's awesome," I say firmly, not wanting him to feel bad for his choices. I'm not trying to make him feel guilty, that's for sure. And I really don't want to bring up that lame pact we made either.

Though I am surprised he's not looking for a relationship. Josh is all about relationships—or at least, he used to be. "But I want to have sex with someone I trust. And even if the actual experience is disappointing, *we* won't be disappointed because it happened between us, you know? The metaphorical us," I quickly correct, because I don't want Josh to think I'm talking about him.

Because I'm afraid I'm starting to think…

I really am talking about him.

Chapter Eight

EDEN

"So…" I'm at work, folding a pile of bright pink sweatshirts that are hideous and will probably sell like crazy. I opened the store today by myself with Matilda coming in a little later, and I'm scheduled till three, so that's not too bad. Molly and I never really talked about last night, so she stopped by with coffee from Java Hutt and promised conversation.

"So." The mysterious smile curving Molly's lips just before she takes a sip of her mocha tells me she has something promising to say, which is a good thing because I've got nothing.

Well, that's sort of a lie. I could tell her about my conversation with Josh last night and how weird it got with all the sex stuff. But then she'd start asking me questions, and I might end up confessing my…yearning for Josh. Which isn't a real thing, but I'm toying with the possibility, and that's something I've never done before.

Like ever.

If I told her I might like Josh as more than a friend, she'd tell me I was crazy for even considering something with him. It's probably best to keep my mouth shut. Though maybe it wouldn't hurt to have my one best friend tell me I'm insane for wanting more with my other best friend…

"What happened between you and the college guy last night?" I ask, desperate to push all the Josh thoughts out of my brain. On the ride home last night, none of us talked much. It was like we were all too inside our own heads, which is kind of weird. The four of us are pretty talkative people.

"Nothing much." Molly shrugs, her gaze landing on the pile of ugly sweatshirts. "Those are awful."

"Tell me about it." I stop folding and focus all my attention on her. "Come on. Spill."

Molly rolls her eyes and starts to follow me over to the register counter. "I talked to that one guy for most of the night."

I slide behind the counter so I can face her. "And his name again?"

"Kirk." Molly giggles. "Ridiculous, right?"

"Sort of." I don't want to tell her how Josh thought he was totally rude and that the gold chain he wore was super cheesy. "But is he nice? And cute?"

"The answer is yes to both. He's very muscular. Nice bulky arms. Told me he plays baseball."

"Sporty?" I raise a brow. "That's not your usual type, Mol."

"I have no type, and you know it. I will take pretty much whatever I can get. I don't want to sound desperate but—I'm desperate." She starts laughing, and I do, too. "He did ask me for my phone number. And we added each other on Snapchat."

"Aw, see. I told you that was going to happen."

"Whatever." Molly waves a dismissive hand, but she's still

smiling. "He hinted at taking me out sometime. Let's see if he follows through."

"That would be awesome if he did. I can see it now, you forgetting all about us since you're going out with the hot college guy." I mean every word. I want Molly to find a guy she's happy with, one who's totally in to her. She's never really had a boyfriend before. Plenty of crushes that always caused a lot of confusion and Molly ended up with a broken heart.

"Don't jump ahead of yourself," Molly warns with a tiny smile.

"But what about Abraham?" I still can't believe she told me she liked him yesterday. I never even had a clue. This Thanksgiving break has been full of craziness, and it's hardly started.

"I don't know what to think about Abraham." Molly sighs and shakes her head. "He virtually ignored me last night, after he told me I was looking good or that I was sexy or whatever. Then he hooks up with that one chick, which was sort of gross. You know he had sex with her."

"I know," I agree with a mock shudder. It was very obvious Abraham had been up to no good last night, not that I'm judging. He can do whatever he wants, as long as he's not chasing after me. That just complicates things and makes it weird. "I didn't expect him to do that."

"Me, either."

"Supposedly it meant nothing, though. I heard them talking." Right, one person did end up talking a lot on the drive home last night, and that person was Abraham. He went on and on about his one-night stand. His fling. His hookup. His one and done.

When he made that last remark, Josh corrected him.

"Technically—and according to you—you and Nicole have been together twice. So she's definitely not a one and done," Josh had pointed out.

That remark sort of pissed Abraham off. Heaven forbid he's with the same girl twice. It's almost like he has sincere player aspirations.

"What about Josh?" Molly asks me, knocking me from my thoughts.

My heart starts to pound, and I remind myself to act normal. "What about him?"

"He told me he has a date with Taylyr this afternoon."

Oh. Taylyr. God, I hate even thinking about her, and not for the reasons you'd assume. My biggest problem is the way she spells her name. Who uses two y's like that? It looks wrong. I'm being totally petty, right? But I can't help myself. She spells her name in the dumbest way possible.

"They're meeting for lunch." I try to sound nonchalant.

Molly raises her brows. "Lunch? How grown up of them."

"We're off school, it's the perfect time to go to lunch, right? Doesn't scream too serious, yet it's still officially a date," I explain.

"Oh, I get it. The thing is I didn't realize those two were interested in each other."

"You didn't?" Oh, yeah. Molly doesn't know Josh's plan. I'm not allowed to tell her, either, which is slowly killing me. "They make sense as a couple, don't you think?"

"I guess. They're both athletic. Both driven. She's his usual type."

Uh huh. And I'm not his type. Not even close. Though I guess you could say he's not my type, either, because he's not. Not really.

"Do you like her?" Molly asks me.

"She's okay," I answer.

"Really."

Uh-oh. "Why do you say 'really' like that?"

"Like what?" Molly's face is pure innocence.

"Like that." I point at her. "Come on. Out with it."

Molly sighs, sagging against the counter. "I don't like her."

"Why not?" I'm surprised. Molly usually likes everyone. Of the two of us, she's the nice one. I'm the mean one. Not that I'm mean, but compared to sweet Molly, I'm a horrible, hateful person.

"She's always been bitchy toward me. Like blatantly rude, when I haven't done anything to her."

"Really? She's always been okay toward me."

"I had chemistry with her last year, and we were assigned partners. Do you remember?" When I shake my head, she continues. "That was rough. I basically carried the workload the entire year, and when our grade was kind of crap on some of the experiments, she'd flip out and ask me where *I* went wrong. But she never actually contributed anything."

Ugh. "She sounds like a terrible partner."

"More like I think she's a terrible *person*."

"Huh." I'm quiet for a moment, my mind racing. "Do you think I should warn Josh?"

"Warn Josh about what?"

"That Taylyr is a terrible person." Well, she's a terrible person when it comes to school. Maybe she's okay otherwise?

Doubtful, but I can hope.

"Oh, I don't know. He'll figure it out eventually, right?" Leave it to Molly to let Josh figure out if Taylyr's nice or not, on his own.

"Do you really think she's that bad?"

"Yeah, actually I do. She's not a nice person, Eden. She thinks she's all that because she's sporty, and fine, I'll give her that. She's a great athlete. But she's also rude and likes to talk about herself all the time. She doesn't know how to be a genuine friend."

"Wow, tell me how you really feel," I tease her, but all I get is a dirty look in return.

"I'm being serious. She's kind of—backstabby." Molly wrinkles her nose.

"Is that even a word?"

"I just made it one." Molly is glaring at me again. "She doesn't really have any friends. Don't you think that's a sign?"

I go quiet again, thinking about Taylyr. Molly's right. She doesn't hang out with a big group of friends. Or even a small group. I always figured she was a one-on-one type of girl, but maybe it wasn't that at all. Maybe she really is backstabby and a bad friend.

"She likes hanging out with guys, but I never see her with girls. That's a bad sign, too," Molly adds.

"Are you slut shaming her, Mol?" I'm totally teasing her, but then again I'm not.

"Of course I'm not. I'm saying that girls don't want to be around her because she's mean. And she is. She's super mean and rude and arrogant. I had to deal with her all last year in chemistry, and I was miserable."

"Why didn't you ever tell me this?"

"I sort of did. I just never wanted to name names." Molly shrugs when I send her a look. "What? It's true."

"I even forgot she was your chemistry partner."

"Listen, she wasn't worth complaining about, that's why I kept my mouth shut. Why waste time thinking about her when she's such a bitch?" Molly takes another drink of her coffee. "Josh can figure this out on his own. Either he sees her for what she truly is, or he bails as fast as he can. If he's smart, he'll bail before he gets in too deep."

Gets in too deep. Fitting words for what Josh wants to potentially do with Taylyr. Ew, but seriously.

"She could be nicer to guys," I point out.

"True. But still. Why would he want to be with someone who has such an evil soul?"

I laugh at Molly's serious tone, but she does have a point.

Josh doesn't want to be with someone who has an evil soul. I should warn him. But not right now, before he goes on his date. I don't want to seem like I'm jealous. I'm the one who pushed him to go for Taylyr, and now here he is going for her, and I'm backtracking.

That's not cool.

"You'll have to tell me how their date goes," Molly says as she walks over to the trash can and pitches her empty cup inside. "I'm sure he'll FaceTime you tonight, eager to tell you all about it."

"Yeah, he probably will."

"Don't you ever get tired of hearing all about his many dates with many girls?" This isn't the first time Molly has asked me this question.

"I hate it when he goes into graphic detail, but for the most part, no. I don't mind if he tells me things." At least he's still willing to tell me what's going on, instead of cutting me out. I take that as a good sign.

"I don't think I could take it. I overhear some of his conversations with you, and sometimes they make me want to freak out."

After she leaves, I think about what Molly said. Are Josh and I *too* familiar with each other? Have we crossed so far into the friend zone that now there's no turning back? If that's the case, then there's probably no hope for us. He would only see me as a friend and that's it.

Wait a minute. Why the sudden change of heart on my end? Do I really look at him as more than a friend?

No. Only lately, what with all this sex talk and finding Josh a girl. Of course, that's going to change my perspective.

Honestly? That's the way I need to focus on him. He's just a friend, and nothing else. So what if Josh is incredibly good looking and smart and attentive and fun? Just because he's a great friend, that doesn't mean he will be a terrific boyfriend.

I need to remember this.

But I can't help but think about him for the rest of my shift. It's continuously busy all morning and into the early afternoon, yet any free moment I have, my mind goes straight to Josh. Wondering about his date, wondering if he liked her, wondering if they went anywhere else. Has he already kissed her? Like, with tongue and wandering hands and bodies pressed close? God, what would it be like if they had sex and he ends up telling me *all* about it? Like every stupid, awful detail?

I could just tell him to shut up. Yeah, that would be smart. But it's like I can never tell Josh no, which is ridiculous.

This entire situation is ridiculous.

My thoughts are torturous and I regret agreeing to help him lose his virginity.

Yeah. I'm regretting it big time.

• • •

JOSH

Taylyr texted me earlier saying I couldn't come pick her up after all, but that she'd meet me at the restaurant instead. So I amble up to the front of the Coast Café just after noon to find Taylyr already waiting for me. She's leaning against the side of the building, concentrating on her phone, and when I say her name, she nearly jumps a mile.

"You scared me!" She rests a hand on her chest, looking sort of…pissed? Her eyes are narrowed, and her lips are tight. "Don't *ever* do that again."

"Okay…" I say slowly, hating the doubt that's already creeping in. So I force it out and concentrate on having a good time. "I hope I didn't keep you waiting."

"You didn't. Well, not for too long." She shoves her phone into the pocket of her black Adidas track pants. "I'm always early."

That's a good habit. Can't hold it against her.

She continues, "It's like…I never want someone to beat me, know what I mean?"

Huh. That's…

Weird.

"Let's go inside," I tell her, and she falls into step beside me, the both of us entering the busy restaurant. It's one of those places where you order at the counter, go find a table, and someone brings your food to you. It's a popular café that's been around for years, like way before I was born, and they have really great seafood.

"What are you going to get?" I ask as we wait in line and study the menu on the wall above the registers.

"I don't know. I don't really like seafood."

Well, shit. "Are you serious?" When she turns to look at me, I forge on. "I would've chosen somewhere else to go if I knew you didn't like seafood."

"It's okay. We're surrounded by it living here, you know?" She shrugs and resumes looking at the menu board. "I think I'm gonna have a grilled cheese. But with no fries."

"Why no fries?"

Taylyr wrinkles her nose. "Too fattening. I'm trying to watch my weight."

I surreptitiously check her out. She's tall with broad shoulders, yet lean, though I can't tell too much since she's wearing a light gray Nike sweatshirt. I'm pretty sure I own the same exact one. It looks good on her. "Watch your weight?"

"Yeah." She shrugs. "I work out all the time, and I try to watch what I eat, too. Though a grilled cheese probably isn't the best option."

There aren't many other options on the menu if she's watching her weight. Even the salads are loaded with some sort of seafood. Lobster salad. Shrimp Louie salad. Crab salad. "You can order a salad and say hold the lobster or whatever."

"Yeah. Maybe. Though I think I just want a grilled cheese."

That's the end of our conversation. She pulls her phone back out and starts scrolling again, and I wait anxiously for the woman behind the counter to finish up with the family ahead of us so she can take our order. Once they're done, I order a grilled cheese and a water for Taylyr and clam chowder in a bread bowl with seafood topping for me, plus an extra large Coke.

Screw it. I never bother watching what I eat.

We find a small table way in the back and make small talk. Chatting about sports and how she's currently playing basketball, just like me. She bitches about her coach and her teammates, and I try my best to keep an interested look on my face, but she's starting to lose me.

It's not that I don't like talking about sports, because I live for that. Seriously, it's one of my favorite subjects. But it's the *way* Taylyr's talking, like everything she's saying is a complaint. There's nothing I like better than complaining sometimes. I'm not a saint.

But this girl is just…nonstop bitching. And it's not cool.

Once our lunch arrives, she smiles dutifully at the girl who's brought our food, murmuring a thank-you as she sets the plate in front of Taylyr. Once the employee is gone, though, Taylyr is studying her sandwich like a bug just crawled out from between the bread and crapped on top of it.

"What's wrong?" I ask before I dive into my clam chowder. I'm starving, and it smells incredible.

"It looks sort of burnt, don't you think?" Taylyr points at her sandwich.

"Looks like an even golden-brown to me," I say, then take another bite. I seriously don't want to sit around and criticize her sandwich. Talk about lame.

"Huh." She picks it up and starts eating despite her complaints. "You want to come over to my house after lunch?"

I'm so surprised by her question I almost drop my spoon on the ground. Is she for real? "Uh, I can't. I have practice." Which is true. I just have it a little less than three hours from now.

The disappointment on her face is obvious. "I was hoping I could show you my thirty-person spa."

"You have a thirty-person spa?" Why would she have such a huge spa? For like...orgies or whatever?

I can't believe my mind just went there. Though then again, I sort of can believe it. Sex is all I've been thinking about lately.

Well, and Eden. I bet she wouldn't complain about a sandwich. She'd probably make me split it with her so we could both suffer and end up laughing about it.

"Yeah." She nods, her eyes lighting up. "My parents got it a couple of years ago, when they remodeled the backyard. My dad is a doctor."

"Nice." I knew this little fact, about her dad being a doctor. "So you're rich."

"Not really." A giggle escapes her. "Okay fine, we totally are."

This chick is something else.

"Must be nice," I tell her because I have no idea what else to say.

"It's pretty great actually." She takes a sip of her water. "Are you sure you don't want to come over and hang out in the spa?"

"Wish I could," I say with a dramatic sigh. "But like I said, I have practice."

"Not until three."

Wait, what is she, a stalker? "Yeah, after we have lunch, I need to run a few errands. For, uh, my mom." All lies, but what do I say? No, I don't want to check out your thirty-person spa because you drive me nuts? That's not cool.

"Oooh, like what sort of errands?" She seems truly interested, which is weird. Just two seconds ago she didn't want to let me talk, and now she wants to know about my fake errands?

"Um, I gotta pick up a few things for her at the store."

"Awesome! Maybe I can come?" Her expression is full-on hopeful.

Shit. Like, double shit. I can't say no. How can I get out of this?

"Yeah, sure," I agree, my voice weak.

"Yay!" She claps her hands like a little kid and eagerly leans across the table. "I've had my eye on you for a long time, Josh Evans. I'm so excited we're actually going to make this happen."

Make what happen? I asked her to lunch. That's it. Yet she acts like we're going to actually get together and become a couple or whatever.

Freaking Eden thinking that Taylyr and I together is a good idea. More like the worst idea ever. It's all her fault I'm with Taylyr on this stupid date.

Can't wait to tell her all about it later.

Chapter Nine

EDEN

The FaceTime call comes around eight-thirty, and I let it ring a couple of times before picking it up. Josh's face appears in the tiny screen, and he's scowling, his hair tousled and damp, and I would bet big money he just got out of the shower.

That makes me think of Josh. In the shower. Naked. With hot water spraying all over his body and…yeah. I absolutely cannot go there.

"Joshy," I say in the baby voice that annoys him. "What are you up to?"

His scowl deepens, and he runs his fingers through his hair, tousling it worse. He just got that stuff cut but maybe not short enough after all. "Reminiscing about my date today with Taylyr."

My heart sinks into my toes, and my entire body goes shaky. "Oh really? So it was that good?" *But she has an evil soul!* I want to yell that so bad.

Of course, I don't.

He remains quiet for a while, making me want to lose my mind before he finally speaks again. "It was that *bad,* Edes. Like super awful, spectacularly bad."

My heart now feels like it wants to leap out of my chest in pure, radiant joy. I shouldn't be so happy his date was a total failure. I shouldn't.

But I am. Does that make me a bad person?

Probably.

"That's too bad," I say in the most sympathetic voice I can muster. "What happened?"

"She complains too much. About everything. And then she sort of invited herself to go with me while I ran bogus errands."

I frown. "Bogus errands?"

"Yeah, I told her I couldn't come over to her house to check out her thirty-person spa because I had practice. But she called me out on it because she actually knew what time I had practice, which is weird, Edes. You gotta admit that's pretty weird."

"She has a thirty-person spa?" That's a lot of people in a Jacuzzi or whatever. Seriously, *thirty?*

Josh makes an irritated noise. "That's not the point."

"Okay, sorry. Carry on."

He sighs. "So I tell her I have errands to run. For my mom."

I start to laugh. "Your mom would never trust you to run errands for her. You'd screw it up, bring her the wrong thing."

"I lied to her, Edes. I was trying to get out of spending more time with her, okay? So she asked if she could go with me, and I had no choice but to say yes. Then we drove around and I took her to Target and the grocery store." He starts to laugh, that dirty laugh of his that always makes me laugh, too.

"What's so funny?" I ask him when my laughter dies off.

"I bought some crazy shit. I was trying to scare her and

make her think Mom and I are a bunch of freaks."

"What did you buy?"

"The biggest bottle of Pepto Bismol I could find. I told her my mom and I had serious bowel issues." He starts laughing again, sounding downright hysterical, and I can't help but laugh, too.

"Joshua." I'm trying to chastise him, but it's too funny. "You really said that?"

"Yeah. I bought a pack of Depends, too, and when she asked me if they were for my mom, I just gave her a look."

"What kind of look?"

"One that could mean they're for my mom or for...me." More laughing. He finds himself extra amusing tonight.

"What if she spreads rumors around school that you wear Depends?" I would be mortified if that happened to me.

"Who cares? Like anyone would believe her."

I envy his confidence. "What else did you do?"

"Picked up prunes and fiber bars at the grocery store." He nods, looking pleased with himself. "For our bowel problems."

"What's so scary is you seem to know what can help your supposed bowel problems," I point out, not that he cares.

"Yeah, Mom says I have to eat the prunes."

Gross. "Is she mad at you?"

"Not really. I told her the story, how annoying Taylyr was on our date." He sighs and shakes his head. "I don't think I want to go out with her again. No red rose for her."

I'm frowning. "What do you mean?"

"It's a *Bachelor* reference. Get it?" He shakes his head. "Never mind."

"No, I get it, I get it." Josh knows way too much about *The Bachelor*. "So she wasn't a good match for you." I decide not to tell him about Taylyr's evil soul and Molly's hatred for her. There's no need to bring it up now.

"Yeah, you picked wrong." He smiles, and I know he's teasing me. "Though really she should've been the perfect match for me, don't you think?"

"I did think, but maybe that's where I made my mistake. Taylyr's like all the other girls you've gone out with."

"Yeah, she is. Though she complains way too much. And she's a little more—intense."

"Too intense?" When he's quiet, I fill the silence. "You did mention that before."

"Yeah. She's not chill. Like, not at all." He's quiet once more, and I'm about to open my mouth when he starts talking again. "Not like you, Eden. You're totally chill."

I don't know what to say. A week ago this would've been no big deal. I would've laughed and agreed with him. Now it's just—confusing. His simple compliment is making me flushed and awkward and unsure. Like…what does he mean by that? Is there something more behind his words? Is he comparing me to Taylyr and letting me know he thinks I'm—better?

No. That can't be possible.

"Maybe that's just because we've known each other for so long," he continues. He gets up from wherever he was sitting, and I can tell he's moving about his bedroom, doing whatever it is he does when we FaceTime like this. We'll talk for hours sometimes, either totally focused on each other the entire chat or we'll walk around, hang up on each other, make fun of each other, whatever.

"Yeah. Probably." I sound sad, so I clear my throat and force myself to be happy. "I've known you a long time, Evans."

"Right back at ya, Sumner." He reappears in the little square, and he has a baseball cap on, and he's wearing it backwards.

My secret weakness. Boys are so cute when they wear a baseball hat backwards.

"I scored a new hat." He flips it around so I can see the

front. It's black with the orange San Francisco Giants logo on it. "On clearance at Target."

"I like it."

He flips it backward once again. "Yeah, Taylyr said I looked dope in it."

Ugh. Taylyr. "Did she really say dope?"

"No, I did." He laughs, and it's not quite as dirty sounding as usual. "She said I looked good."

I'm sure she did. "She likes you, huh."

"Yeah. She's pursuing me pretty heavily."

"But you're not interested? Really?"

"No, not really. Not at all. Like I told you, she complains too much. It's annoying. And she's persistent. Like, she doesn't take no for an answer."

"Neither do you," I point out.

"And maybe that's the problem. Maybe we're too much alike, and she's getting on my nerves because she reminds me of—me." He mock shudders. "Yeah, I don't want to do myself."

"Oh my God, Josh." I start laughing.

"What? I'm serious. I don't want a girl who's just like me. Opposites attract, right? Though I do want some common ground, I don't want her to be my duplicate in female form."

"This conversation is veering way off track."

"Like usual," he retorts. I study him sitting there with the hat on backward. He's chewing on a straw, and I zero in on his lips. They're full—like women pay good money to have their lips injected to look like Josh's. And of course, completely kissable. Why haven't I ever noticed this before?

You have noticed this before. You just always push those thoughts out of your brain because they're wrong. Wrong, wrong, wrong.

"I think I'm gonna go for Whitney," Josh suddenly says, startling me from my Josh-has-kissable-lips thoughts.

"Whitney?" I ask weakly.

"Yeah. She's hot. Flirty. I bet she'd be down."

"Down for what?" I'm still focused on his lips. His upper lip is very full. Almost pouty. He's chewing on the end of that straw, and it's kind of...

Hot?

"Down for...you know, Edes." He leans forward until it's just his sexy lips filling the screen. "S-e-x. As in g-e-t-t-i-n-g l-a-i-d. Or you know, f-u-c—"

"Eden." My bedroom door slams open, and in strides my mother, acting like she doesn't have a care in the world. I shriek when she enters, worried she might've heard Josh starting to spell that last word, but she's either completely oblivious or a great pretender. "I'm going to the grocery store, and I need your help."

"Hey, Mrs. S," Josh calls from my phone.

Mom walks over to my desk and leans into the screen, smiling. "Hello, Josh. What are you up to?"

"Talking to Edes. Telling her about my crap date I had today."

Mom frowns and sends me a look. "Crap date with who?"

"Some girl. She doesn't matter," Josh tells her.

"Mom, I hate to interrupt your conversation with my best friend, but why do you want me to go to the store with you?" I ask.

"It's going to be busy since it's almost Thanksgiving, so I need you to keep me on track." Mom works from home. She's a graphic designer and super creative, and most of the time she gets so involved in her work, she sits for hours hunched over her computer. She's a bit of a daydreamer and always lost in thought, so she's probably being 100 percent truthful when she says she needs me to keep her on track.

She's pretty forgetful a lot of the time.

"Did you make a list?"

"Sort of." Mom frowns. "Help me with the list before we leave."

"It's so late, Mom." I'm whining, but the last thing I want to do is go to the store.

"Better we go now than tomorrow. The day before Thanksgiving is always a nightmare."

"If I was there I'd take you to the store, Mrs. Sumner," Josh says.

"Suck up," I tell him, making him smile.

"I'm sure you would, Josh," Mom says. "Hey, what are you doing for Thanksgiving? Are your brother and sister coming home?"

"No, not this year. We're supposed to go over to my mom's boyfriend's place." Josh makes me a face. He's not a huge fan of his mom's boyfriend. "I don't want to go."

"Oh, you should come to our house for Thanksgiving dinner," Mom suggests. "We'll have a lot of family over so it'll be complete chaos, but you're more than welcome to join us if your mother doesn't mind."

Noooo. No, no, no. I don't want Josh here. We'd hang out together the entire time. I'd have to fend off endless questions from various family members asking if Josh and I are a thing. Listen to him laugh and say, *no way would I ever date Eden. She's my best friend.*

Before, this would be no big deal. Now, I don't know if I could take it.

And that's weird, right? It's totally weird. I need to get over this newfound Josh crush. I'm just thinking about him like this because we're always talking about sex. And this makes me think of having sex with Josh. Like, he's going to ask me to participate in the pact we made, and I'm probably going to enjoy myself because hello, I'd bet he'd be a great kisser and he has nice, big hands and …

"Yeah, I'd love to." Josh sounds sincerely thrilled at the

offer. "Thanks, Mrs. Sumner. I'll talk to my mom."

Oh my God, I really need to control my thoughts. Like big-time control them. I swear I feel faint.

But I stare at his face on the phone and I realize, I don't want him to hook up with someone else. I want him for myself.

"Tell her to call me if she has any questions. And I don't want her offended or think we're stealing you away," Mom says, knocking me from my thoughts.

"She won't think that. My mom loves Eden," Josh says, his voice deep, making me shiver at his choice of words. *Ugh.*

What the heck is wrong with me?

I think I have Josh fever.

"You never know." Mom turns to look at me. "You ready, Eden?"

"Gotta go, Josh. Talk to you later." I end the call before he can say another word. I'm torturing myself right now, I swear.

"Eden Marie Sumner, that was very rude," Mom says. "You hung up on him."

I shrug and grab my hoodie, tugging it over my head, desperate to change the subject and leave this house. "We hang up on each other all the time."

"You don't mind that I invited Josh over for Thanksgiving, do you?"

"No, of course not."

"Who's the girl he was dating?"

I slip on an old pair of Uggs. I'm all class going to the market tonight, looking like I just rolled out of bed. "They weren't really dating. More like just one date. He didn't like her. Said she complained too much." I am way too relieved that he doesn't like Taylyr.

"What's her name?"

"Taylyr Howard." I hesitate and decide to go for it. "With

two y's."

Mom frowns. "Two y's? That's ridiculous."

And this is why my mother is so cool. She gets me. "Tell me all about it."

• • •

JOSH

"Thanks for letting me come over so late," Abraham tells my mom as he enters my house. It's past ten, and Abraham called me on the landline—a rarity—asking if he could stop by for a little bit.

"Are you okay, Abraham?" Mom asks, sending me a concerned look.

"Yeah, I'm fine. Just—anxious." His hand is in his hoodie front pocket, and he's jingling his keys. It's the most obnoxious sound in the world.

"Let's go to my room," I tell him, pausing by the kitchen. "You want anything to drink? Or eat?"

"Nah." He follows me into my room, and the moment I close the door, he's collapsing on my bed, staring up at the ceiling. "I messed up."

"What do you mean?"

"With Nicole. I kept texting her, like ten times, asking what she's doing and she never answered me. Not once. I don't know how to play it cool with girls I have sex with." He turns his head, his gaze meeting mine. "I'm a total failure."

I withhold the sigh that wants to escape me. He's being pretty dramatic. "You're not a failure," I reassure him as I lean against the edge of my dresser. "But I can't lie. Now you might seem...desperate."

"Great." He covers his face with his hands and moans. "I'm a desperate failure."

Guess there's no talking to him tonight. "You're not.

Just…relax. Focus on something else."

"I can't think about anything else. All I can think about is her and what happened between us last night."

"What exactly happened?"

Abraham drops his hands from his face. "What do you think? We did it. Twice."

"Twice?" Seriously? He must finish quick.

"Well, she gave me a BJ and then we had sex. And uh, it um—happened. Twice."

I get what he's saying. "Gotcha."

"And it was amazing. That girl rocked my world."

"Uh huh." I hesitate. Wait a minute. "What about Eden?"

Abraham frowns. "What about her?"

"I thought you said you liked her?"

"Oh, I was full of crap. Trying to get you jealous so you'd go for Eden instead." Abraham covers his face once more. "Damn it, I wanna talk to Nicole. Just for a few minutes at least," he complains, his voice muffled.

My head is buzzing. Like full-blown buzzing as if it's filled with a million angry bees. "What did you just say?"

Abraham drops his hands yet again and sits up. "That I want to talk to Nicole again?"

"No, the other part," I say through clenched teeth. Is he for real?

"That I faked liking Eden so I would make you jealous and push you to go for her? Yeah, that's all true." Abraham shrugs. "Didn't work. You still went out with Taylyr."

"Yeah and that date was a disaster. I have no interest in seeing her again." I'm trying to wrap my head around the fact that Abraham *faked* liking Eden to push me into making a move on her. Is he for real?

Apparently.

"That bad, huh? She's too much like you." Wish I would've had Abraham around earlier to tell me that. "Plus, she can be bitchy sometimes. You need to forget any other girl and pursue Eden."

"Are you serious right now? I can't 'pursue' her." I even added air quotes with my fingers like a complete jackass.

"Why the hell not? She's everything I said she was. Gorgeous, funny, fun. You two are totally into each other."

"We're best friends."

"Best friends who can make out and do the nasty yet still be best friends. That's the best kind." Abraham shakes his head. "Why wouldn't you want to hit that? You already know you're compatible. Despite you claiming you want a quick hookup, you like having commitment strings. You told me that yourself. You say you want a girlfriend, but dude. You pretty much already have one. Her name is Eden."

I collapse on the bed beside him and stretch out, my head hitting the pillow. I stare up at the ceiling fan, the words Abraham just said running through my brain on an endless loop.

You say you want a girlfriend, but dude. You pretty much already have one. Her name is Eden.

Is that for real? Like, for real for real? Does Eden think of me in that way? Could she want to go out with me? Make out with me? "Do the nasty" with me?

Damn it, Abraham's stupid words are invading my thoughts.

"I don't want a girlfriend," I say, my voice, my words hollow. "We're going to graduate soon. Why would I want a girlfriend?"

Abraham makes a dismissive noise. "Whatever, dude. Keep telling yourself that."

He doesn't sound like he believes me. I don't really believe myself. My mind is churning, full of thoughts of…

Eden.

"You think Eden likes me?" I ask, my voice hoarse, like I

just ran a thousand miles. My heart is beating so hard it *feels* like I just ran a thousand miles.

"I don't know. Why don't you ask her?"

I sit up just as he stands. "I can't just ask her that."

"Why the hell not?"

"It would be weird."

"No, it would be a freaking relief for the both of you. I can hear you two now." He clears his throat and starts talking in a low voice. "Oh hey, Edes. Uh, I really like you. As in, I want to strip you naked and lick you everywhere. Will you let me?" He clears his throat again, and this time his voice comes out a high falsetto. "Oh, Joshua, I thought you'd never say those sweet words! Let's do it." The falsetto voice is gone, replaced by regular Abraham voice. "Then the two of you will finally kiss or whatever. Seal the deal. Live happily ever after and amen. No more torturous flirting."

His imitation isn't too far off the mark, which is annoying. "You think our flirting is torturous?" We flirt? Okay yeah, we definitely flirt, but we know it's not going anywhere so it's harmless.

But then again, maybe it's not.

"I think the two of you pretending you're not into each other is torturous. It's stupid, man. You two are made to be together. Can't you see it? Eden and Josh. Josh and Eden. Everyone at school already thinks you're a couple. Go ahead and make it happen for real." Abraham checks his phone yet again, shaking his head. "She is never gonna respond to my texts. Like ever."

"Of course she isn't. You're a desperate seventeen-year-old only after one thing, and she knows it."

"Thanks for pumping me up. Making me feel positive." Abraham is glaring now. "You're a dick."

"So are you, for trying to make me jealous over Eden." I'm not really angry with him, though, and I know Abraham isn't mad at me, either. This is just how we are sometimes.

"Nothing else was working, so I had to stoop to desperate actions. You should be thanking my ass for helping you realize your real feelings." Abraham actually sounds offended.

"Thanking you? Forget that." I shake my head. "I can't think of Eden that way. Like in a—girlfriend way." I'm lying. I'm so lying. I can think of her that way, I just choose not to.

She doesn't think of me like that, either. We've always said we're just friends. She's into guys like Cole. And while I like my friend, I think he's bad boyfriend material. When they split up, Eden was devastated. I think she still is devastated. She never talked to me about their breakup, and I didn't want to ask questions.

Maybe I didn't want to know how he broke her heart.

"Why not?"

"It'll ruin everything."

"Like what?"

"Abraham, if we ever break up—and we might because no matter how hard I try, my relationships end—our friendship is over. Done. I will lose her forever. I can't…" My voice trails off, and now I'm the one clearing my throat. "I can't risk it. I like having her in my life. We talk every single day. Sometimes for hours. I need her to be there for me, and I like being there for her. Turning our friendship into something more will just lead to our downfall."

"You might not break up," Abraham starts to point out, but I cut him off with just a look.

"And then again, we might. It's only November. Things can change in a few months, a few weeks. Hell, a few days." I flop backward on the bed again and stare up at the ceiling. "I'd rather keep her in my life as a friend than risk going out with her. It's the right thing to do."

Losing her would hurt too damn much. I need to keep her as a friend and keep my so-called relationships string-free. No more commitments. Hookups are the way to go.

"Whatever, man. Your loss." Abraham shakes his head. "When she comes to school one day telling us about that hot guy she met who's gonna take good care of her, you're going to regret it. So fucking hard."

I'm about to protest when Abraham's phone buzzes, and he checks who the notification is from. "Holy crap, it's her." He's reading the text or whatever. "She wants to meet me."

Look at that. Abraham's getting lucky tonight after all. "You going to go meet her, then?"

"You think I should?" His fingers are already flying, so I assume he's made up his mind.

"It can't hurt."

"Cool. Done." He sends the text and grins at me. "I'm out of here, man. Thanks for helping me in my time of need."

I walk him to the front door, my mind still spinning with thoughts of Eden. "Tell me the truth. You really were faking it about liking Eden?"

He stops just before he's about to open the door and turns to face me. "Yeah, I was. She's cool as hell, she's beautiful, she's smart, but she's not for me—she's for you. I've always thought the two of you belonged together."

"Really?" His words are officially blowing my mind.

Abraham nods. "Really. I find it hard to believe you never thought of her like that."

"Well, I have. I can't lie. I just always figured that would be a mistake."

"I think the biggest mistake is you not even giving it a try." He grabs my shoulders and gives me a little shake. "Talk to her. See what she says. See how she feels. And if she's not into you, then at least you tried, right?"

But what if she rejects me and our friendship is ruined? I can't let that happen. I just…

I can't.

Chapter Ten

JOSH

"Hey, you finally made it." Eden smiles and opens the front door wider. "I was starting to get worried."

Guilt swamps me and I try to ignore it, but it's difficult. I don't like disappointing or worrying Eden. "Sorry I'm late." I walk inside her house and glance around while she closes the door. There is a bunch of unfamiliar people sitting in the living room watching the football game on the giant flat screen, all of them talking and shouting over each other. The house seems extra warm and smells like turkey and spice and pumpkin. I hear the clank of dishes, Eden's brother Travis singing some song off key, and their mother telling him to *please* stop singing.

It's another happy Thanksgiving at the Sumner house.

"Where have you been?" Eden asks after she shuts the door. I let my gaze roam over her, taking in what she's wearing. She looks good in tight jeans and an oversize black sweater, the neck slipping off one shoulder and revealing a bright pink lacy bra strap. Her dark hair hangs long and straight, and she flips it over her shoulder as she studies me, her delicate brows scrunched in concern.

"After my mom and her boyfriend left this morning for his parents' house, I, uh, I fell back asleep," I explain.

Her mouth drops open. "You slept most of the day then?"

"Yeah. Sorta." I shrug. That's a lie. I did end up taking a nap after noon and slept too long, so yeah, technically that's why I'm late. But I spent most of last night and this morning Snapchatting Whitney, and I'm not sure if I should tell Eden that or not.

Because I'm also pretty sure I have Whitney halfway convinced she wants to hook up with me. Soon.

What about Eden? What Abraham said has stuck with me. Made me realize that being with Eden, like the two of us as a real couple, would be…awesome.

But what if it's not? What if she's not into me like that? What if we tried to get together and then it fell apart? I'd lose her forever. I can't stand the thought of her not being in my life.

So maybe I should just stick with her as my friend. That way I'm guaranteed never to lose her.

"Oh, well I'm glad you made it." Eden smiles and grabs my arm, leading me deeper into the living room. "Hey, everyone, you remember my friend Josh?"

I wave when they all say hi, and a bunch of them give us that knowing look. The one that says, *yeah, right you're just friends.*

"You missed dinner," she tells me as she drags me toward the kitchen. "My mom made a plate for you."

"She didn't have to do that for—"

"There you are!" Eden's mom appears in front of me, a giant smile on her face. She's wearing an apron that has fall leaves, turkeys, and pilgrims scattered all over it, and she wraps me up in her arms, giving me a big hug. "I thought you weren't going to show."

"And miss your cooking? No way." I withdraw from her embrace, smiling down at her. Mrs. Sumner is cool. She reminds me a lot of Eden. Not only do they look alike, but they also have the same laid-back personality.

"You flatter me." She smiles and waves me toward the granite counter where the bar stools are. "I saved you a plate when we worried you weren't going to make it."

The guilt is back, even heavier now with what Eden's mom said. Not that she's trying to make me feel guilty. I shouldn't have taken that nap. I should've manned up and showed up on time.

Problem is Abraham freaked me out last night. Bad. With all that talk of Eden and me belonging together and how she's essentially my girlfriend already so why don't I just make it happen. She's not my girlfriend, though. I've never even kissed her. Not a friendly kiss on the lips, the cheek, nothing that would give off a boyfriend-girlfriend vibe. We've hugged. Brief hugs that never linger. Oh, we cuddled on that lounger at the frat party a few nights ago. We've cuddled a few other times, too, but I never thought of her in *that way*.

Okay, fine. I've thought about her in that way. Like with the sex pact. And the occasional sex dream. And the weird feeling in my stomach when I used to see her in her cheer uniform. Or when she smiles at me in a certain way. But it means nothing, you know? Or it meant nothing.

Now it means…

I don't know what it means.

Yeah. I don't like Eden like that. Nope. Can't do it. I'm going to focus on Whit instead. She's down for whatever. She basically told me that last night when we were texting. Sent me a few sexy Snapchat photos that were set to about four seconds so I only caught a glimpse of bare skin and cleavage but it was enough to get me interested.

Because that's all I'm looking for. A quick lay. A girl to help me lose my virginity and that's it. At least, that's what I tell myself.

Yet here I am at my best friend's house, checking her out as she moves about the kitchen. The sweater keeps slipping off her shoulder, revealing that lacy pink bra strap, and I'm curious. What exactly does the bra look like? Since when did Eden start wearing neon pink bras? I bet she looks smokin' hot in that bra and nothing else. Like super hot.

Don't freaking go there.

Eden gets me something to drink while her mom fawns over me, making sure the food is to my liking. I sit at the kitchen counter and dig in, suddenly starving. I consume pretty much everything on that plate and ask for seconds on the mashed potatoes and gravy and another roll.

"Watch your carbs," Mrs. Sumner tells me when she hands over another warm roll.

Eden rolls her eyes. "Josh doesn't have to watch anything. He eats like a pig and never gains weight."

I pause mid-chew. "I eat like a pig?" I'm slightly offended.

"You eat everything in sight, and you know it. Yet you never gain an ounce. It's annoying." Eden smiles and pushes the butter plate closer to me. "Go ahead, you know you want some."

I don't take any of the butter on purpose and tear the roll in two, dunking one half in gravy before I shove it into my mouth, offering her a closed mouth smile with my cheeks full of bread. Eden just rolls her eyes and starts moving about the kitchen, helping her mother clean up.

"Hey, Josh, glad you finally made it. They thought you weren't gonna show up." Travis appears in front of me, a big smile on his face. He holds his hand up, and I give him a high five, which of course causes Eden to roll her eyes. "What's up, man?"

"Nothing much. Just enjoying your mom's cooking."

Travis grimaces. "It's all right." He's a picky eater. Eden figures he'll live on hamburgers and Dr Pepper for the rest of his life. Not a bad way to live, I've told her, which only irritates her further.

"Where's your girlfriend?" I glance around the kitchen, but Travis is alone. The dude always has a girlfriend—the current one is named Isabella, and they've been going out for about three months. Eden says they seem serious but we'll see. Travis isn't the most serious guy I know.

"With her family. They go out of town to her grandparents' house in Palm Springs every year for the holiday." Travis grabs a handful of tortilla chips out of a bowl that's sitting on the counter and shoves them in his mouth. "When's the pie getting served, Ma?"

"Stop calling her Ma," Eden says irritably. When I send her a look, she explains. "He's been calling her Ma lately, and it sounds so stupid."

"I watched a *Little House on the Prairie* marathon a few weeks ago, and they called their parents Ma and Pa. I like it," Travis says with a shrug.

"Who watches *Little House on the Prairie*?" Eden asks.

"I loved that show when I was a kid," Mrs. Sumner adds as she opens the refrigerator and starts pulling out one pie plate after the other, setting them on the counter.

"That makes sense considering that show was actually popular when you were a kid," Eden says, turning her glare on Travis. "Why you're into it now makes absolutely no sense."

"Whatever. I was bored. It helped me kill some time." Travis flicks his chin toward the pie dishes. "Is it pie time, Ma?"

"In a few minutes. Let Josh finish his dinner first."

"I don't want to hold up dessert," I start to protest but Eden's mom sends me a look.

"Hush. Eat your food, Josh. When you're done, then we'll serve pie."

"Hurry up, Josh," Travis says.

"Shut up, Trav," Eden snaps.

"Eden Marie. We don't say shut up in this house," her mom tells her, her voice calm.

I chuckle under my breath before shoving another forkful of mashed potatoes into my mouth. This right here feels normal. Eden and Travis arguing, their mom telling them to stop, me always observing. Laughing. Enjoying the moment. My older brother and sister are gone, and though we all drove each other crazy when they were still at home, now that it's just Mom and me in the house, I miss them.

Not that I'd ever admit it. But I envy Eden's relationship with Travis, even though she says most of the time he makes her completely insane.

"Don't rush because Travis wants pumpkin pie," Eden says, her voice low as she settles onto the barstool next to mine. "Take your time. Drive him crazy."

"I'm not the one who wants to drive him crazy," I tell her. "You are."

"Oh, that's right." She sighs and looks at me, her gaze meeting mine. There's a faint smile curving her lips, and I stare at her mouth for a little too long. She has a great smile. A great laugh. She tucks her hair behind her ear, her fingers playing with the two tiny studs in her earlobe and I watch, momentarily fascinated.

What if I did tell her we could make a great couple? What would she say? Would she agree with me? One simple discussion and we'd be together? Is that all it would take? Then I'd have every right to touch her. Tuck her hair behind her ear, my fingers lingering on her skin. Touch her earrings, trace them. Touch her neck. Kiss her there. Hold her hand. Capture her laughter with my lips. Make her hum in surprise. Make her moan—

Eden leans in closer, her lips practically touching my ear. My skin prickles with awareness. "The turkey was too dry."

A shiver moves through me at her whisper. I turn to look at her, and our faces are so close. Too close. Kissing close. "I drowned mine with gravy so I couldn't tell," I tell her, then clear my throat.

"Lucky you. That was the smart choice." Her smile grows, and her blue eyes sparkle. Shiiiit, she is so pretty. And it's like she realizes I just realized that, because the smile fades and she slowly pulls back, her eyes wide with shock or something like that.

Yeah. Stay back. Keep away from me. I'm trying to keep this simple. No more complications, no more strings. I don't need these weird thoughts screwing with my brain. I'm leaving soon. Kiss this town and everyone else in it good-bye. I need to focus on my future, and not on Eden.

But the weird thoughts are still there. Like I can't shake them. Can't shake her. And I can't. I don't want to. She's my best friend. There's no one else that I'm closer to, that I want to be closer to. Just Eden.

• • •

EDEN

Josh is studying me weirdly. Like that way Molly does sometimes, as if she can see into the depths of my soul. It's bad enough when Molly does it, and it's super disconcerting when Josh does it, too. It's like I want to cover myself and throw up a protective shield, what with the way he's examining me.

"Is there something on my face?" I ask when he doesn't say anything.

"No." He slowly shakes his head. Sets his fork on top of his now empty plate and pushes it away from him. "You look good today, Edes."

My skin warms at his compliment, and I tell myself it means nothing. "You do, too." He's wearing new jeans and the blue flannel shirt unbuttoned over a white T-shirt, and his mom is right—the color does bring out the blue of his eyes.

He glances down at himself. "Thanks." Lifting his head, his gaze meets mine once more, and his expression turns serious. "So. I talked to Whit last night."

My hopes come crashing down. Just like that we're back to him looking to get laid—with another girl. Anyone but me. "Oh yeah?" I try my best to keep my voice casual.

"Yeah, we talked a lot actually. She's a huge flirt, lots of fun." Josh smiles, but there's something about it that seems a little off. "I think maybe she's the perfect candidate after all."

"Candidate for what?" Travis asks, suddenly appearing on Josh's other side.

"Nothing," both Josh and I say at the same time.

Travis sends us a suspicious look. "You two are up to no good."

"More like he's up to no good." I point at Josh. It's so true. He just wants to have sex with a girl and nothing else. Maybe that's my problem. He looks at me and sees serious. But he likes relationships, too. He's never been a casual hookup type of guy. So what changed?

"Hey. Thanks for making me look bad," Josh jokes, knocking me from my thoughts.

"Ma, Josh is finally done eating. Let's have pie," Travis practically pleads. He's so annoying with the Ma crap and wanting pie so badly.

But then again, everything's bugging me lately. I feel tense. Wound up. Nervous. I blame Josh.

Correction. I blame my sudden, confusing feelings for

Josh.

"If you want pie, then go ask everyone in the living room what kind they want. Get a count and then you can help me pass the plates out," Mom says, making me smile. Guess I got out of that one.

Travis grumbles and leaves the kitchen. Mom heads out to the garage to get the whipped cream out of the other refrigerator, leaving Josh and me alone.

"So you gave up on Marin?" I ask.

He blinks at me, like he doesn't recognize the name at first. Jeez. "Oh yeah. Marin. She still hasn't opened my Snapchat, and I sent it days ago."

"Scratch her off the list then." Why can't he scratch everyone off the list and consider me?

Ugh. I know why. I'm not in it for a quickie, especially after what I told him. About wanting to be with a guy I'm in love with when I finally do have sex for the first time. And that's true. I really do want that. All these years, all the time I've spent with Josh, and here I am, wanting to actually be with him.

It's weird.

"I already did scratch her off the list. Besides, Whitney is totally down. She sort of hinted around about the two of us hooking up this weekend." He hesitates before he says, "Actually she *did* ask me if I wanted to hook up with her this weekend."

"Hook up as in…" I brace myself for his answer. My heart is racing. Like it feels like it wants to jump out of my mouth and run away from my body.

Josh sits up straight. "Well, I won't move *that* fast, because that would just make me an asshole, don't you think?"

"I don't know. Maybe not, if that's all you want and that's all she wants." I cannot believe I just said that. That I'm actually encouraging him to hook up with this girl like the pimp that I secretly am. This is all so screwed up. What I'm doing, what Josh is doing, and how I'm helping him.

"Are you serious, Eden?" He looks shocked. And he actually said my full name, instead of calling me Edes. That's rare.

Slowly I nod. Maybe if I convince him I believe this, I'll convince myself, too. "Well, yeah. You're looking to get laid, and she's willing to help you out with that, so..." I subtly glance around the kitchen. Where the hell is my mom? How long does it take to grab a couple of cans of whipped cream?

"You're right." He's nodding, like I just gave him the permission he needed to hear. "There's no emotional connection with her. I'll just—do it with Whitney, and then it's over."

"So romantic," I say sarcastically, like I can't help myself, which I can't.

"Yeah, yeah. I know you're looking to do it with a guy you care about and all that, but that's too much hassle." He waves a hand.

Too much hassle. He's so funny. And blind. So freaking blind. Why doesn't he realize that the two of us together would make total sense? That he's the guy I would willingly give up my virginity to because I trust him implicitly. Like there's no one else I'm as close to as Josh.

No one.

It hit me last night when I tossed and turned, unable to fall asleep. I've been fighting it all along, and I was fully ready to tell him how I felt at this very moment but...

He wants Whitney. Not me.

"You should go for it," I say firmly. "Get together with Whitney. See what happens. If she is ready and willing to do it, then—perfect. It'll all work out just how you want."

Saying those words leaves a bitter taste in my mouth, and I swallow hard. Why can't I tell him the truth? Why am I pushing him to get together with Whitney?

"Just how I want," he echoes, his expression almost… forlorn.

And now I'm confused. Why does he look sad? He's going to get everything he wants. What more could he ask for? Please don't tell me it's still about that pact. I forgot about it. I thought he had, too. People say stupid stuff when they're fourteen and desperate. That's who we were then.

We're not those people now. Even though I would willingly be with Josh, I'm not about to do him because of a pact.

That's just tacky. There's more to our friendship—our *relationship* than a sex pact.

"Edes." He clears his throat, his gaze locking with mine. Without warning he reaches for my hand, holding it loosely in his. My fingers tingle from his touch, and that's never happened before. Not that I've ever noticed. "I want to ask you a question."

My entire body breaks out in chills. "About what?" My voice is soft. My heart is racing. This feels like it could become a moment. Like a life changing, forever different kind of moment.

"I don't know how to say this exactly." He laughs and shakes his head. "Abraham and I were talking last night, and he told me the craziest thing. Do you know that he—"

"Found the whipped cream!" Mom strides into the kitchen clutching two cans of Reddi-wip in her hands, her cheeks pink and her hair windblown. "Sorry I took so long, was talking to Mrs. Hankins next door."

Josh drops my hand, focusing all his attention on my mother, his question for me forgotten. Just like that. "What kind of pie do you have, Mrs. Sumner?"

"Pumpkin, apple, and pecan. All homemade." Mom is beaming proudly. She loves baking pies, and she's good at it, too. "Want a slice of each?"

He leans back in his chair, patting his flat stomach. "I'll just stick with a big slice of pumpkin, please."

I'm this close to losing it over Josh not finishing his question, and he's acting like it's no big deal. All he cares about is getting a piece of pumpkin pie.

Whatever.

Mom looks right at me. "What about you?"

"Um, I'm not hungry," I say weakly, earning a weird look from her. I'm always hungry for pumpkin pie, and she knows it.

"All right, whatever you say." She pauses, her brows furrowed in concern, and I pray she doesn't ask me what's wrong. "Where's your brother?"

"Right here, Ma. Got the list." Travis enters the kitchen, holding up his phone.

"Let's get to work," Mom says with a smile.

I watch them buzz around the kitchen, waiting until they aren't as close before I talk to Josh again.

"What did you want to ask me?"

He smiles, but it's a nervous attempt at best. "I'll talk to you about it later. Promise."

Chapter Eleven

EDEN

Josh never talked to me about that mysterious question, and I never asked again, either. It was like he couldn't bother to bring it back up, and I was too scared considering I'm a total chicken. So instead, he devoured my mother's pumpkin pie, finished the slice she forced on me, then moaned and groaned the rest of the time he was at my house about his full stomach and how tired he was.

Finally, I told him I was tired, too, and basically kicked him out. He looked hurt, Travis protested his leaving, but I wasn't having it. I needed Josh out of my house.

After the last couple of days, I'm wondering if it would be better to have Josh out of my life. For good.

Yeah, right. Like that could ever happen. Like you'd actually want *that to happen.*

I worked Black Friday, which wasn't that bad considering I'm employed at a gift shop in a touristy area versus a store in a mall. Saturday afternoon has been pretty easy, too. The customers have been steady, and I'm scheduled to close at six. It's almost five now, and I'm counting down the minutes until I get to go home, take a quick shower, and dive under my covers, where I'll hide out for the rest of the night.

Yeah. I'm so over this break. Over helping Josh with his girl problems—really got myself tied up into a mess with that one. I need to get back to school and focus on other stuff. Other people.

No more Josh.

"Eden. I had a feeling you'd be working."

I turn at the familiar male voice to find my ex-boyfriend Cole standing in front of me, a faint smile curling his lips. I return the smile and give in to sudden temptation, going in for a hug. "Cole. What are you doing here?"

He gives me a brief squeeze before withdrawing. "My grandparents are in town, and they wanted to go to the beach. So we've been walking around looking at all the shops down here."

"Are you bored yet?"

"You know it," he says with an easy smile.

Everything was always easy with Cole—until it wasn't. He's like a light switch. Most of the time he's on and it's great. But when he shuts off, forget it. He freezes you out, refusing to turn back on. Once he's done, he's done.

And he's frozen me out twice now over the years. I'm not a believer in that three times a charm saying, either.

A customer approaches the counter, and I go to ring up her purchase, carefully folding the T-shirts she chose before I stuff them in a bag. Cole lingers by the counter, thumbing through a bowl of colorful polished rocks, and when the customer finally leaves, he's standing in front of me once more with a nervous smile.

"So what are you up to?" he asks.

I glance around the store before my gaze meets his. "Uh,

working?" He's sort of annoying me. But ever since we broke up, he's sort of annoyed me. I understand what I saw in him. He's cute with his floppy brown hair and his light brown eyes, his mischievous moods, and his easygoing personality.

But we argued a lot. He was jealous of my friendship with Josh. I was jealous of his flirtatious ways. He broke up with me twice because he thought he found someone better, and I realized after the second time, I would never measure up to his standards.

Maybe that's my problem. I don't measure up. I'm okay as a friend, but not good enough as girlfriend material.

Ugh. I've never had major self-esteem issues, so what's my deal now?

"What are you doing later?" When I frown, Cole continues. "Tonight."

"I'll be at home, I guess."

"Want to go to dinner with me?"

I cross my arms. "Why?"

He starts to laugh and shrugs. "Why not? It could be fun."

"I don't know, Cole. Haven't we done this before already? Like twice?" I drop my arms, feeling a little helpless, a lot confused.

"Maybe we should do it again." He leans across the counter and grabs hold of my hand. "I've missed you, Eden."

My brain is telling me *oh hell no*. My heart is telling me maybe? Some other part of me keeps asking a question on repeat.

What about Josh?

"Have you missed me?" Cole asks when I still haven't said anything. He squeezes my hand, his expression hopeful.

I withdraw my hand from his and take a step back. "You know I missed you. You were the one who broke up with me."

"Biggest regret of my life so far," he says with absolute

certainty.

The temptation to roll my eyes is strong, but I keep it in check. "Yeah well, you've made your point. And to be honest, I really don't think we should do this again."

He stuffs his hands in his pockets, his expression contrite. Cole is really good at laying it on thick in order to get what he wants. I've fallen for this sort of thing before. I'm hoping I'm smart enough—and strong enough—not to cave right now. "Just…give me another chance. I've been thinking about you a lot lately, especially this last week. And I've realized I miss you a lot. Life isn't the same without you in it."

My heart perks up in that hopeful way it does when Cole says the right things, and I mentally tell it to calm down. We've been down this road before.

"We're still friends, Cole," I say gently.

"It's not the same, and you know it. We don't really talk. You barely look at me." His jaw firms, and his lips tighten. "I'm surprised you and Josh didn't get together after we broke up."

My mouth drops open. Where did that come from? "What? Are you serious?"

"Well, yeah. I figured it was only a matter of time. Feels like Josh has been lying in wait for years."

"That's—that's not true." I'm shaking my head, totally in denial, but come on. Why does this keep happening? Can't I just be friends with the guy? Why does everyone think Josh and I somehow belong together? Is this some sort of sign from the universe? Have we both been blind all this time and now all of a sudden, I realize that we could be perfect together?

Yeah. Maybe.

"You really believe he just wants to be your friend?" Cole is practically sneering.

"Yes, I believe he *is* my friend, and that's all he wants. He's my best friend, and you know it. Josh has never tried to make a move on me. Ever," I say firmly, because it's freaking true. We've only ever been friends. Josh never tried to touch me inappropriately. He's never tried to kiss me or said anything to me that would imply he was interested in me sexually.

And for all these years, I've felt the same. Until all this "help me find a girl to have sex with" stuff came up, and now my mind is a mess and my emotions are everywhere.

It sucks.

"You're just blind," Cole says irritably. "He's totally into you."

"And you're just jealous. You always have been," I throw back at him. "I can't even believe we're having this discussion right now while I'm at work."

"You avoid me everywhere else. It's the only place where I knew I could talk to you."

"What do you mean? I don't avoid you." Well, I sort of have. He Snapchats me. I leave him unopened. He texts me; I send him minimal replies back. Yes, we're friends but most of the time our conversations are awkward at best.

Like now. This conversation is off the charts awkward. In fact, it's not even a conversation.

It feels like a fight.

"You do avoid me." His expression softens, and he comes around so now he's standing behind the counter with me. "And I don't want us to treat each other like this, Eden. I want you back in my life."

"Cole, I just...I can't do this right now." I glance around the store, wishing a customer would walk in. Anything to get me out of this conversation.

"Can we talk later? I'll take you to dinner." He smiles, his entire face lighting up. "What time are you off here?"

"I can't..." My voice drifts, but he's not having it.

"Come on, it's just dinner. It'll be fun." He grabs my hand again, interlacing our fingers together. "Like old times."

"Isn't your family looking for you?" I ask weakly, hating how good it feels when he rubs his thumb across the top of my hand.

"I'll go find them in a minute. Just say yes, Eden." He squeezes my hand. "Please."

I stare into his familiar brown eyes, reminding myself that it ended so badly between us before. Yet, I'm drawn to him still. I have no business giving Josh any crap over Kaylie. I'm just as bad with Cole. "Fine," I finally murmur. "I'll go to dinner with you."

This will probably be a huge mistake but…

Cole beams and leans in, giving me a quick kiss on the lips. I'm so startled I can't even find the words to speak. "Want me to pick you up here or at your house?"

"I'd like to go home and change first, so pick me up at the house. Maybe around seven-thirty?" I can't believe I'm agreeing to this.

"I'll see you at seven-thirty then." He kisses my cheek this time, squeezes my hand, and then he's striding out of the store.

I slump against the counter, my mind spinning. What did I just do? What did I just agree to? Am I trying to banish my weird, confusing feelings for Josh by refocusing on Cole? That's the worst idea ever.

Ever.

Grabbing my phone, I open up Snapchat and start typing.

• • •

JOSH

Want to come over tonight?

I stare at the five words that show up in my chat with Whitney, blinking at them. Trying to comprehend them. Talk about moving fast. I asked for Eden's help last Friday.

Eight days later and I have a girl who sounds like she's ready, willing, and able.

So why am I sitting here like a dumbass staring at her text when I could've already answered her and been halfway to the shower by now?

Looking up, I glance around my room, tapping my fingers against my knee. I'm sitting on my bed, and only a few minutes ago I was bored out of my mind. I'd tried messaging Eden, but she didn't respond. When I reached out to Abraham, he told me he was at dinner with his family. I hadn't talked to Cole all week so I sent him a text, but he didn't respond, either. I even sent a Snap to Molly, and she sent me one in return almost immediately.

It was a selfie of her giving me the finger. Nice, right?

I stare at my phone screen once more, chewing on my lower lip. What do I say? Am I ready for the hookup? What the hell is wrong with me that I'm questioning myself? Why wouldn't I be ready for the hook-up? Whitney is hot. She's single. She wants me to come over to her freaking house tonight. This is everything I ever wanted. One night to shed my virginity, and then it's done. I can feel worthy in the locker room. I can feel worthy when I graduate high school and eventually go to college.

"Screw it," I mutter and start typing.

What do you have in mind?

Whitney responds quickly.

Whatever you want. :)

My eyebrows shoot up. If that isn't an open invitation, I don't know what is.

What time?

Around eight? My parents are gone. They won't come back till late.

I'm going to do this. I'm really going to do this.

Sounds good. I'll see you at eight.

Can't wait. :)

I leap off the bed and go to my dresser, pulling open the top drawer and grabbing a pair of underwear. I check the black boxer briefs for holes, then immediately decide I need to wear something different. Not the usual old boxer briefs.

So I dig to the back of the drawer and grab a pair of blue and white checked boxers I've only worn once, then slam it shut. I'll pick out what I'm going to wear later. First, I gotta take a shower.

For a solid fifteen minutes I soak under the hot water and wash everything at least twice. I jerk off because I don't want to be like Abraham and come twice within a forty-five-minute span if that. I need to prolong this. I've had enough experience and read enough articles on Cosmo the last couple of years to know this.

Once I'm out of the shower, I dry off, towel dry my hair, shave, and deodorize. I spray myself with the subtlest cologne I own, and then I stare at my reflection in the still fogged up bathroom mirror.

Not bad. I look pretty good. I glance down at my chest, scratch my finger lightly along a zit that's somehow popped up. Spot a few hairs curling in between my pecs and wonder if I'll get more. I've grown another inch over the past year, putting me at a little over six-foot, and it's weird because you think you finish all that growing up stuff during the typical puberty spurt at age thirteen or fourteen, but you don't. Sometimes it keeps happening.

I run my fingers through my hair until it looks decent, slip on the boxers, then grab my dirty clothes and hightail it out of the bathroom in a mad dash toward my bedroom.

Of course, my mother intercepts me in the hallway.

She sends me a look. "Where do you think you're going tonight?"

"It's Saturday, Mom." I try to keep the irritation out of

my voice, but it's there, lurking just beneath the surface. She hears it, too. I can see it in her face, the way she crosses her arms in front of her chest, like she's ready to interrogate me.

"So you're going out."

"Yeah." I nod, feeling weird standing in front of her with just my boxers on. "I won't be out too late though. Promise."

"What are you doing?"

"Going over to a friend's house."

"Who's?"

"You don't know her. She's a friend of Eden's." This is sort of true.

Mom smiles. "Will Eden be there?"

Wouldn't that be awkward as hell? Though Mom will get off my case if she thinks I'm going to hang out with a few friends versus just one girl she doesn't know. "Yeah, she'll be there. Molly, Abraham, and Cole will be there, too."

God, I'm such a liar.

"Nice. Well, have fun. Don't stay out too late." She pats me on the arm before she walks past me.

I go into my bedroom and shut the door, leaning against it with a big sigh. Got past that potential barrier, thank God. I grab my new jeans and the new black button-down shirt and put them on, then check myself out in the mirror. Eden liked how I looked in this outfit. I remember at the store when she unbuttoned my shirt, her fingers brushing against my skin for the tiniest moment, and the shock on her face when our eyes met. Like maybe she felt something when she touched me. Because I know I did. I always seem to. I just push it out of my mind, since I can't go there.

Frowning at my reflection, I finish buttoning the shirt. I need to stop thinking about Eden. Tonight isn't about her. It's about Whitney. Hot, blond, willing to do anything Whitney. I'm freaking excited. Nervous, too. Apprehensive. I've messed around plenty. I don't want to screw this up or finish too fast—my biggest fear. I need to make sure and put the condom on right. Need to make sure I actually have condoms with me. This is nerve-wracking stuff, especially since I have a feeling Whitney's done this before. Maybe more than a few times.

Not that she's a slut. I don't slut shame. Eden taught me that term and told me I need to live by it, too.

Dude. Forget Eden.

I go to my bedside table and open the drawer, pulling out a single condom and stuffing it into my wallet. Then I grab another one just in case. I shove the wallet into my back jeans' pocket, then grab my phone, opening it up and checking out my notifications.

They're all Snapchats from Abraham, Cole, Molly, and one from Eden.

I open them in the order I received them.

Abraham's is a text in chat.

What are you up to tonight, player?

I answer him, telling him where I'm going.

Cole's is a photo taken from behind the steering wheel of his car, with a caption.

Going to pick up my girl.

Frowning, I send him a quick pic back without a caption. Who the hell is his new girl?

Molly's is another selfie, her scowling into the camera like she's got full on hate for me. There's a caption, too.

Eden is going to dinner with Cole tonight. *gag*

What the ever lovin…

I send her back a photo with my own caption.

Are you serious?

Then I open Eden's, already starting to feel angry.

It's a selfie with no caption and she looks…beautiful. Hair straight and hanging past her shoulders, a big smile on her face, showing off those straight teeth that took two years of braces to fix. I've never seen her look prettier.

And she got pretty for some other guy.

Not just some other guy, but Cole, her ex-boyfriend. The douchebag who broke her heart and made her cry more than once.

I think she's trying to drive me crazy.

Stupid freaking lucky ass Cole, who's my friend, but hasn't she done this already? She's as bad as Kaylie and I.

I take a quick selfie and send it to her. Just as I do, my phone lights up with a call from Abraham, so I answer it.

"Bro, you're going to Whitney Gregory's house right now? Someone I know is getting laid tonight," Abraham crows as his greeting.

"Jesus, keep it down," I mutter, making Abraham burst out laughing. "Aren't you with your family right now?"

"I'm alone, chill." He starts laughing harder when I growl at him in irritation. "This is gonna be sick, you hooking up with Whit. I've heard good things."

"You've heard good things?" I almost don't want to know what he's heard.

Or do I?

"I heard she's good. And that's all I'm going to say about that."

Since when does Abraham keep quiet about anyone or anything? "Are you serious? You're not going to tell me who your source is?"

"No. I was sworn to secrecy."

"Are you the one who did Whitney Gregory?" I sound like a jackass. Eden would probably hit me right now if she were here.

Abraham snorts. "In my dreams. Naw, it wasn't me. But you know this guy." His voice lowers. "Swear you won't say anything."

"I swear," I say immediately. Abraham isn't about

keeping secrets. Not that he blabs, but he always tells it like it is.

"Okay, because this is messed up, and I hate that I know, so I'm dragging you into this with me." Abraham clears his throat. "Remember when Cole broke up with Eden last time?"

"Yeah." Icy cold dread slithers down my spine. That was a bad moment last year. Eden had been a wreck. She thought things were going well with Cole, and then out of nowhere—at least according to Eden—he dumped her. Pulled one of those, *it's not you, it's me* lines on her and was out. It took her a while to recover.

"It's because he hooked up with Whit when he was still with Eden. At some stupid party where he got drunk and claims he didn't remember what happened. Whit lost her shit and threatened to tell Eden if Cole didn't break up with her, so he did. Then he goes to Whitney thinking they're going to become a thing, and she blows him off. Acts like she never went off on him, like he was the crazy one," Abraham explains, sounding disgusted. "She's kind of psycho, dude. But I think maybe she's worth it because look what Cole did to Eden just to get another piece of that."

I think I'm going to be sick. I know it sounds like an exaggeration, but I lived through that breakup. I was there for Eden when she cried over Cole. I went and yelled at Cole on Eden's behalf, and he told me I wouldn't understand why he broke up with her.

Now I get it. I totally get it. What a mess. And Eden is going to dinner with Cole tonight, while I'm going over to Whit's house to get laid.

What the hell am I doing? What the hell is Eden doing?

"Molly told me Eden and Cole are going to dinner tonight," I say through clenched teeth.

"They are? Tonight?" Abraham sounds shocked.

"Yeah. Can you believe it?"

"Actually, I can. Cole always regretted breaking up with her last time. Said it was a huge mistake on his part."

"He's an asshole."

"We're all assholes. It's what we do." Abraham pauses for a moment. "You're not going to tell Eden about this, are you?"

"No, I promised I'd keep it secret." Though it's going to kill me to keep it from her. Cole cheated on her with Whitney. *Cheated.*

If Eden knew, she'd be devastated. If she knew, she wouldn't be going to dinner with that asswipe right now. If she knew, she'd tell him to kiss her ass and never speak to him again.

But I can't tell her. She's still hung up on her ex-boyfriend. I have to let her go out with Cole. And I'm going over to Whitney's.

My earlier excitement evaporates, just like that.

"Okay, good." Abraham breathes a sigh of relief, then he starts chuckling. "Forget about Eden and Cole. It's not our problem, you know? Just concentrate on Whitney tonight. I'm so jealous."

"Where's your college girlfriend?" I need to change the subject, focus on Abraham.

"She promised we're gonna sext later. Gotta go. Don't forget to use a condom." Abraham ends the call before I can say anything else.

I shove my phone into my back pocket and then look at my reflection yet again. Should I even go through with this? What Whit and Cole did has nothing to do with me. I shouldn't worry about it.

I can't worry about it.

But I can't help but think about Eden and Cole on that stupid dinner date my entire drive over to Whitney's house.

Chapter Twelve

EDEN

The conversation between Cole and me during dinner is slow and almost painful. At first I tried to be bright and cheery and told myself it was just like old times, but it's not. As the minutes tick by, all those old resentments start to build within me, bubbling in my stomach, rising to my throat, ready to shoot straight toward Cole in a barrage of ugly words.

But I contain myself. I can get through this. I won't let him win me over with his usual charm and the sweet things he says. He knows how to flirt. He knows how to say or do just the right thing to make a girl go *awwww*. He's always used that to his advantage, and most of the time, it's harmless.

He doesn't feel harmless tonight. For some reason, it's like he's trying so hard, it's actually turning me off. Tempting me to run in the opposite direction. He's showing off about his grades, his potential for getting into Stanford, his parents promising to buy him a new car before the end of the year.

Like for real, he's going to get a car for Christmas. How

spoiled is he?

"What type of car do you want?" I make the mistake in asking.

Cole's eyes light up, and he literally rubs his hands together. "I'm hoping for a brand-new truck, one of those Ford F-150s. They're so freaking nice, especially when it's fully loaded with all the extras and tricked out. Dad is on board, but I don't know if Mom is."

His dad is a doctor. His mom is the vice president of a bank. Cole is an only child, so to say he's spoiled is putting it mildly.

"What color?" I take a sip of my water and silently will our server to bring our dinner. We ordered almost twenty minutes ago, but the restaurant is so packed everything seems to be taking extra long tonight.

"White or silver. Probably white, with black tinted windows. Won't that look dope?" He's nodding and smiling, and I can't help but think of Josh. He always says dope. It's like his signature word. I used to give him crap over it, but then had to stop when I realized the word had become a part of my daily vocabulary.

Ugh. I push Josh out of my mind.

"I'm sure it'll look awesome," I tell him with my politest smile.

Cole frowns, tilting his head to the side. "You okay?"

I keep the smile in place. "I'm fine."

"Are you sure? You look a little...down." He leans forward, his voice going lower. "Is something bothering you? You can tell me you know. I'll always be here for you, Eden."

Leave it to Cole to keep digging. Why can't he accept my answer at face value and continue talking? My smile slips, and I give up the pretense. "No, really. I'm okay. Just hungry."

"I told you we should've ordered appetizers." When we were finally seated at our table at the Italian restaurant downtown, that was the first thing Cole wanted to do. But I told him I didn't want to ruin my meal, considering Italian food is always so heavy, and he told me I was acting like an old lady, which sort of pissed me off.

Not the best way to start off our date, right? And it feels like it's just been sliding downhill ever since.

The server miraculously appears with our plates in hand, and he sets mine in front of me first, then Cole's. "Sorry for the delay. We're extra busy tonight," he says.

"No problem," I tell him with a polite smile while Cole scowls.

"Maybe you should comp us some appetizers to make up for our wait," Cole suggests.

I send him a look, but he's ignoring me.

"I could do that for you, no problem." The server smiles. "What would you like?"

"The bruschetta plate sounds good." The smug expression on Cole's face is super annoying.

And kind of embarrassing.

Once the waiter leaves, I lean across the table, my voice dropping. "We don't need free appetizers."

Cole frowns. "Why not? It's the least they can do for making us wait."

"It hasn't been that bad of a wait," I start, but he cuts me off.

"This place is always fast. Tonight, they're not. They owe us something for the inconvenience," Cole says firmly.

I don't want to fight about this, so I dig into my pasta dish. It's delicious, and I concentrate on that, feeling full after only a few minutes, nearly groaning when the server sets our appetizer plate in the middle of the table with a flourish. No way am I going to be able to eat one of those, no matter how yummy they look.

"Enjoy," he says with an overly fake grin, then dashes off.

"That guy is a jerk," Cole grumbles as he reaches for a bruschetta topped with tomatoes, prosciutto, and cheese.

"You were being a jerk, too," I point out.

He shoves the appetizer in his mouth, glaring at me as he chews. "Are you pissed at me, or what?" he asks after he swallows.

I'm surprised by his question. "I'm not mad at you. Why would I be mad at you?"

"Did you talk to Abraham?" He looks away, like he can't meet my gaze and my suspicions rise.

What does Abraham know that I don't?

"I talk to Abraham all the time," I say carefully.

"So he told you then." Cole's lips go thin. He's still not looking me in the eye.

"Told me what?"

"About me and Whitney." Cole shakes his head, his gaze finally locking with mine. "I'm tired of pretending it never happened. I promised myself I would tell you tonight."

Now I'm confused. Why did he mention Whitney? "What are you talking about?"

"I can't lie to you anymore, Eden. If we're going to give this a go again, I need to tell you the truth." Cole takes a deep breath and lets it all out in one gusty exhale before he says, "When we were together, I might've...cheated on you."

The words echo in my head, over and over again. "You might've *what?*"

"You didn't know?" When I furiously shake my head, he nods, his expression grim. "I didn't mean for it to happen. It was a stupid mistake. I never meant to hurt you when I broke up with you, but I felt so guilty and I couldn't live with myself for what I did. So I thought it was better to just end it with you and walk away."

"You cheated on me? With who?" Whitney. He said Whitney. "Whitney Gregory?" My voice is shrill, and I swear someone at a nearby table turns to look at us.

Cole winces. "It was a one shot thing. I was at a party and I was drunk, and we were flirting pretty heavily. Next thing I know she's led me to a bedroom, and we're naked and then we were—yeah. We were doing it. But it was a mistake. I realize that now. You are the best thing that's ever happened to me, Eden. And I messed it all up by screwing a girl I don't really know when I was drunk."

I'm in shock. I must be. The only thing I keep thinking is what a cliché. My life, what Cole did to me, is such a total cliché it's not even funny. Though he might've been laughing behind my back. I'm the idiot girlfriend who had no clue what he did to me.

And all along I thought *I* did something to drive him away. I'd always wondered exactly how I screwed up our relationship. When he dumped me, I vowed I would never let another boy hurt me like Cole did again. Then I came up with a mental list of all the things I must've done to make him not love me anymore.

So lame.

Turns out it wasn't me. He was right.

It really was all on him.

"I promised that if we were going to start over, I would be honest with you," he says, reaching across the table to touch my hand. I let him. I don't want to cause a scene in the middle of the restaurant. And really, couldn't he have told me this later, after I finished my dinner?

Clearly this isn't bothering me as much as I thought it would.

"You weren't honest before when you broke up with me," I finally say, slipping my hand from beneath his and folding it into my lap. "What's making you want to be honest now?"

Cole has already shoved another bruschetta into his mouth, and I wait for his answer, impatient as he chews and chews and finally swallows. "If we're really going to get back together, I needed to tell you everything. It's been hanging over me, eating me up inside, what I did to you when we were together. I'm sorry, Eden. I'm sorry for hurting you, for breaking up with you without giving you a reason, for breaking your heart. I didn't know how else to do it."

He didn't know how else to do it. I don't even know what he means by that statement. He didn't know how to hurt me? Didn't know how to be honest? Didn't know how to keep his dick in his pants? There are so many things swirling in my brain right now, and I can't focus on any one of them.

My appetite is gone. It's disappeared with Cole's confession. I push my pasta away from me and bring the red cloth napkin to my face. I wipe my mouth, then drop the napkin on top of my barely touched plate. "I should go."

"What?" Cole is frowning. He looks majorly confused. "You can't just leave. We're on a date."

"Yeah, I think this date is done." I bend down, grab my purse off the ground, then stand. "I'm leaving."

"Where are you going? I'll drive you home. Come on, Eden." He stands, too, but I say nothing as I slip away from the table and start walking toward the front entrance.

I pick up speed and can hear Cole following me. It's funny how after such a big revelation, such a huge, hurtful betrayal, I don't feel like crying. Not even close. I'm numb as I walk through the restaurant, as I pass the tables full of people talking and laughing and having a great time. I smile at the woman standing behind the hostess stand, my gaze wandering over the people waiting for a table in the front lobby, and then I'm pushing open the door, walking out into the cool, dark night. The door shuts, sealing off the sound from inside, and it's quiet. So quiet, I can almost hear the waves crashing against the ocean shore that's only a few miles away from where I'm standing.

But maybe that's just my imagination.

Cole doesn't follow me outside, and I'm relieved. The server or hostess probably stopped him, must've thought he was trying to dine and dash or whatever, and that's kind of amusing. Cole would never do something like that.

Of course, I never thought Cole would cheat on me, either. So maybe he would do something like that.

Glancing both ways for traffic, I hurry across the street, annoyance flashing through me when a car suddenly speeds by, the driver honking at me. I walk down the sidewalk toward the pier, the salty scent of the ocean lingering in the air, and I glance at my phone, contemplating my next move.

I'm not sure what I should do, but I know I don't want to end up with Cole driving me home. Forget that. I can find someone to pick me up. I know I can.

The old bowling alley with a giant arcade looms ahead, the large building wrapped in garish bright pink and blue neon lights and I duck inside, lurking by the large window that faces the street so I can see if Cole approaches. The place is full of people, most of them teenagers younger than me, and the music is loud and obnoxious. I'm sure Cole would never think I'd hide from him in here.

I'd bet money Cole would think I'd never hide from him, period. The arrogant ass.

I check my Snapchat, but there aren't many notifications from close friends. Guess they're all busy on a Saturday night. I send a quick text to Molly, but she's on a date—an actual date—with the college guy Kirk, so I don't expect a response. I text Josh, but there's nothing from him, either.

The disappointment that crashes through me is near overwhelming. Then I remember he mentioned going out with Whitney, the girl who Cole cheated on me with, and I immediately want to throw up.

How does this girl keep creeping into my relationships?

Deciding to hell with it, I text Abraham and ask what he's doing. Of course, like he always seems to do, he calls me.

"Aren't you on a date with Cole?" he asks after I answer.

"How do you know?" Who told him?

"Josh told me that Molly told him." Ugh, Molly. I bet she was complaining to Josh about it, too. "So what happened?"

I really don't want to get into this right now at the arcade with the loud music and the strangers standing nearby. "I realized Cole is a total asshole."

"Took you long enough," Abraham mutters.

"And I walked out on him at the restaurant."

"What? I bet that made him madder than hell." Abraham is now laughing.

I can't help but start laughing, too. "He wasn't too happy with me, but he can't complain. He confessed he cheated on me."

Abraham is silent. And Abraham is never silent. His silence tells me he knew this, though Cole already brought up Abraham's name earlier.

"He cheated on me with Whitney Gregory," I finish, her name leaving a bitter taste on my tongue.

"Yeah." Abraham sighs. "He recently mentioned this, and it was killing me that I couldn't tell you."

"It's okay," I say, because it is. Cole was his friend first, way before I ever came around.

"So he told you in the middle of the restaurant while you guys were eating dinner?" Abraham sounds incredulous.

"Yes, he did."

"That's insane. But also sort of smart, because then you can't throw a huge fit."

"I threw a minor fit," I say with a smile. "I walked out on him, remember."

"Where are you now?"

"I'm at the bowling alley, close to the pier."

"Damn, where did he take you to dinner?"

"Lorenzo's. They have great food. Too bad I couldn't eat much of it." I pause, hating that I want to ask the next question, but I do it anyway. "Do you know where Josh is?"

Abraham remains quiet again, which is a bad sign. He knows exactly where Josh is, he just doesn't want to tell me. "Um, maybe."

I sigh and lean my forehead against the wall, closing my eyes. "Just tell me."

"He's over at Whitney Gregory's house. Said he was going to get some tonight. No one's home so those two are all alone."

My heart aches. Seriously, this is so stupid. I'm the one who suggested he give Whit a try. I pushed her on him when he said he wasn't interested, and now he's over at her house, probably having sex with her as we speak.

"Oh." The word sounds as hollow as I feel.

"Eden." Abraham clears his throat. He sounds uncomfortable, like he knows he was just the bearer of some major bad news. "You want me to come get you and take you home? I can. I'm not doing anything."

"Would you? I hate to ask, but I have no one else and I don't want to call my parents or Travis." Travis is probably on a date with his girlfriend so it's not like he'd run to my rescue. A realization hits me. "But I don't want to lead you on, not after what you told me earlier—"

"Don't worry about that," he says, cutting me off. "Whatever you think you know about me, you're wrong."

"Okay." That was super confusing. What is he talking about?

"Give me fifteen minutes, and I'll be there, okay?" Before I can offer up a thank-you, Abraham's already ended the call.

• • •

JOSH

Whitney's house is huge. She lives in one of those private subdivisions near the ocean, and while they're not on the side of the street closest to the Pacific, her house definitely has ocean views. Plus, they have a massive circular driveway and a perfect front yard with a giant fountain that looks straight out of a magazine. I pull into the driveway in my beat-up, old Toyota truck that belonged to my dad, and shut off the engine. It ticks loudly in the otherwise quiet night, and I glance around, staring at the looming house in front of me.

Damn. The girl is loaded. I should've known with a name like Whitney Gregory. It just sounds rich, you know?

I climb out of the truck and lock it, then go to the front door. When I hit the doorbell, it sounds like a thousand dogs just started barking within the house, and I take a step back, fully prepared for a pack of wild dogs to rush out at me the moment the door opened.

But when the door swings open, all I see is a tiny, golden fur ball Whitney's clutching in her arms.

"Yay, you made it," she says with a smile, squeezing the dog closer to her, so the dog's face is practically nestled in her cleavage. "I thought you might chicken out."

Chicken out? Why the hell would she say that? "I'm here," I say, my voice gruff. I nod toward the dog in her arms. "Who's your friend?"

She brings the dog's face up to hers, pressing it against her cheek. "This is Lala. She's a Pomeranian. Isn't she adorable?"

I make eye contact with that dog, and I swear it bares its fangs at me. What a stupid name. I can hear Eden complaining now. She hates ridiculous names. "Yeah, cute," I say, my voice faint.

"Come on in." Whitney opens the door wider, and it's when I walk inside that I notice what Whitney's wearing, and it's not much.

Tiny white denim shorts that show off long, thin legs and a cropped black top that reveals most of her stomach. Her belly button is pierced, a pale pink stone glittering in her navel, and her skin is so tan I wonder if it's fake.

She shuts the door behind me and turns the lock, the sound sending dread slamming into me. I need to get over myself and all the gloom and doom I'm currently feeling. Seriously, I'm about to get laid for the first time, and I'm acting like I'm going to freaking die.

"Nice house," I tell her as I look around, hoping she can hear the sarcasm. This place is freaking amazing. The ceiling soars about three stories above me, and my voice literally echoes.

If it was Eden, she would know I'm being sarcastic and say something in return.

But Whitney doesn't.

"Isn't it nice? We only moved in about two years ago." She smiles at me, gives the dog a kiss on the forehead and then lets the little fluff ball go. It scampers after us as Whitney leads me into the living room, the dog's claws clicking against the marble floor. "You want anything to drink or eat?"

"Nah, I'm good." I'm also too nervous to eat, not that I'd ever tell her that.

Whitney smiles and makes her way around the living room, going to the giant entertainment center that takes up one whole wall and pushing a few buttons. Music suddenly spills out of invisible speakers and she turns that bright smile on me, flicking her wavy blond hair over her shoulder. "I love this song."

I don't recognize it, but I go along with her. "It's good."

"Do you like music?" She sits on the giant L-shaped couch and pats the empty spot beside her.

"Yeah, who doesn't?" I take a few steps toward the couch

but don't sit down yet. It's like I'm trying to draw this out.

"I don't know, some people don't care about music. But I love it. I listen to all kinds. Pop, rap, classical, country. New age, oldies, whatever's playing usually makes me happy because I love it all." She tilts her head to the side. "Are you going to come sit by me? I swear I won't bite. Unless you want me to."

I laugh because she's giggling, but I'm sort of sweating this. Nothing usually fazes me. I can handle anything—or at least, I think I can. But I guess I can't really handle a cute girl ready to jump me on a Saturday night.

"Josh," she says when her giggles dry up. "Come over here."

Without a word I go to the couch and sit down beside her, leaving a few inches of room in between us. She gives me a look that says she knows exactly what I'm doing, and then she's grabbing one of like twenty remotes that sit on the coffee table in front of us.

"Forget the music. Want to watch a movie?" she asks as she hits a button that shuts the music off, then she grabs another remote and turns the flat screen TV on.

"Sure."

"I'm in the mood for something scary." She shoots me another look, one that says she has a plan and I nod in agreement. "Do you like scary movies?"

Usually I do, because it means the girl is going to leap into my arms and clutch me close when she sees something that freaks her out. "Yeah, I do."

"Good." She opens up the Netflix app on the smart TV and starts scrolling. "Hopefully we'll find something we both haven't seen."

My body sinks into the couch, because it's made of the softest, most comfortable fabric I've ever sat on. I throw my arm up against the back of it, right above where Whitney's sitting, and she sends me yet another one of those knowing looks before she settles on a particular movie I've never heard of before. Something about sexy vampires who are feeding on guys in their high school, I didn't even catch what it's called.

Within minutes the movie is rolling and there are naked boobs bouncing on the big screen. Whitney giggles, her gaze meeting mine. "This movie might be kind of sexy. Hope you don't mind."

Mind? No way would I normally mind. I'm all about movies with nudity in them, because let's be honest, I love staring at the naked female body. But it doesn't feel right, being here with Whitney. Sitting next to her on the giant couch, supposed teenage vampires with huge tits on the TV, knowing that when this movie is over—or hell maybe halfway through, maybe only twenty minutes through—I'll have my hand up Whit's shirt and her hand will be on my junk and then the next thing you know…

My phone buzzes, yanking my mind from my dirty thoughts, and I pull it out of my pocket to see a text from Abraham.

She knows.

Frowning, I chance a look at Whit, but her eyes are glued on the TV. "Mind if I call someone real quick?"

Whitney shrugs. "Yeah, sure. But don't take too long. You don't want to miss the movie."

Eden would pause the movie for me. Eden would ask who I'm calling.

But this girl isn't Eden.

"I'll be right back," I tell Whitney as I stand and walk into the kitchen. I find a door that leads to the backyard and sneak through it, closing the door quietly behind me as I dial Abraham's number.

"Who are you talking about? What does she know?" I ask him when he answers.

"Eden. Freaking Cole took her to dinner and told her he cheated on her with Whit over the main entrée." Abraham sounds thoroughly disgusted. "Is he a dumbass or what?"

I can't believe Cole told her—and while he was out to dinner with her, too. That's cold. "Why'd he choose now to tell her?"

"Eden said he wanted to come clean if they were going to try and make this work. All he did was make her mad, and she walked out on him. Right in the middle of dinner."

"How do you know all of this?"

"She just called me and asked if I'd pick her up from the bowling alley," he says, as if that should all make sense. "Do you want to go get her?"

"What do you mean, the bowling alley?"

Abraham sighs, like I'm annoying him. "She walked out on Cole in the middle of their date. She's at that Italian restaurant downtown, and she ended up in the bowling alley across the street."

"Why didn't she call me?" I'm kind of offended that she didn't.

"She said she sent you a text or whatever, but you never responded. And I told her that's because you were with Whitney."

"You told her that?" Shit. Now I feel like a total sleazebag.

"Yeah, what's the big deal? I thought she knew you were all up in that."

God, sometimes the way Abraham says things. "Is Eden okay? Was she crying?" I hate it when Eden cries. It makes my freaking heart hurt, not that I'd ever admit that to anyone. But it's like her pain becomes mine, and all I want to do is make her smile again.

"Surprisingly enough, she wasn't crying. At least not when I talked to her. Said she was sort of numb to it all now, I guess." He hesitates. "You never answered my question. Do you want to go pick her up or not?"

I glance toward the house. "I can't just ditch Whitney." Why the hell not? I barely know her. Eden needs me.

But she called Abraham. Not me. She didn't want to interrupt my time with Whitney. I'm overthinking this. She doesn't like me like that. She went on a date with Cole—yeah it didn't go quite as planned, but she'll be okay.

Right?

There's this need deep inside me, though. I want to go get her. Make sure she's okay. I'm worried about her. How will I be able to concentrate on Whitney tonight when all I'll do is worry about Eden?

You don't like Whitney, you dumbass. It's Eden that you like. Eden is the girl you want.

"No problem," Abraham says easily. Almost too easily. "I've got it. I'm gonna go get her now."

"Should I text her? Make sure she's okay?" I'm starting to sweat, and I'm feeling sort of dizzy.

I can't stand the thought of not being with Eden right now.

"Nah, she knows where you're at. Don't even bother. Text her tomorrow. She'll understand."

Yeah, no. This doesn't feel right. I can't let Abraham rescue her. That's my job. "I'm picking her up," I say, my voice firm.

"Are you sure?"

I've never been more sure in my life. "Yeah, I want to. Don't worry about it. I'll take care of Eden." I try to ignore the warm feeling that washes over me at saying those words, but it's difficult. I *want* to take care of Eden.

I end the call with Abraham and then I go in search of the text from Eden. I find it in Snapchat. She sent it to me about an hour ago.

Hey, are you busy?

I hesitate for only a moment before I send her one back.

Are you okay? I talked to Abraham.

She answers almost immediately.

It's been a rough night, but I'll survive. A's coming to get me.

I can't believe what Cole told you.

He's a cheating douche.

Yeah he is.

He ruined my dinner. I'm starving.

I chuckle to myself. She doesn't sound too broken up over this.

I'll pick you up. And if you're lucky, I'll bring you some food.

Wait. Aren't you on your date with Whitney?

Yeah. Whitney. I lift my head and stare at the house once again, see the flickering light from the TV illuminate the interior. I should go back inside and sit next to Whitney. Pull her into my arms and let her snuggle in close, let her pretend that she's scared of what's playing out on the screen so she can bury her face against my chest. It's what I'd normally be down for.

Tonight, it's not.

And I need to answer Eden. Truthfully.

Yeah, I am. But I don't wanna be here.

:(Why not?

Maybe I'll explain it to you when I come get you.

Josh you don't need to do that.

But I want to.

I really want to.

Then come to the bowling alley and pick me up.

Okay I will.

Chapter Thirteen

EDEN

It's late, past ten when Josh and I walk into the house. My parents went to bed a while ago, supposedly exhausted over setting up the artificial Christmas tree earlier this afternoon that's now sitting in front of the window facing the street. It's lit up but not decorated yet. We're saving those fun times for tomorrow.

I lock the front door as Josh heads toward the kitchen carrying an In-N-Out bag in each hand. Leaning against the door for a moment, I think of our drive from the bowling alley. Not many words were said. I watched him pull up in front of the building, and I went to his truck, thankful that he showed up so quickly. He didn't mention Cole, and I didn't mention Whitney. There wasn't much said at all, but it didn't feel awkward.

Funny thing is, it never feels awkward with Josh.

Pushing away from the door, I follow after him, stopping in the doorway as he moves about my kitchen with the ease of someone who's been here countless times before.

And he has. He's spent a lot of time in this house over the years. On the way home, I texted Mom to let her know Josh was coming over, and she acted like it was no big deal. Mom just warned me not to stay up too late with Josh and that was that.

If they only knew my weird thoughts about Josh lately, they might reconsider their feelings about him coming over so late.

"Want a plate?" Josh asks, pushing me out of my thoughts.

I nod and go to the cabinet to get them for us, opening a door to grab a couple of paper plates. Josh goes to the fridge and grabs a bottle of ketchup and two Cokes, and then we're sitting at the kitchen counter, Josh divvying up the food and me biting into that cheeseburger like I haven't eaten in years.

It tastes like heaven, even though it's not as hot and fresh as I prefer it. Doesn't matter. I can feel Josh watching me with what I'm sure is amusement, and I give him the finger before I shove a handful of fries into my mouth with the other hand. "So. Freaking. Good," I say, my mouth full.

"You weren't lying when you said you were hungry," he says, his deep voice tinged with amusement.

"Cole ruined everything. I love pasta." I hold up my cheeseburger. "But I love In-N-Out, too, so you did good."

We continue to eat in companionable silence, neither one of us bringing up what happened tonight. Still nothing mentioned about Cole, nothing mentioned about Whitney. I'm curious, yet I don't want to know. He doesn't look any different, though I suspect when he eventually does have sex with someone, it's not like he's going to walk around with a sign around his neck proclaiming I DID IT in big, bold letters.

I sort of wish he did, just so, you know, I'd realize when it happened. But do I want to know? Or is it easier to be oblivious?

"If he hadn't told you what happened with uh—the cheating thing, would you have reconsidered going out with him?" Josh asks after he finishes his Double-Double.

I study him, my gaze meeting his. Did he know about the cheating thing with Whitney? Ugh. I barely know the girl and thought she was sweet, and now all I want to do is barf every time I hear her stupid name. "I wouldn't have reconsidered our relationship. It didn't feel right, being with Cole tonight. Something was off."

Josh nods, like he understands. "It felt off with Whit, too."

Wait. What? "What do you mean?"

He shoves a bunch of fries in his mouth, chews fast, and swallows. "I went over there fully prepared to—you know—and from the moment I arrived, it felt weird. Like I didn't belong there. I wasn't interested, and she's hot, Eden. She has a badass house, and she had on some sexy scary movie with topless teenage vampires sinking their teeth into their boyfriends right in the middle of sex. She was totally setting the scene, and I just wasn't feeling it. At all."

I hate hearing him describe Whitney as hot. Worse, I hate the doubt creeping into my mind. If Abraham knew about Cole cheating on me with Whit, then maybe Josh knew, too. Does that mean he kept it from me? I understand Abraham doing that, but not Josh. Never Josh. "Did you know?" I ask, my voice quiet. "About Cole and Whit?"

With a sigh, Josh drops the fries he just picked up. "Abraham told me about it a few hours ago."

The relief that washes over me is strong. "Abraham told me Cole confessed to him last week."

"I guess it's been bothering Cole a lot lately."

"Guess so. Only took him what? Like nine months to finally confess?" I'm so irritated by the entire situation. What did I ever see in Cole anyway? "So you didn't know until today."

"Like literally only a couple of hours ago, tops. I had no

idea Cole did that to you. If I had, I would've kicked his ass."

I 100 percent believe him. That's Josh, always bailing me out. "I know. And I appreciate that."

Josh smiles at me and ducks his head.

"What about Whitney? Why didn't that happen?" I ask.

"Felt too forced. I kept thinking about what you said. How it should happen naturally. How it should be with someone special." He's still not looking at me, and it's the fact that he can't look me in the eye that's making me nervous. "I thought I wanted a casual hookup, but I don't even know that girl, and I was going to have *sex* with her."

His words make me so happy, yet I have to act like they're not affecting me at all. "So you couldn't go through with it."

"No, I couldn't." He shakes his head and finally lifts his gaze to mine. "I told her I had to go help a friend out, that it was an emergency, and she said she understood. She's nice."

I make a face. Right, she's so nice she'll have sex with my now ex-boyfriend and then keep it a secret. Whatever.

"But she's not you, Eden," Josh adds, his voice so low I almost don't hear him.

We stare at each other, my stomach doing dips and loops, my breath coming a little faster. What does he mean by that? Am I reading too much into his words?

"I hope I didn't ruin everything with you having to run to my rescue yet again," I say, trying to lighten the mood.

But that serious expression remains on his face as he continues to watch me. "I'd run to your rescue any time you asked, no matter what."

Oh. I don't know what to say, don't know what to do, don't know how to react. I just stare at him, blindly reaching for my Coke, and take a long, noisy sip out of the straw. The air seems to shift between us, crackling with a charged energy I've never felt before, and I leap to my feet, gathering the empty wrappers scattered all over the counter and shoving them back into the bag.

"I'm going to throw this away," I tell him, heading for the garbage can on the opposite end of the kitchen.

He doesn't answer and that's fine. I'm too focused on trying to even out my stuttering breaths, calm my racing heart. Once I dispose of the trash, I go to the sink and wash my hands, my skin prickling with awareness when he does the same, joining me by the sink. He pushes up the sleeves of his shirt, adds a couple of pumps of foamy soap into his palms, and starts washing them. When he dunks his hands under the water, they brush against mine, sending tingles of awareness shooting straight up my arms. I suck in a breath, wondering since when did washing hands become such an intimate act.

Clearly I'm overreacting.

"Do you need to head home?" I ask once we've dried our hands, and now we're left staring at each other in the middle of the kitchen.

He shrugs those broad shoulders, and my gaze roams over his chest, that black shirt he's wearing. He looks good tonight. Clearly, he dressed up for his so-called date with Whitney. Yet somehow he ended up with me.

And that shouldn't give me even a glint of satisfaction, but it does. It so does. I love that he's not with her, and that he's with me.

Only me.

"I can stay a while longer if you don't mind," he says with an easy smile.

"Yeah, you should. Let's go watch some TV." I head for the living room, and Josh falls into step directly behind me, so close I can feel the warmth from his body, the light scent of his woodsy cologne. I go sit on the couch, and he joins me, sitting right next to me when usually he's kicked back in my dad's recliner on late nights when we do this sort of thing and my parents are already in bed.

I keep my gaze fixed on the TV as I lean forward to grab the remote and start searching the guide for something to watch. Josh is so close our thighs are pressed together, and I glance over my shoulder to find him already studying me. "Anything in particular you want to watch?"

"No." He reaches for my hand. "Come here."

I let him take it. He removes the remote and sets it somewhere else, I don't know where and I don't really care. The TV is stuck on some lame channel with an infomercial playing, the volume turned down so low I can't even hear what they're saying. The Christmas tree glows with multicolored lights that gently flash, illuminating the room, and when I stare up at Josh, the lights cast shadows across his handsome face.

He slides his fingers through mine, our palms pressed together, and I swallow hard when he squeezes my fingers. Our linked hands feel so good together, so right. My heart starts to thump extra hard. "Eden."

All he says is my name, and I want to say something back, but it's like I can't speak.

"Edes." Josh smiles, and he looks so nervous. So incredibly nervous and adorable, too. "I want to tell you something."

I swallow again, my throat dry, my thoughts going haywire. I want to hear what he has to say, but I'm also scared. This is a huge moment that could change everything. Either make our relationship great or ruin it completely. "Wh-what is it?"

With his free hand he touches my face, drifts the back of his hand across my cheek. Tingles spread across my skin, and I feel like I can't breathe. "When I was at Whitney's, all I could think about was you."

I frown, hating that he went to her house, but there's nothing I can do to change that. "What do you mean?"

"I was fully intent on going over there to have sex with Whitney, yet all I could think about was you. I didn't want to be with her. I wanted to be with you, Edes." He cups the side of my face, his fingers gentle against my skin, and then he's leaning in, his mouth landing on mine tentatively just as I close my eyes. His kiss is a question, his lips gentle as they test mine, and before the kiss has even started, he's already pulling away.

"If you want me to stop, I'll stop." His voice is firm, and I crack open my eyes to find him watching me. He looks just as dazed and confused as I feel, and I know he means what he says. "I don't want to ruin our friendship Edes, but I'm willing to…"

I don't want to hear his excuses. Instead I cut off whatever he was going to say with my lips.

• • •

JOSH

Holy shit. Holy. Shit. Eden is kissing me. Kissing *me*. And I'm kissing her back. I cup her nape, my fingers tangling in her soft hair as I tilt her head to the side and deepen the kiss. Her lips part, and I touch my tongue to hers.

And that's all it takes. The kiss instantly goes wild, Eden wrapping her arms around my neck, me slipping my other arm around her waist. I haul her into me, until she's sprawled across my body, and we kiss like this for what feels like minutes. Hours.

Days.

She fits perfectly in my arms. The sounds she makes, the way she tastes, how she touches me, it's like everything I've been searching for but never found.

I've found it now. I've found it with Eden.

After long, lips-and-tongue-filled minutes, I break away from her first to catch my breath, kissing a path down her neck, smiling when I feel her shiver. I slip my fingers beneath the hem of her long-sleeve T-shirt, touch the bare skin at her waist, and there's another shiver. This one accompanied by a whimper.

"Josh," she whispers, and I open my eyes, lifting away from her delicious neck. She's watching me with slumberous eyes, the lights from the Christmas tree flashing across her pretty face. "What are we doing?"

"I don't know," I whisper back. "But let's not think too hard about it tonight, okay?"

Eden nods, her lips parting, her tongue sneaking out to streak across her upper lip. I groan and press my mouth to hers once more, capturing her lower lip with mine and giving it a tug. She makes this tiny whimpering sound that's like a shot of electricity throughout my entire body, and now I'm going on pure instinct. Pure want. I wrap both arms around her tiny waist and haul her in as close as I can, her legs going around my hips, her hands diving into my hair. One hand slides down, along the side of my neck, down the front of my shirt and then—holy shit—she's unbuttoning my shirt. One button. Then the next, and the next...

A different type of light flashes through the room, and then Eden's pushing away from me, climbing off my lap. I open my eyes once more to find her standing in front of the couch, tugging at the hem of her shirt down, then reaching up to smooth out her messy hair.

"My brother's home," she whispers frantically. "Go sit in my dad's recliner!"

I do as she tells me, throwing myself into her dad's chair and pulling the handle so it reclines.

"Oh my God, fix your hair," Eden says before she stretches out on the couch and tugs a blanket over her. "Looks like my hands were in it."

"Your hands *were* in it." Felt damn good, too. Everything she did felt good. And now Travis is totally interrupting us and ruining everything.

For once, I'm sort of hating on him, and I never hate on Travis. That's always Eden's job.

A key sounds in the front door as he undoes the lock, and then Travis pushes the door open, closing it behind him with a quiet click. He turns and his eyes go wide when he spots us sitting in the living room, our gazes focused on the TV.

"Oh, hey." He shoves his hands in his front pockets, rocking back on his heels. "What are you two up to?"

"More like what are you up to?" I throw back at him, taking the spotlight off us.

"Where have you been?" Eden asks, sounding like the stern older sister, though I swear there's a quiver in her voice, too. Our gazes meet. Linger. She looks away first, and her cheeks go pink.

I carefully touch the corner of my mouth. I feel marked, like Eden's hands are still all over me, her mouth fused with mine. My lips are swollen, and they tingle, and I swear I can taste her...

"I went to the movies with Isabella." Travis tilts his head to the side, his gaze on me, going to Eden, then coming back to me again. "What are you two doing?"

"Watching TV," I say, thankful Eden grabs the remote from where I discarded it earlier on the couch.

Travis looks over at the flat screen. "Infomercials?"

Eden immediately starts changing the channel. "We were looking for a movie," she says.

"With no volume on?" Travis's eyebrows shoot up.

I remain quiet, and Eden hits the volume button until we can finally hear the TV. "We were—talking," she says.

"Uh huh." Travis sounds doubtful. "Well, don't let me disturb your *talk*. I'll see you guys later." He starts to leave the living room. "And hey Josh, your shirt is unbuttoned," he adds as he walks down the hallway toward his bedroom.

Damn it. I immediately glance down and grab at the front of my shirt, doing up the buttons that Eden undid a few minutes ago. "Jackass," I mutter.

"Finally you're on my side," she says, tossing a throw pillow at me. It glances off the side of my head, and I catch it before it drops to the ground, throwing it back at her. She dodges it just in time before it hits her, and the pillow smacks the wall, then lands on the ground.

"He totally knows what we were up to," I say, hoping it doesn't freak her out. I'm not freaked out. No, more like I feel lit up from the inside, which is the corniest shit *ever.*

But it's true. That kiss with Eden was everything.

She chews on her pinkie nail. "You really think so?"

"Oh hell yeah, did you see that knowing look on your brother's face?" I kick the recliner into place and rise from the chair, then stretch my arms above my head, my spine giving a satisfying crack. "I'm sure he suspects something's going on between us."

"Oh my God." She sounds panicked. "What should we do?"

"We don't have to do anything." Because nothing's really happened yet, I want to say, but don't. That one kiss rocked my world, but we don't need to tell anyone our private business.

I'd rather keep this between us. At least for a little while.

"Yeah, okay. You're right." She exhales slowly, staring down at the floor. "It's no big deal."

But it was a big deal to me. I can't deny that. So she can go ahead and say what she needs to convince herself that everything's going to be all right. That our friendship won't become royally screwed if we end up getting together only for everything to fall apart.

Without another word, I go stand in front of the couch and hold out my hand to Eden. She takes it and I pull her to her feet, then pull her into my arms. She leans into me, her face pressed against my chest, her soft hair brushing my jaw. I close my eyes and just hold her, savoring the feeling of her in my arms, taking advantage of the moment. I don't think I've ever held her this close for this long before. Her arms sneak around my waist, and she runs her hands up and down my back while I lean my head on top of hers. She's short. I'm a full head taller than she is, yet somehow we fit together like two pieces in a puzzle.

"I should probably go home," I whisper against her hair.

"Yeah?" Her voice is muffled against my chest.

"It's late."

"Not too late."

I'm quiet for a moment, thinking. "What time is it?"

"Around eleven."

Mom doesn't even have a curfew on me anymore. Most of the time, she's not home, especially on a Saturday night. She's always over at her boyfriend's house, leaving me on my own.

"I can stay for a while if you want me to."

Eden lifts her head away from my chest, our gazes meeting. "You should stay for a little bit longer."

"Okay." I just agreed way too quick, probably sound too eager, but Eden doesn't even notice. I think she's glad I want to stay.

"Maybe we can watch TV in…" Her voice drifts and her gaze drops from mine. "In my room."

My entire body tightens. Is she suggesting what I think she is? "You sure?"

She nods and lifts her head, a little smile curving her lips. "Yeah."

"Then let's do it," I murmur just before I kiss her.

I'm guessing those words have more than one meaning tonight.

Chapter Fourteen

JOSH

"What's going on? Why do you look so spooked?"

These are the first words Abraham says to me when I arrive on campus the Monday after Thanksgiving break. And yeah, I'm feeling pretty spooked, but I don't need to get called out on it, you know? That makes me feel even sketchier.

"Rough weekend," I tell him as I head straight for my locker.

Abraham follows me. "Are you serious? You hooked up with Whitney Gregory, and you call that a rough weekend? What the hell is wrong with you?"

That's right. I didn't talk to Abraham so he doesn't know what happened. And that's because I didn't talk to anyone about what happened this past weekend. It's no one's business but ours.

"I didn't hook up with Whit," I tell him just before I swing my locker door open. I exchange a few books and shut the door to find Abraham standing there, his mouth hanging open.

"Are you serious?" he asks, shaking his head slowly, like he's in a daze. "Why not?"

I take a step closer to him, not wanting anyone else to hear. "I wasn't feeling it. Not with Whit."

Abraham stares at me, his head still shaking from side to side. "You are a crazy asshole," he finally says. "I don't understand you."

"Trust me, I don't understand me, either." I start walking, and again, Abraham falls into step beside me. Usually, I'm glad to have him around. For once, I want to be alone and wallow in my own thoughts.

And every one of my thoughts right now is zeroed in on Eden.

As we walk down the hall toward our first period class, Abraham is talking to me, but I don't hear a word he says. I'm too busy searching the faces passing us by, desperate to catch a glimpse of Eden.

"Winter formal's coming up." Those particular words Abraham just said caught my attention.

"Still going to ask Eden to the dance?" I ask, my entire body stiff as I wait for his answer.

"Hell no, I told you I was trying to make you jealous and push you to go after her." Abraham shakes his head. "Too bad that didn't work."

He has no idea, and I'm not telling him, either.

Or should I?

I finally spot Eden. She's walking down the hall from the opposite direction, chatting and laughing with Molly as they head right for us. Every once in a while Eden looks around, like she's searching for someone, and I'd bet everything I've got she's looking for me.

"Yo, Molly. Eden," Abraham calls out in greeting as they draw closer.

Molly smiles, her cheeks pink. "Abraham."

"Hi, Abraham," Eden says. Her gaze lands directly on mine. "Joshua."

I tip my head toward her, barely able to contain the smile that wants to break free. "Eden."

They walk past us, and I turn my head as they go, watching Eden from behind. She's got on an oversize sweater and black leggings, black Converse on her feet. Bummed out over the sweater since it's covering her ass, and she's got a great one.

I should know. I had my hands all over it Saturday night.

"Did you just check out Molly?" Abraham asks.

I start to laugh. "No, asswipe."

Realization dawns, and Abraham's expression is downright hilarious. "You were checking out Eden?"

"Yeah, and keep it down." I'm smirking. I can feel it. "We sort of—hooked up over the weekend." Guess I'm not keeping us a secret after all.

"What the hell?" Abraham is practically shouting. "Seriously?"

I nod, trying to keep my cool.

"So you two are a thing now?"

"Sort of," I hedge. We never talked after Saturday night. I left in the middle of the night, sneaking out of her house like a criminal. We exchanged a few casual Snapchats to keep up our streak like normal, and that was it. But I have a perfectly good excuse. I slept most of Sunday since I was exhausted, and the next thing I knew it was Sunday night and I was working on my homework that was due, Mom giving me a lecture about procrastination and how I'll never make it in college if I keep that crap up. I ignored her and finished my government assignment, took a shower, and then collapsed into bed.

Abraham is frowning at me. "What do you mean, you're sort of a thing? What does that even mean? Either you are or you aren't."

"Are you and Nicole a thing?" I throw back at him.

"Uh, I don't know." The frown is gone, replaced by an expression filled with confusion. "We hook up and that's about it."

"Right, so don't give me any shit since you're in the same situation as me," I tell him as we keep walking. I feel sort of like a jerk, how I just said that. But whatever just happened between Eden and me is…fragile. Plus, it's awesome and amazing and mind blowing and scary.

Yeah, it's definitely scary.

"Nah, man, you two are different. You're like best friends, and now that you two have done—whatever, it changes everything, right? Like now you should act like a couple of disgusting lovebirds who make kissy faces at each other and drive us all totally insane with your over the top love for each other."

I send him a sideways glance. "Are you a closet romantic, Abraham?"

"What? Me? No freaking way." Abraham makes a dismissive noise. "I'm just stating the truth, bro. You know it's gonna happen."

I have no idea what's going to happen with Eden and me, and that's the scary part.

We're walking and talking—make that Abraham's talking—and I'm not paying attention to where I'm going. My thoughts are Eden-filled and I'm wondering if we'll sit together at lunch. Or better yet, maybe we'll go off campus somewhere for lunch and make out instead. Which makes me think of Eden's lips. And her hands. And the way she kissed my neck and bit my ear and—

I run into someone. Hard. Reaching out, I grab slender shoulders to keep her—because she's definitely a her—from falling. I hold her away from me and realize it's Kaylie. I ran into Kaylie. My ex-girlfriend.

And she's smiling at me like I'm her absolute favorite person.

Uh-oh.

"Josh," she breathes, her smile growing. "How are you?"

"Good, good." I remember how she ignored me in the parking lot when we walked by each other Friday afternoon before break, but I decide not to bring it up. "How was your break?"

"Oh, you know. I did the usual stuff, going to my uncle's for Thanksgiving, having to babysit all the time for my parents. It sucked." Kaylie is the oldest of six, and she's always watching her younger siblings. She hates it.

"Sounds fun." I glance over at Abraham, and he's got this bemused expression on his face. Like he's loving watching me squirm while talking to Kaylie. "Gotta go to class. See you around, Kaylie," I say, trying to get away from her.

We start walking again, but she follows after us, calling my name. I pause and Abraham keeps on walking, like he knows some bullshit is about to go down and he doesn't want to be around for it.

Some friend he is.

"What else is going on?" I ask, just to make conversation, because I'm not a rude bastard. I'll talk to her if I have to, but I'm done seeking her out or wanting to try things again with Kaylie. Especially after what happened with Eden Saturday night.

Kaylie and I move out of the way of oncoming hallway traffic, and we both stop. "Nothing much. But I, uh, wanted to ask you a question." She bites her lower lip, a thing I used to love when she did that, but now when I see her do it, I feel nothing, like absolute zero interest. My mind is 100 percent Eden filled. "Um, do you have a date to the winter formal yet?"

She can't seriously be asking me this right now.

"Because if you don't, I was hoping maybe we could go together." The nervous yet hopeful look on her face makes me feel bad. Like really bad.

I part my lips, ready to offer up a firm *hell no* as my answer when the bell rings.

"Don't say no yet," Kaylie says. She lets go of my arm and starts walking away. "Tell me your answer later," she calls over her shoulder.

I watch her go, stress turning my stomach into a jumble of nerves.

Great. Now Kaylie thinks I'm considering going with her to winter formal when there's no chance in hell that's gonna happen.

. . .

EDEN

"You've been acting weird all morning," Molly observes. We're sitting in our student council class, everyone working on stuff for the upcoming holiday festival the school holds every year. Molly and I are designing a flyer, but I can't concentrate for crap and she knows it.

All I can think about is Josh.

"I'm fine," I tell her, my voice robotic as I stare at the laptop screen.

"You don't sound fine. You sound like a weirdo." Molly punches me in the shoulder. So hard I yelp and turn to glare at her. "I mean, I get that you're not into my stories about Kirk. And that's fine if my best friend isn't enthusiastic about my dating choices, but at the very least, you could at least pretend that you care? Just a little? Maybe?"

My shoulders sag, and I grab hold of her, giving her a big hug. "I'm a shitty friend," I murmur against her hair.

Molly slowly pulls away. "You forgot, huh."

I nod, hanging my head. "I did." And I feel like crap for it, too. But I had a lot of drama happen on Saturday, and I was a little distracted.

"Well, it wasn't that great of a date, but I'm going to give him another try." She leans in close and whispers near my ear. "He's sort of boring."

"Why?" I rear back so our gazes meet.

"He always talks about himself." Molly wrinkles her nose, making me laugh.

"I hate it when people do that."

"Me too." Molly's eyes narrow, and she does that *I'm staring into your soul* thing she usually does. "So. What's going on with you?"

"What do you mean?" I turn away from her so she can't peer into the depths of my brain or whatever magic voodoo she works to get me to confess my sins.

"Like I said, you've been acting weird all morning. Does this have to do with Cole? You never did tell me what happened on your dinner date," Molly says. "I'm still sort of mad at you that you went on an actual date with him. What he did to you before was so awful, I don't know why you'd want to put yourself through that again."

Oh my God, that's right. I can't believe I didn't tell her. So I launch into the entire story, starting from the very beginning of the date at the Italian restaurant, to when Cole confessed he cheated on me with Whitney, to the moment when I texted Abraham and he asked Josh to pick me up from the bowling alley instead.

"You texted Abraham first?" Molly sounds shocked. "What happened to Josh?"

"He was busy."

"Too busy for you?"

"Well no, considering he did come and rescue me."

"Right, because he *always* rescues you."

I contemplate telling her about what happened with Josh. I can still barely believe it myself. It's not like we went all the way or anything, but we messed around. In my bed. Lots of sloppy kisses and sexy murmurs and hands everywhere, buttons unbuttoned with fumbling hands and a bra unsnapped with too assured fingers and…

Yeah. It feels like a dream. Like it really didn't happen. Seeing him in the hall before school started was kind of weird. He just looked like—Josh. Normal-every-day-Josh. But now he's also the Josh who kissed me for hours. The Josh whose hands were all over my body. The Josh who touched me in a particular way and literally made me see stars.

My entire body goes hot just remembering.

"Wait a minute." Molly's words knock me from my thoughts. "You actually like Abraham now, huh. And he likes you! I should've seen this coming." She buries her face in her hands.

I pull her hands away from her face and stare into her eyes. Maybe if I look hard enough, I can see into the depths of her soul, too. "Listen to me. I don't like Abraham. He's not my type. Besides, I would never do that to you."

"Right. I know that." She's nodding, but I don't know if I have her convinced. Molly's not the most confident girl in the world when it comes to boys. Everything else in her life, she's fine. More than capable. Beyond capable. Boys? They freak her out.

I'm quiet for a moment, contemplating what I should say next, and then I just blurt it out. "Josh and I hooked up."

Molly's eyes go so wide it's almost comical. "What did you just say?"

I lean in closer, glancing around to make sure no one is listening to us. "Saturday night, Josh and I were together. And we sort of—messed around."

"Ohmygod. Did you have sex with Josh?" she breathes, her eyes ready to bug out of her head.

"No." *Not yet.* "He was over at Whitney Gregory's house before he came and picked me up from the bowling alley."

"Ew. She sucks. So bad." Spoken like a true loyal best friend.

"Right. Well, Josh went to her house fully planning on hooking up with her, but then he ended up picking me up from my disastrous date with Cole instead."

"And so Josh ended up at your house and you two hooked up?" Molly shakes her head. "Are you sure you're not just his...sloppy seconds?"

"Ouch, Molly." Her words hurt. I know she's watching out for me, but I never once viewed myself as his second choice of the night.

Or was I? Maybe he lied about not feeling right with Whitney to save face? Maybe Whitney wasn't in to him after all and so he ended up with me?

Ugh. I hate that Molly just put major doubt into my head.

"I'm sorry, I hated saying that, but I'm just trying to be real. I don't want to find out that he's settling for you or whatever and then he ends up hurting you," Molly explains.

"*Settling* for me?" Ouch again. She's slinging the insults today, isn't she? "I don't think that was the case. He said he couldn't stop thinking about me."

"Of course, he would say that. He's trying to get in your pants."

Okay, before I was hurt. Now I'm just...mad. And I never get mad at Molly.

"You're being really mean right now."

"I'm trying to be really *real* right now. I don't want you to get your hopes up only for them to come crashing down when you find out that Josh didn't mean it."

"Mean what?"

"Whatever it is he's telling you!" Molly is full on yelling now. A few people are looking over at us and I know they're trying to overhear what we're saying.

"Lower your voice," I tell her, keeping mine low too. "Seriously, people are totally eavesdropping."

Molly sighs and looks away, staring out the window that faces the campus quad. "I don't want you to get hurt, Eden," she says, her voice so low I have to lean in closer. "I know you claim you've never felt that way about Josh until now, but I don't know if I believe you. I think you've been in love with him forever."

"So not true," I immediately retort, grabbing my backpack off the ground and slinging it over my shoulder as I rise to my feet. "He was my best friend and now things have totally shifted. I don't know what's happening. I don't think even he knows what's happening. But I do know this."

Molly lifts her chin, her expression stony. "What?"

"I'm totally disappointed that my other best friend can't be happy for me." I walk away from her. She calls my name, but I don't turn around. Instead, I go to the advisor's desk and ask Mrs. Watters if I can go to the bathroom. We're ten minutes away from lunch, and I'm pretty sure she'll let me leave.

"Of course. You don't have to bother coming back if you're done with your work for the day," Mrs. Watters tells me with a faint smile.

"I am. I'll finish the flyer tomorrow. Thank you, Mrs. Watters." I buzz out of the classroom before Molly can stop me, and I head for the bathroom, locking myself in a stall and taking a few deep breaths before I handle my business.

But my brain is full of jumbled thoughts, every one of them confusing. Annoying.

They're even a little dark and depressing.

Like maybe Josh isn't into me after all. Maybe I was

second choice. He could've been lying about the entire Whitney Gregory thing. She might've rejected him and he came to me looking to hook up with me instead.

He'd seemed so sincere though, telling me how he couldn't stop thinking about me. The way he kissed me and held me and touched me…he likes me. He has to.

The bell rings for lunch, and within seconds girls are storming into the bathroom. One voice rises above the rest, and I recognize it immediately.

Kaylie. My friend. Josh's ex-girlfriend. She's always been loud. She told me a long time ago it's the only way she can be heard in her house, and considering her noisy brothers and sisters, the theory makes sense.

The problem is that she's talking so loud about something I both want and don't want to hear.

"I asked Josh to winter formal," she says to whoever's with her.

Say what?

"Josh Evans?" I don't recognize the voice, but she sounds shocked.

"Yes, my Josh."

I hate how possessive she sounds. He's not her Josh.

"What did he say?" the other girl asks.

"I told him to think about it. He seemed like he wanted to go. I kind of want to go find him right now so we can talk, but I don't want to be too pushy," Kaylie says.

Oh God. Is he seriously considering going to winter formal with Kaylie? What about me?

I smack open the stall door and go to the sink so I can hurriedly wash my hands, then go find Josh. Kaylie is standing nearby with her friend—I recognize her vaguely, she's a junior on the softball team with Kaylie—and I offer them both a quick smile.

"Eden," Kaylie says, turning to study me. "Have a good

break?"

"Had a great one," I say truthfully, though I should also add the words confusing and weird to my break description. But I don't. Instead, I smile at her and her friend, dry my hands, and yell out a cheery, "See ya!" as I bolt out the door.

I head toward the senior parking lot, hoping Josh will already be out there. I have to beat Kaylie. I have to get to Josh first. I have to—

"Eden."

I whirl around to find Cole standing in front of me, a scowl on his face. *Crap.* Could this get any worse? "Hey, Cole," I greet him weakly, my gaze darting everywhere in search of Josh. I wonder if Cole is going to apologize for what he said—more like how he said it—on Saturday night.

"What happened Saturday was total bullshit," he says, the disgust clear in his voice.

My mouth drops open. Did he really just say that?

"You shouldn't have walked out on me like that, Eden. I was trying to apologize to you for what I did," he continues.

I snap my lips shut. "My walking out shows you how much I value your apology, Cole."

His expression turns downright thunderous. "So that's it? You're done? You're over me, over us?"

Glancing around, I make sure no one's paying any attention to us. This is the last place I want to have this conversation, in the senior hall during lunch. There are so many people around, but I don't think they're listening. "Cole, it was over a long time ago," I say gently. "When you broke up with me last time. I think it's best we don't revisit our relationship anymore."

That was the kindest way I could think of putting it, and he still manages to look furious. There's no pleasing him.

"So all the history, all the time we've spent together, you're willing to just throw it away," he says.

"You threw it away by cheating on me!" I throw my hands up in the air for emphasis, but I don't know if he gets it. "There's too much history between us, Cole. Too much built up resentment and old hurt feelings for us to make this work again. Can't we just be friends?"

With an impatient shake of his head, Cole doesn't say a word. He stomps off instead, pushing through the double doors that lead to the parking lot with a violent shove, letting in a blast of cold air before the doors slam shut behind him.

Sighing, I look over my shoulder to find Josh a few locker rows behind me.

And Kaylie's with him.

Ughhh this is like the worst teen movie I've ever seen, I swear.

I lean against the nearest locker and blatantly watch them, not caring if I get caught. She says something to him, twirling a strand of golden-brown hair around her finger, her dark brown eyes sparkling and her smile wide. The flirtation is painfully obvious, and I'm half tempted to walk over there and call her out on it.

But I don't, because Kaylie is my friend. And Josh is my friend, too. He's just turned into a friend with...benefits, I guess. Which makes everything weird and uncomfortable, and I don't know what to do about it.

So I handle my troubles in the best way I know how.

I run away from them.

Chapter Fifteen

After school, I got a ride home from Abraham of all people. It's so weird, but since I don't have my own car—that will happen when I go to college next fall—and I'm mad at Molly and avoiding Josh, that leaves me relying on Abraham.

And he steps up, too, readily agreeing to take me home. We talk about miscellaneous stuff on the drive to my house, until he hits me with a Josh question when we're still about five minutes from my neighborhood.

That's when things get a little sketchy. At least, on my part.

"Josh was looking for you at lunch." A hesitation, then Abraham decides to go for it. "Were you avoiding him?"

I stare straight ahead, not looking at Abraham. "Did he say he thought I was avoiding him?"

"No, but I wondered if you were." Another hesitation. "I saw you in the hall right when lunch started, watching Kaylie talk to Josh."

I sink lower in my seat, still keeping my gaze fixed on the windshield.

"He talked to her for like, less than a minute, which you'd know if you'd stuck around. Josh doesn't like her," Abraham adds. "He likes you."

"How do you know?" I turn to look at Abraham but he is, of course, driving and paying attention to the road. "Did he tell you? Oh God, did he tell you what happened between us?"

"Sort of." Abraham has the decency to look uncomfortable, which makes me uncomfortable. "He didn't give me any details, so don't worry."

I cover my face. Josh is the king of giving up all sorts of details, so Abraham is lying through his teeth. "I'm so embarrassed," I mumble against my palms.

"You have nothing to be embarrassed over. He never said anything to me beyond the two of you hooking up. I have no idea what exactly happened between you two. Your secrets are safe."

Whatever. I want to believe him, but it's hard. I know Josh. He loves to talk about his love life, share painfully intimate details so he can dissect every little thing in order to figure out what he should do next. He told me so many things about the girls he's been with over the years, things I never wanted to hear. Things those girls would die over if they found out I knew. So no way is he keeping our little moment from Saturday a total secret.

Josh must've told Abraham *something*.

"He's totally into you, Eden. He has been for years; he just never realized it until now," Abraham says, as he turns right and onto my street.

My curiosity gets the better of me. "What about…" Oh, God. I can't do this. I can't.

I have to.

"What about what?" Abraham sounds confused.

"Um, you." My voice is small. I bet he didn't hear even me.

"What about me?"

Ah crap, he did hear me. "I thought." I swallow hard and close my eyes for a brief moment. Saying this isn't easy. "Josh told me that—you liked me."

Abraham starts laughing. Like downright hysterically. I let him get it all out, becoming madder and madder with every second that passes.

"What's so funny?" I ask once his laughter starts to die. I cross my arms. "Is it that hilarious, thinking you might actually like me?"

"Eden, you're taking this all wrong. Seriously." He pulls over, directly in front of my house, and kills the engine. "I don't like you like that. I never have. I said that on purpose to bug Josh."

"What? Why?"

"I was hoping he'd finally make a move and end the suspense. We've all been waiting for the two of you to get together."

"So he only hooked up with me because he thought you liked me?" I'm bewildered. A little insulted. I don't know what to think.

"No, no. His feelings for you finally bubbled close to the surface, I guess. I don't know what exactly pushed him, but I don't think it was me. He knows I told him I liked you to get a rise out of him anyway," Abraham explains, his gaze meeting mine.

My heart is sinking, and my mind is spinning. "Can I be honest? I'm doubting everything that's happened between us," I whisper. I hate the doubt that's creeping into me, but I can't help it. Seeing him talk to Kaylie at lunch shook me. Barely a week ago he was sort of admitting he wasn't over her. I even pushed her on him, adding her to his list, though that made him mad. Will he toss me aside for Kaylie? They do have a lot of history between them.

Plus, we might've fooled around, but we didn't have actual sex, and that is his ultimate goal. Maybe he's ready to move on from me. Maybe he's eager to get back with Kaylie and have that quick hookup he so desperately wants. Not that I would call Kaylie quick hookup material but…

You never know.

And if he is willing to give Kaylie another chance, where does that leave me?

All alone and sad and crying and feeling sorry for myself.

Ugh, I need my thoughts to stop being so dramatic.

"If you're doubting everything, then you should stop avoiding Josh and go talk to him about it," Abraham says.

"You make it sound so easy." I sort of groan. Man, I'm pitiful.

"It is, if you'd just open your eyes. You and Josh talk all the damn time, Eden. What's the big deal about this particular conversation?"

It's the biggest deal ever, I want to tell Abraham, but I keep my mouth shut. This particular conversation will put our entire relationship on the line. I know what I want—Josh. But does he want me? Or is he realizing that maybe he wants Kaylie more?

If he goes back to Kaylie, that will kill me.

"Talk to him, Eden. Stop wasting your time sitting here with me when you could actually go be with him."

My mouth pops open. "But…"

"Go. Get out." Abraham waves an impatient hand at me before he starts the car. "I mean it. Go talk to him."

I reach out and punch his upper arm, making him yelp. I'm surprised at how muscular he is. My knuckles hurt. "Why don't you drive me over to his house then." It's only a few blocks away.

"Deal." He puts the car in drive and off we go, my stomach going into full on nauseous mode the closer we get to Josh's house. It doesn't help that Abraham doesn't say a word. He remains quiet the entire drive and by the time he pulls into Josh's driveway, I'm sweating.

"Thanks," I murmur as I reach for the door handle.

"You've got this," Abraham tells me, briefly squeezing my shoulder. I glance back, offering him a faint but nervous smile. "Go get your man."

I burst out laughing. "Why are you being so supportive?"

"Because you make our friend happy," Abraham admits, his voice quiet. "Because the two of you are good together, even if you dumbasses never even saw it. I've been seeing it for years."

I'm speechless. I wouldn't know what to say even if I could speak.

"Get out of my car, Sumner," Abraham says, chuckling.

I do as he says, slamming the door extra hard, earning a scowl from Abraham for my efforts. He pulls away as I head up the walkway, my footsteps slow, my stomach churning. I tell myself this is no big deal. Josh and I talk every single day. Josh and I have had countless conversations over the years. Josh and I have kissed and touched each other only a few nights ago, and now we're ready to take our friendship to the next level.

The door swings open before I manage to walk up the porch steps, and he's standing there wearing black basketball shorts and a dark gray Nike sweatshirt. In other words, he's wearing a typical Josh outfit. So why does he look extra good? Why do I want to run up the steps and tackle hug him?

I'm about to when I notice the scowl on his face, his defensive stance. He looks...

Pissed off. And kinda hot, too.

"Hi—" I start to say but he cuts me off.

"You've avoided me all day." His tone is accusatory, making me take a step back.

"No, I haven't," I say quietly. But he's right. I have avoided him.

"Don't lie to me, Edes. If this," he waves a hand between the two of us, "makes you uncomfortable, then tell me now so we don't completely ruin our friendship."

I slowly walk up the three porch steps, my gaze never leaving his. His expression is wary, he's got his defenses up, like he's afraid I'm going to hurt him, and I stop just in front of him, tilting my head back so I can look into his handsome face. "You're right. I have avoided you all day," I admit.

He looks taken aback by my confession but recovers quickly. The mask is up, one I recognize. I've seen that look before, when he's trying to pretend he can handle whatever's thrown at him, even if he's scared shitless. "Why?" he asks gruffly.

"Because now I don't know how to act around you, Josh. It feels…weird between us."

"Good weird or bad weird?"

I smile since that question is so Josh-like. "Good weird. Confusing weird."

His lips curve in the faintest smile. "I know what you mean."

That's all he says, yet it's enough. He gets it. He gets me.

"I've missed you today," he says, his voice soft, his gaze hot as it skims over me.

My heart starts racing at his confession. "I've missed you, too."

"Come here." He takes me in his arms before I can say or do anything else, and he tugs me close. I go to him easily, wrap my arms around his waist, bury my face against his chest so I can inhale his woodsy, masculine scent. He feels good. Warm and solid and—dare I think it—all mine. I banish all negative thoughts from my mind when he slips his fingers beneath my chin and lifts my head up so our mouths can meet in a sweet kiss that turns hot within seconds.

I have no idea how long we kiss on his front porch, but a car honking as it zooms past on the street is finally what makes us spring apart from each other. Josh's hair is wrecked by my fingers and his cheeks are ruddy, his mouth swollen. I can't help but grin at him, and he beams at me in return.

"You're a mess, Edes."

"So are you, Joshy," I say in my awful baby voice.

He bursts out laughing and turns toward his front door, pushing it open. "Want to come inside?"

I hesitate, sinking my teeth into my lower lip. Walking inside Josh's house right now ensures something is going to happen. Possibly something major. Do I really want to do it on a cold Monday afternoon after school? When we have to hurry since we're worried Josh's mom is going to walk in the house at any moment?

No thanks.

Plus, there's the Kaylie thing. I should ask him about it. But will I look like a possessive psycho if I do? I have no right to question who he talks to. It's not like I'm his girlfriend.

"Want to come over to my house?" I suggest.

He frowns and pulls the door shut. "Isn't everyone home?"

Yes, that's why we should go there, I want to tell him. "Travis bought a new video game."

"The Street Fighter revamp?" Josh rubs his hands together.

I nod. "That's the one."

"Let's go then," he says, already heading toward his truck. I fall into step behind him.

Thankful for the distraction.

• • •

JOSH

You know how things feel like they're going so good it's almost…too good?

Yeah, that's what's happened these last few days. Ever since Eden and I first sort of hooked up and sort of confessed our feelings for each other, everything had been going great. With the exception of that one blip on Monday, when Edes avoided me all day at school.

Her avoidance became worth it with the hot way we made out on my front porch, which is ridiculous if you think about it, because come on. We put on a show for the neighbors, and Mom would've died if she knew what we were up to, but no one ever said a word.

It was our little secret.

And that's how it felt this past week, you know? Eden and I aren't really together, but then again, we are. We hang out during school whenever we can. I held her hand in the parking lot when we walked to my truck yesterday. I kissed her for almost an hour after basketball practice last night, when she came by to bring me the sweatshirt she borrowed.

She never borrowed my sweatshirt. She used that as an excuse to come over so we could sneak into my backyard and make out in the gazebo.

Today is Friday, and I'm feeling on top of the world. I want to ask Eden to be my official girlfriend this weekend, but I worry that's moving too fast. Considering we've been best friends for years, I guess nothing feels fast anymore, but I'm full of doubt. Worry. Nerves.

My plan to get laid quick and easy with a girl who doesn't really matter to me? Not even on my radar anymore. I can't think about getting with anyone else. Just Eden.

So when Kaylie corners me right before lunch with an expectant look on her face, I know it's time for me to actually talk to her and get it over with.

"I haven't seen you all week," she says accusingly after she stops me in the hallway as I'm on my way to my locker.

"Yeah, sorry. I've been really busy." I can barely look her in the eye, which makes me feel like a total jackass.

"With Eden?" Her tone is snide, a single eyebrow raised in question.

Slowly I nod, taking a step away from her. "We've gotten closer." I'm not telling her anything. Kaylie has always been jealous of my friendship with Eden. Just like Cole was always jealous of our friendship, too. After the last few days I've spent with Eden, I've realized we were the last ones to see just how good we are together.

"You never did answer my question." Kaylie smiles.

Her quick change of subject throws me. "What about?"

"Winter formal, silly." Her smile grows. "Will you go with me or not?"

I look at Kaylie and it's like our past rushes through my brain, reminding me of the good times, and there were a lot. I also remember the bad times, which were numerous, too. I don't want to hurt her feelings. I have a hard time saying no—even with Taylyr, it was hard to tell her no.

"Come on, Josh." She moves in until she's invading my personal space and rests her hands right on my chest. "Just say yes. You know you want to."

I hear a gasp, and I glance up to find Eden standing there, her mouth hanging open and her eyes wide. I step away from Kaylie so her hands drop from my chest, but it's too late. Eden's already running in the opposite direction.

"Edes! Wait up!" I call after her, catching up to her with ease because she has short legs and she's not the fastest runner. She just keeps walking, never glancing my direction and I keep pace with her, silently willing her to look at me.

But she won't.

"Let me explain," I finally say.

"There's nothing to explain." She pauses. "I saw everything."

"You saw nothing—" She cuts me off with a look and we both come to a stop at the end of the hall.

"I saw Kaylie put her hands on you," she whisper hisses.

"It was nothing."

"She asked you to winter formal, right?"

How did she know? "Uh, yeah."

"You didn't bother telling her no the first time she asked you. How about this time?" She stops walking and whirls on me, her eyes dark and full of anger.

I can't believe she's pissed at me. Worse, I can't stand how she's trying to make me feel guilty. I did nothing wrong. "I'm not going to winter formal with Kaylie."

"Did you tell her no?"

I didn't. And my silence is answer enough I guess.

"That's what I thought," she says, her tone smug, like she wants me to mess up just to prove her right. She rests her hands on her hips, glaring at me. "What are we doing, Josh?"

"What do you mean, what are we doing? I think we're arguing." This is nothing new, yet it feels different.

Truthfully? It feels ominous. Like something major is about to happen. Something majorly bad.

"We are arguing. Over Kaylie." She's quiet for a moment, making me antsy. "Do you still want to be with her?"

"No. Hell no," I say vehemently. I can't believe she just asked me that.

"She was on your list."

"My list?" Realization dawns, and I shake my head. "You put her on my list. And let's forget about that stupid list. It doesn't matter anymore."

"It matters to me," she points at her chest, "since I wasn't on the list."

"You weren't on it because you're the one who created it."

"Right. But I was never your first choice. I was never even an option."

"That's not true."

"That's what it feels like."

I frown. "Are you being serious right now?" I can't believe she's saying this. Bringing up the list. Acting hurt because she wasn't on it. What the hell is she doing?

"Of course I'm being serious! The list, helping you try to find someone to have sex with, I should've never have done any of that. Talk about the dumbest idea ever. I just set myself up to fall for you, even though I knew you'd hurt me in the end."

"Fall for me?" Had she really fallen for me? I know I've fallen for her.

She ignores my question. "I'm surprised you didn't hold me to the pact. Why didn't you?"

I can hardly keep up with what she's saying. "That was just stupid kids' stuff, Edes. I only mentioned it as a joke," I explain, my voice soft. I'm trying not to get angry, but the more she says, the madder I get.

"So now I'm a joke." She crosses her arms in front of her. "Great."

"I never said that—"

"This was a mistake."

"What was?" Eden's talking so fast she's making my head hurt.

"All of this. You and me. Us. Saturday night. Helping you, making that list, trying to get you *laid*. I'm so stupid." She shakes her head, and I swear I catch a glimmer of tears shining in her eyes, but maybe I'm wrong. Right now she's acting too heartless to actually cry. "We should've never happened."

Her words feel like a knife driving into my chest over and over. "You really believe that?"

"Yes." She takes a deep breath, exhales loudly. "I do."

And with those words, I stop. Stop talking, stop thinking, stop functioning. It's like I just got body slammed and the wind was knocked out of me. I can't believe she just said that. Worse?

I can't believe she meant it.

• • •

I sulk for the rest of the afternoon. Mom comes home from work around six with Chinese takeout from our favorite restaurant, and when I tell her I'm not hungry, she rushes straight over to the couch where I'm sprawled out, pressing the back of her hand against my forehead.

"Are you sick?" I can't tell if she's joking or not.

I push her hand away. "Stop. I'm fine."

She rests her hands on her hips, her lips thin. The usual look she sends me when she suspects something's wrong. "You're not hungry for Mr. Wu's? Seriously, Josh. Something must be wrong."

Sighing, I stretch my legs and arms out, then rise to my feet. "Fine, I'll eat. Only because you're making me."

"Uh huh." She sounds skeptical but doesn't say anything else. Just hustles over to the kitchen and grabs plates out of the cabinet and silverware from the drawer. I grab a Coke and a bottle of water for her, and we sit at the kitchen counter, Mom doling out the food while I grab a pot sticker, dunk it in the sauce that came with it before shoving the entire thing in my mouth.

"You are disgusting," she says mildly, reminding me of

Eden. Sounds like something she'd say. If she were here, I'd take another one and shove it in my mouth too just to make Eden laugh or squeal or roll her eyes in disgust. Any type of reaction from Eden always makes me happy.

The pot sticker turns to sawdust in my mouth, and I choke it down, then crack open the soda can and take a big drink. I set the can on the counter with a loud clunk and push away the full plate Mom just set in front of me.

"You're really not hungry?" Mom asks as she cracks open her water bottle. "Is something bothering you?"

Should I tell her? "Just having uh, relationship issues."

Mom frowns. "With who?"

"Eden," I mumble, taking another swig of my Coke.

"Eden? Are you guys fighting?" Mom gives my arm a squeeze. "You two never fight."

"I know. We've, uh, we've kinda complicated things." I duck my head when I can feel Mom staring at me. "Now it's a big mess."

Mom starts rubbing my back. "Aw, I always knew this would happen."

Immediately irritated, I shrug away from her touch. "You knew what would happen?"

"You and Eden, finally getting together."

"Yeah, it's not working out that way though. She called us a mistake." I feel like the saddest little baby, crying to his mama, but I can't help it.

"She did?" Mom sounds surprised. "I bet she didn't mean it."

"Sounded like she meant it when she told me to my face that she thought we were a mistake."

"Aw, sweetie." Mom pushes her plate away, too. "I'm sorry. I'm sure you guys will work it out eventually. You have too many years of friendship to just throw it all away over a minor fight."

"It's not minor though." I can't tell her what happened. What Eden and I did in her bed Saturday night. How we kissed until my mouth and jaw were sore and I'd touched her in places I never thought I'd get the chance to touch. She shuddered in my arms and touched me everywhere and gasped my name and it was...

Incredible.

The last week with her has been incredible.

And according to Eden, it was all an incredible *mistake*.

Damn, that hurts.

"Maybe you should go talk to her."

I'm still not ready.

"Josh, don't be stubborn." Mom knows me too well.

I pull the plate back in front of me and dive in, desperate to occupy my thoughts with something other than Eden. "Let me eat in peace, Mom."

She goes quiet and starts eating, too, and I'm so freaking thankful she's not saying anything else. I need the quiet.

I need to think.

Chapter Sixteen

"Go with me to winter formal."

"What? No." I shake my head, making a face. I don't want to go to winter formal with anyone. I don't want to go to formal at all.

I'd rather stay home alone and sulk.

"I mean it. Just—go with me." Abraham puts his hands together like he's praying. "Come on, Eden."

It's lunchtime on the Wednesday after the big "this was a mistake" moment, and Josh still isn't talking to me. And I'm not talking to him, either. Abraham is trying his best to play mediator between the two of us, but we're not having it.

At least Molly and I have made up. She apologized to me for being so brutal, and I apologized for being too sensitive. We're all good now. Abraham has been hanging with the both of us when he's not with Josh or playing basketball, and we even went to a game last night to watch him.

Well. Molly watched Abraham. I couldn't take my eyes

off Josh. Of course. So irritating, how I couldn't stop watching him. We made eye contact once, when he first ran out on the court and the game was just about to start. His eyes were cold when they met mine, his expression pained, and when the buzzer kicked off the first quarter, he went into high gear, practically showing off every second he was in the game.

And of course, he played perfectly, scoring the highest out of anyone on the team. They won by a landslide, and everyone treated Josh like he was some sort of hero, his teammates high-fiving him, his coach literally hugging him, and the entire gymnasium erupting in cheers, chanting his name over and over again.

I found the entire night both irritating and amazing. I was proud of him for playing so well, yet irritated that he had to show off for me. Because the way he played felt like it was all for me—one big, fat F-U aimed straight at Eden Sumner, thanks so much for asking.

It hurt, too. How easily he cut me from his life, how it doesn't seem like he's suffering, while I feel like I'm on the brink of crying twenty-four/seven.

Though, really, I'm not being completely honest with myself. He's suffering. I saw it in his eyes that night at the game. I see it in the way he holds himself at school. He's suffering, but he's also defiant. Almost angry.

The only one he can be angry with is himself.

"Why don't you ask Molly to go to winter formal with you," I suggest, glancing around to see if she is nearby. But I don't see her, and usually she's sitting with us by now.

"Nope." Abraham shakes his head, smirking at me. "She's asking Josh to winter formal."

"What the hell?" My voice is extra sharp and draws the attention of more than a few people sitting at the tables near us. I lower my voice almost to a whisper. "Are you serious?"

"We have a plan, Eden. Just roll with it." He smiles, going

for innocent angel face but I know that's crap. "Say yes."

"Please don't try and pair us together. It won't work, and you know it." Josh and I haven't talked since that big blow-up on Friday. This is the longest we haven't spoken to each other since we became best friends. Yes, we've argued before. Yes, we've been so mad at each other, we gave each other the silent treatment, but never for more than a few hours. It's almost like we couldn't stand to be apart.

And yes, I still feel that way. I miss him so much, my heart aches every time I spot him. In class, in the hall, during lunch, after school in the senior parking lot, driving by my house in the morning when he goes to school, driving by my house again in the afternoon when he's on his way home. I've been working less lately since business slows down by the pier during the winter months, and I've been busy with school stuff, mainly student council and the holiday festival that's happening tonight, but still there's no Josh in my life.

It's weird.

"Next weekend is the dance, Eden. We can't keep putting this off," Abraham says, trying to use his logical voice on me. "Say yes."

"You're not going to let me get out of this, are you?" I sigh wearily when he grins, like he knows he has me. Which he does. "Fine, I'll go."

I can't believe I just agreed to this.

"Seriously? *Yes*." He actually does a fist pump in the air. "Now Molly has to come through on her part and we're golden."

"You're trying to set us up."

"So what if we are?"

"It won't work. Josh and I are over."

"You two are being so freaking ridiculous, it's almost laughable."

"Yeah, no. It's not that laughable." It hurts, that he won't talk to me. He won't hardly look at me. I go to Snapchat him and remember we're not talking. Travis and I got into a huge fight Sunday night and I wanted to FaceTime Josh so bad but I couldn't. I knew he wouldn't pick up my call so I refused to make myself look stupid.

We're both being so ridiculous neither one of us is willing to give first. It's stupid. But I'm remaining stubborn and so is he.

Josh is the king of stubborn. And I guess I'm the queen.

"No, it really is, Eden. But whatever, we've got a plan." Abraham rubs his hands together and Molly shows up just in time to see him act like a greedy villain hell bent on total destruction.

See? There go my overdramatic thoughts again.

"He said no." Molly barely spares me a glance, she's too focused on Abraham. "What should I do?"

"I can't even believe you're discussing this right in front of me." I go to stand but Molly's grabbing my arm, forcing me to sit back down before she slides onto the bench next to me. "Of course he said no. He's probably going to winter formal with Kaylie."

Oh, I sound like a jealous bean, but screw it.

Molly sighs, like I just sorely disappointed her. "Josh is *not* going with Kaylie. He already told her no. He doesn't want to go period. Not even with me."

"What did he say when you asked him?" Abraham asks.

"He asked me if you put me up to it." Molly points at Abraham. "And then he told me he wouldn't go to winter formal with me even if I paid him a million dollars and guaranteed him a spot with the Golden State Warriors."

"What a prick." I sound shocked because I really am shocked. I can't believe he said that to Molly. "Seriously, that's so freaking rude."

"Yeah, well, he's pissed off and acting like a wounded

animal." Molly is totally sincere when she says this, which is blowing my mind. "And you know how wounded animals are. They snap and bite and snarl at innocent people. That's Josh right now."

"Are you saying he's a wounded animal because of— *me?*"

They both just stare at me, saying nothing.

"This is stupid." I swing my legs over the bench and rise to my feet, glancing around the cafeteria until I spot Josh sitting on the opposite side of the building, at a table all by himself.

He looks pitiful. And mean. People pass by him and if any of them are too close, he sends them a murderous look that would make pretty much everyone else run.

Not me. Nope, I'm headed straight toward him.

"Where are you going?" I hear Molly call after me. Then I hear Abraham laugh and that just spurs me on even further.

I march up to the empty table Josh is commanding and slap my hand on the table surface with a loud smack, making Josh startle. He glares at me and I glare at him back, the both of us silent for what feels like hours but probably only lasts about thirty seconds, if that.

"You're being a dick," I tell him, my voice low. Being this close to him, my entire body is trembling. I wish I could sock him in the face.

Or kiss his stupid, perfect mouth.

He raises a brow, and oh my damn it, he looks so freaking sexy doing that. He's angry. I can feel the tension vibrating from his body, and he's wearing the blue flannel shirt that brings out his eyes.

His icy cold yet absolutely mesmerizing blue eyes.

"How exactly am I being a dick, when we're not even talking?" His voice is in full-blown snotty mode. I didn't know he could even sound that snotty.

"You're not being a dick to me." I stand up straight, looking down my nose at him. "You're being a dick to Molly, and that's not cool."

He shrugs one broad shoulder. "Abraham made her ask me to winter formal. I don't know what he's got planned, but I'm not falling for it."

"That still doesn't give you the right to be a jerk to Molly. You know how sensitive she is."

His lips curl and he presses them together. But they curl again, they're almost wrinkling, and I know he's trying to hold back his laughter. Sighing, I cross my arms in front of my chest and wait him out.

"Give me a break," he finally says after about a minute of that awful dirty laugh of his. "She's not sensitive."

"Whatever." I wave a dismissive hand. "You being angry with me doesn't give you the right to act like an asshole to everyone else."

"Oh, so now I'm an asshole." Both eyebrows are up, practically in his hairline. "Nice to know you think so highly of me, Edes."

My chest hurts at hearing him call me that. No one else calls me Edes. Just Josh. "Lately I'm not thinking so highly of you, Joshua."

"Yeah, well, right back at you." He's glowering. His brows are back to normal, and his jaw is tight. He has a great jaw, too, have I mentioned that? I've kissed that jaw. I've kissed those lips. Why are we acting like this again? I don't even remember what started this argument in the first place.

Oh right, we messed around with each other and he started talking to Kaylie again and I got upset. So. Stupid.

I can't fall back into that trap. To mess around with Josh is just that—messing around. He's become anti-commitment, what with college on the horizon. I can't put my heart back on the line, just for him to smash it into tiny bits.

He already did that. I can't let him do it again.

"Just go with Molly to the stupid formal," I tell him, letting my irritation shine through. "It won't kill you to put on a suit and take Molly to a dance."

"I hate Molly." He makes a face.

"No, you don't."

"She hates me. She's already chewed me out twice over this entire thing."

"What entire thing?"

"Us." He points at me. "Don't play innocent. I'm sure you put her up to it."

"I haven't put *anyone* up to *anything*," I stress, his words like a physical blow. "Why bother when I know you're going to act like this?"

"Act like what?" That familiar confused expression on his face makes my heart pang. The realization hits me, just like that—I'm in love with him. It's the worst time ever to have this life-changing moment, yet here I am, ready to lay into the boy I love.

I can't help it. I'm in love with him, but I'm also so incredibly angry at him, too.

"Act like an asshole!" I practically yell.

Okay. Yeah, I did yell. People are looking. Including the vice principal, Mr. Jackson. In fact, he's headed this way and my legs get wobbly and it feels like our side of the cafeteria slid into this uncomfortable hushed silence that's making me nervous.

I swear, I hear Josh chuckle. The bastard.

"Miss Sumner. Is everything okay over here?" Mr. Jackson is standing directly in front of me. He's not even looking in Josh's direction. Like he knows the only one in the wrong is me.

"Yes, everything's fine, Mr. Jackson." I nod, smiling as politely as I can.

Josh coughs into his hand. I'm pretty sure he muttered bullshit against his fist.

"Are you sure about that? Seems like there was a minor disturbance." He sends a quick pointed glance in Josh's direction.

"No, just having a healthy argument with my best friend here." I point at Josh.

Mr. Jackson swivels around to study Josh. "A *healthy argument*, Mr. Evans? Is that what you two are up to?"

"Guess so," Josh says with an easy smile. His entire demeanor is like he doesn't have a care in the world.

I sort of wish I could punch him.

"Make sure you keep your voice down," Mr. Jackson says, his gaze aimed right at me. "Wouldn't want any foul language being heard in my cafeteria. Understand, Miss Sumner?"

"Understood," I say with a nod.

Mr. Jackson smiles and walks away without another word.

I nearly sag with relief. "Close one," I murmur, forgetting myself for a moment. Forgetting that I'm pissed at Josh and the reason I almost got in trouble in the first place is because I called him an asshole.

"Yeah, it was," he agrees, like he just forgot himself, too. "You were sweating bullets, Edes. I could see it in your eyes."

"I wasn't that scared."

"You so were." He's smirking now, looking smug. "But it's cool. You played it off pretty well. I'll give you credit."

We're smiling at each other, just like we have over the years—with the exception of the past five days—and then we catch ourselves. Our smiles fade at the same time and our eyes go a little wider and I take a step back.

"Just—consider it," I tell Josh. "Going to the winter formal with Molly. It won't be so bad."

"I don't get why you want me to go with your best friend."

He's frowning again. I like Josh better when he's smiling.

"Because I'm going with your best friend." I tip my head toward him. "I think they're forming a plot and trying to fix us."

"I don't know if that's possible," he says, his voice low.

"They want to try," I say, my voice also low. Again, his words hurt, but I push past the pain. He needs to hear me. Actually *listen* to me. "I'm just humoring them. Maybe you should, too."

· · ·

JOSH

Eden is humoring them by agreeing to go to winter formal with Abraham? I didn't even know he asked her. Why didn't he tell me? He's my best friend. He's not supposed to keep secrets like this. And this is a big one.

"Okay." I stand, gather my trash, and shove it back in the brown bag I brought for lunch. I toss it in the nearby garbage can and head toward the table where Abraham and Molly are still sitting. "I'll play your little game."

Eden falls into step just behind me, and I can smell her. That familiar floral scent that drove me crazy not even a week ago when I had her pinned beneath me on her bed. I couldn't figure out its source. Her hair? No. Her perfume? Nope. I finally figured it had to be her body lotion, because I could smell that scent all over her skin, like she bathed in it or something.

I'm veering off track. Typical when I'm with Eden. Being this close to her makes my entire body ache with the need to touch her. Bury my face in her hair. Kiss her angry mouth. Yeah, kissing her would be a most excellent idea. Would that make her stop saying all this crazy stuff?

No. Kissing her is a very bad idea. Yeah, I miss her, but

more than anything I miss our friendship, hearing her laugh, seeking her advice, because Eden never steers me wrong. But maybe it's best if we just stop talking. It's too hard, seeing her like this. Smelling her like this. I need to focus on the here and now, not on past memories and memorable scents.

"Don't be mean," Eden's telling me, but I ignore her. "Seriously, Josh. Don't start anything, okay? They have good intentions."

"I'm sure," I mutter, smiling like a psycho when Abraham and I make eye contact. He tears his gaze from mine and starts gesturing at Molly, who quickly whips her head around to watch my approach. She looks just as scared.

Good.

Not that I'm going to do anything. I'm in the middle of the cafeteria on Friday afternoon and Mr. Jackson isn't too far, watching us. I won't cause a big scene.

"Molly," I say when I'm close enough for her to hear. "I've been thinking."

"Y-yeah, J-Josh?" She is literally stuttering.

"I've changed my mind." I give her my easy smile. The one that says I have no worries, which is a total lie. I'm pretending because it's easier to do that than wallow in the pain of losing Eden. "I think I'll take you up on your offer."

"My offer?" Her eyes are wide, and she's gone pale. I think I've scared her.

This is kind of funny, which means Eden's right. I'm a total asshole.

But I'm still running with this.

"I'll go to winter formal with you," I tell her with all the sincerity I can muster.

She's frozen, and I think Abraham kicks her under the table, because she mutters *ow* under her breath before she answers me. "Oh! Okay, that's great, Josh. I'm so glad you said yes."

"I hoped you would be." I rest my hand on Molly's shoulder and give it a gentle squeeze. She looks at where my hand rests and then up at my face, her gaze meeting mine. "This will be fun, right? You'll have to tell me what color your dress is so I can pick out the right flowers."

Now she's frowning. "Flowers?"

"Yeah, for your corsage."

"Corsage?" I think Abraham kicks her again. She curses under her breath and sits up a little straighter. "Right, a corsage. Make it white. That way you can't go wrong."

"Good idea. Hope you like roses." I give her shoulder another squeeze, actually wink at her, and then let my gaze go to Abraham's. He's watching me with bewilderment. And I have no idea what Eden is doing, but I'd guess she's not happy with how I'm acting right now.

But it's like I can't help myself. It's like I need to prove to her that I don't need her anymore, even if it is a lie.

Secretly, I need her more than ever.

"See you guys later," I tell them, then make a little phone gesture with my fingers, mouthing, *call me* to Molly.

I turn, nearly bumping into Eden. I step to the side, and she does the same. I step to the other side, and so does she. She's not smiling though. No, she looks beyond irritated.

"Want to dance?" I ask, going for teasing her. I'm sort of over being angry at her. At least for the moment.

"Stop." She takes a step closer, and even though she's short, and I can prop my arm on top of her head because I'm that much taller than her, I'm still a little intimidated. I can't lie. "Don't think you can outsmart them, Joshua. I know what you're up to."

Yet again, I'm reminded of how well she knows me. How I can't get away with shit when Eden's around. "I'm not up to anything," I tell her in my most innocent voice ever.

"Whatever." She jabs my chest with her index finger. And

it freaking hurts. "I'm warning you. Don't hurt Molly."

"She's a big girl," I say, batting her finger away from my chest. "She can handle anything I throw her way."

"Josh." Her tone is a warning.

"Edes."

"Don't call me that."

"I can call you that if I want." I pause, feeling like a sadistic jackass. "Edes."

"You're so annoying," she whispers, a flicker of pain in her eyes just before she turns and hauls ass out of the cafeteria.

I watch her go, my chest aching, my blood running hot. I should chase after her. Make sure she's okay. Though she'd probably tell me to go away. And that might hurt more, yet another rejection from the girl I care about more than anyone else in this world.

"More like you're a complete idiot."

I turn to find Abraham standing there, his hands shoved in his front pockets, the glare on his face extra fierce. Do I really want to hear what he has to say? "I don't need your opinion right now."

"No, I think you do," says another familiar voice.

Molly.

"Seriously, you're being ridiculous," she says, stepping closer to me so she can poke me in the chest, just like Eden did. "The both of you are. I'm not falling for your tricks. Just face facts that you miss Eden and she misses you and you're both madly in love with each other."

Her words paralyze me, even though I want to run. Am I in love with Eden? I've loved her like a friend for years. The feelings have grown for sure over the last few months, and they've pretty much exploded these last few weeks.

Meaning, I *am* totally crazy about her.

And now she hates me.

Chapter Seventeen

"Damn girl, you look gorgeous." The low whistle that accompanies the compliment makes me blush so hard my cheeks are burning.

The dress I found for winter formal is simple. Black velvet, form fitting, it hits me about mid-thigh, with long sleeves and a completely open back. Molly called it serious in the front, party in the back.

"Stop," I tell Abraham as I open the small black purse I borrowed from my mom and stow my iPhone inside. I stashed two twenty-dollar bills, my favorite lip gloss, and a tiny mirror in the purse, too. I'm ready for tonight's dance, even though I still don't really want to go.

"I'm serious. That dress is smokin'." Abraham grins. "Josh is gonna lose his mind when he sees you walking in on my arm."

"Oh my God," I groan, glancing over my shoulder to make sure Mom didn't hear him say that. She has no idea what's going on between me and Josh and I don't want to tell her, either.

No use getting her hopes up and then watch them come crashing down all at once.

"Sorry, sorry." Abraham's expression turns serious. "I'll keep up the charade tonight, don't worry."

"Seriously, could you say that any louder?" My parents think I'm going to the dance with Abraham for real. This is going to fall apart before we even leave the house.

"I want photos!" Mom practically squeals from behind us as she enters the living room, making me roll my eyes. Abraham chuckles, waving me over to stand beside him.

"Come on, Eden. Let's pose for your mama," Abraham says with one of those rare, extra charming Abraham smiles.

I go to him, thankful he's keeping up the facade for my parents. Mom positions us just so in front of the fireplace and Abraham hooks his arm through mine as she takes photo after photo of us. I'm smiling so hard I feel like I'm grimacing and when she asks Travis and his girlfriend Isabella to pose in the photos along with us, I want to scream in frustration.

This isn't how I envisioned my last high school winter formal going down, with Abraham as my date, a guy who usually drives me crazy. Of course, it's not like I thought I'd go with Josh, either, so I don't know exactly what I envisioned.

All I know is, it definitely wasn't this.

Mom takes a trillion photos, and Dad gives us a lecture on making responsible choices and not drinking and driving. The talk makes Travis anxious and fidgety, so I'm guessing he had plans that included alcohol tonight.

"Have a wonderful time," Mom says as we finally make our way to the front door. Travis and Isabella already bailed a few minutes ago, saying they had to take photos at Isabella's house, too.

"Make sure you bring our daughter back by her curfew,"

Dad says, his voice stern, his steely gaze directed straight at Abraham.

Abraham literally salutes him. "Yes, sir."

I grab hold of Abraham's hand and practically drag him out of my house. Once the door is shut and we're headed toward his car, I feel like I can let my guard down and I release his hand. "That was pure torture."

"Your parents don't think we're a real thing, do they?"

We climb into Abraham's car and he starts the engine.

"I told them we were going to the dance as just friends, but my mom is always hopeful," I say, checking my phone. I have a Snapchat from Molly and I quickly open it. It's a selfie of her and Josh, and he's ridiculously handsome in his dark gray suit. There's a caption though, that makes me laugh.

He's so grouchy he's like the worst date ever.

"Lean in," I say to Abraham, waving him closer to me. He angles his head toward mine and we smile big for the selfie I'm sending back to Molly. I also included a caption.

My date is extra cheerful tonight.

Molly texts me back as we drive to school, where the dance is being held.

We should swap dates.

In your dreams.

Come on, Eden. You know you want to be with Josh tonight.

Maybe I want Abraham now. He's way nicer.

Lucky. Josh is so grumpy.

Are you already at the dance?

We just got here.

Within minutes, we arrive at the school, too, and walk into the gymnasium arm in arm. There are tables covered in white linen, a few couples sitting at them and chatting. White twinkle lights are strung everywhere, the music is loud, and the dance floor is packed with people dancing to a popular song.

Abraham is literally bouncing up and down, so I know he wants to dance. "Let's go," he tells me just as he drags me out onto the dance floor and we immediately start moving. Surprisingly enough, he's actually a pretty good dancer, which is awesome because every guy I've ever gone to a dance with isn't that great.

But Abraham is fun. He has no shame and soon we have a circle of people around us, most of them yelling and encouraging him to show off his dance moves. As I'm hopping around, I spot Cole dancing nearby and nearly have a coronary when I realize his date is the beautiful, clad in clingy white and silver sequins Whitney Gregory.

Of course she is. She smiles at me and waves, and I wave back. I'll forgive her. She can have Cole. At least she didn't sink her claws too deep into Josh.

My heart pangs just thinking of him.

Turning my back on Cole and Whit, I throw myself into the music, yelling when the song changes to one of my favorites. I have no idea where Molly and Josh are, but I'll find them in a minute. I raise my arms into the air, screaming along with the lyrics, smiling at Abraham when he grins at me. His face is already shiny with sweat, and his fingers are at his neck, loosening his black tie. I grab his other hand and twirl around, ducking underneath his arm, and he lets me go when I'm still spinning so I go flying, running into someone behind me.

Big hands go to my waist, steadying me, keeping me from falling and goose bumps scatter all over my skin. I don't need to see who just grabbed me. I can feel him.

"Careful," Josh murmurs close to my ear, making me shiver.

I glance over my shoulder, my gaze meeting his, and all the air in my lungs seems to freeze. He looks even better in person in the dark gray suit, his jaw freshly shaved yet his hair stylishly messy. His fingers tighten around my waist, and his touch seems to burn straight through the thick velvet fabric of my dress.

"Sorry," I whisper.

He shakes his head, never letting me go. Instead, he leans even closer, his mouth practically touching my ear when he says, "You look so fucking sexy."

Oh God, I want to melt. I thought he was mad at me. Isn't he still mad at me? I hurt his feelings and he hurt mine, and we both have every right to be angry.

But seeing him, having him touch me, makes all those overwhelming feelings flood my body. I miss him.

I'm in love with him.

I finally find my voice. "You look good, too."

Josh doesn't smile. He still has his hands on me. Though he removes one, only to trace his finger along my naked spine. I'm trembling from his touch, the look in his eyes, and it's like everyone on the dance floor has evaporated. Disappeared. It's just me and Josh, staring at each other, his hand still clutching my waist, his fingers touching my bare skin.

"Hey, there you are!" Molly appears at Josh's side, breaking the tense moment, and Josh releases his hold on me, his fingers lingering like he doesn't want to let me go. I take a stumbling step back, smiling at Molly, so grateful when she wraps me up in her arms and gives me a big hug.

"You look beautiful," she tells me as she pulls away, holding me at arms' length.

"So do you." Her dress is a deep red, strapless with a full skirt that stops just above her knee, very modern yet with a vintage feel. "Your lips match your dress."

"Is it too much?" Molly frowns, and I quickly shake my head.

"It's perfect. You look perfect." I nudge her toward

Abraham, who's still dancing like he's never going to stop. "Go dance with Abraham."

Molly turns her concerned gaze on me. "You don't mind?"

"You know you want to swap dates," I tease. "Remember?"

Molly's smile is grateful, and she hugs me again. "You should go talk to him," she whispers just before she pulls away. "He's miserable, though he's trying to put on a brave face."

It's like I can still feel his hands on me, too. Why are we being so stupid again?

I glance around the dance floor, but Josh is nowhere in sight. "Do you know where he went?"

"Maybe back to the table where we were sitting?" Molly shrugs, her gaze locked on the wildly dancing Abraham.

"I'll look for him." I grab Molly's bare shoulders and push her in Abraham's direction. "You go dance."

I leave the dance floor and wander around the beautifully decorated gymnasium, smiling and waving at people I know as I pass them by. But there's no sign of Josh. He's not sitting at any of the tables, he's not near the refreshment area, and he's not by the bathrooms either.

It's like he completely disappeared.

I spot one of his friends from the basketball team and ask if he's seen Josh.

"Yeah, I think he went backstage a few minutes ago." The gymnasium has a small stage, and it's currently where the DJ is set up.

Why would he go back there? Is he making a special song request? I hope he didn't leave already. We didn't even get a chance to talk.

Not that I know what to say to him.

I leave the guy standing there, practically running toward the door that leads backstage. But before I can open it, the music stops, and a familiar deep voice rings out over the speakers.

"Sorry to interrupt the dance, but I have an important announcement to make."

I turn toward the stage to see Josh standing there, a spotlight shining directly on him, looking gorgeous and nervous as he clutches the microphone so tight his knuckles are white.

Then I notice he's holding something else. A single red rose.

"Hey Edes." He's looking right at me, his expression solemn. "Come up here and join me, will you?"

Everyone inside the gym is silent. I glance around the room and spot Molly, who flicks her head at me and mouths, "Go onstage!"

"Don't leave me all alone up here, okay?" He laughs nervously and before he can say anything else, I bolt for the door, dashing backstage and fumbling with the thick black curtain before I find the opening and I'm standing right beside him.

Everyone is watching us. People sit at the tables, couples are still standing on the dance floor, teachers are leaning against the walls, all of them eyeing us with curious interest. Even Cole is watching, his expression narrowed, his arm slung loosely around Whitney's shoulders. I tear my gaze away from them and focus on Josh.

He holds the rose out toward me. "This is for you."

I take it from him, keeping my head bent as I drift my fingers over the velvety red petals. "It's almost too pretty to be real."

"Oh, it's definitely real. Took me a while to find just the right one, too."

I lift my head, my gaze locking with his. "What do you mean?"

"I went to three florist shops in town before I settled on that rose." He nods toward the flower in my hand. "It had to be perfect. Like on *The Bachelor*, you know?"

My eyes widen, and he grins. I know what he's telling me without saying a word. He actually watches *The Bachelor*. He has to since he knows so much. I guess this is his little secret? And am I actually the last one in Josh's rose ceremony?

Bringing it to my nose, I breathe in the rose's delicate fragrance. I don't know why he went to so much trouble, but I'm not complaining. Or why he feels the need to present the rose to me in front of everyone at the dance. "Thank you, Josh. I love it."

"Good. Because I love you." He says this directly into the microphone, and if I thought it was quiet before, you could hear a pin drop now. Mom says that all the time, and I never really understood it before.

Everything inside of me goes completely still. "What?"

"I'm in love with you, Edes. I think I've been in love with you for years, I just didn't realize it until these last few weeks. Nothing else matters, no one else does, not any other girl. You're my closest friend. You've been my best friend for a long time, and I hate it when we fight. This has been a big one, I know, and I'm sorry. I just want it back to the way we were, only better, you know? We're good together. We always make each other laugh. You get my dumb jokes. You listen to me, and I try my best to listen to you, and every time I'm with you, it just feels…right."

I gape at him, my throat dry. I can't speak. I can't freaking think. Josh is in love with me?

"I think I've been waiting for you all this time, like subconsciously or whatever. Saving it special, just for you." He takes my hand and links our fingers together. "There's no one else I'd rather be with. Just you."

"Really?" My voice squeaks, and I clear my throat,

glancing toward the crowd. They are watching us with rapt attention, even the chaperones. This is sort of embarrassing.

"Really. I'm even going to confess my secret love for *The Bachelor* in front of everyone, so I must really love you, because that's pretty damn embarrassing. This little rose ceremony, it's all for you, because you're the one I want to be with. No one else. We belong together, Eden. What do you think?"

Everyone starts clapping until the sound is deafening. They're yelling, words of encouragement, vaguely inappropriate stuff that has the teachers freaking out. I think I even heard Abraham yell, "Get some, Evans!" Molly's laughter following.

The crowd's reaction along with his words touch some deep emotional part of me, and before I even realize it, I'm crying. Tears are slipping from my eyes, sliding down my cheeks, and when he sees them, he makes a pained noise.

"Ah, damn it, I didn't mean to make you cry." His voice is low, just for me, and he cradles my face in his hands so our gazes meet. Gently he captures my tears with his thumbs, brushing them away. "Talk to me, Edes. You're scaring me."

"Don't worry. They're happy tears," I confess, closing my eyes. I breathe deep, his words on repeat in my brain. He's in love with me. Josh is in love with me. He doesn't want to be with anyone else.

Just me.

"I know you said what happened between us was a mistake, but I don't believe you," he says, his voice low. "Tell me the truth, Edes. Tell me how you really feel."

"I'm sorry I said all that stuff. I was just scared." I swallow hard. Here's my big truthful moment. "I'm in love with you, t—" I barely get the words out before his mouth is on mine, capturing my breath, my heart, my soul.

Oh yeah, totally sappy, but I'm allowed to be sappy

tonight.

Since Joshua Evans just declared his love for me.

. . .

JOSH

Eden feels so damn good in my arms. Seeing her enter the gym with Abraham looking so freaking amazing, all the anger and frustration I felt toward her just disappeared. I realized right then and there I was sick and tired of wasting time, and I was so glad I bought that rose to give her. It was finally time. I needed to tell Eden exactly how I felt about her, and I needed to do it in a big way.

Pulling a *Bachelor* move could've been embarrassing, but I don't care. Eden loves me. She's in love with me. I'd do anything for her, even admit that I love watching the stupid *Bachelor*.

I grab her hand and lead her off the stage, pushing through the closest set of double doors so we're outside. Eden gasps when the cold air hits us, and I grab hold of her so I'm leaning against the gymnasium wall. Then I'm kissing her. She's got her arms hooked around my neck, and I press my hand against the center of her back, touching bare, warm skin. She's so soft and smooth, and I remember how I touched her all over.

How much I want to do that again. Take it further this time. I want to give everything to her.

"Josh," she whispers after she breaks away from my lips.

I press my forehead to hers, the both of us breathing a little heavy. "Yeah?"

"Why did you have to give me a perfect rose?"

"Oh. Right." I'm a little nervous over this admission. Maybe more than I was over declaring my love for her. So stupid, but I need to be real with her. That's all she's ever wanted. Why did it take us so long to realize just how perfect we are for each other? "It's uh, it's a reference to *The Bachelor*. Remember what I said onstage?"

Eden pulls away slightly so our gazes meet, her hands sliding down so they're braced against my chest, the rose still clutched in her right hand. She's frowning, but more out of confusion I think. "Yes, but I want you to explain it to me. You really watch *The Bachelor?*"

"Well, yeah." She must think I'm a complete dork. "You know how it works, right? Whoever is the Bachelor or the Bachelorette, they give roses to the ones they want to keep, remember? If you don't get a rose, you're off the show. He didn't choose that girl. Or she didn't choose that guy." I pluck the rose from her fingers and bring it up to her face, tapping it on the tip of her nose. "I choose you, Edes. I want you to be mine."

I drop my hand to my side and hold my breath, waiting for her answer. This somehow feels like the make or break moment. She'll either tell me I'm a complete idiot for the *Bachelor* reference or she'll love it.

"I want to be yours," she whispers, her hand going around my nape and drawing me closer. "I love you so much, Josh."

Our lips meet again, the kiss longer this time. We wrap our arms around each other, and I'm clutching the rose so tight I'm afraid I'm going to snap the stem in half. We're full-blown making out at a school function, and I know the minute a chaperone catches us, we're busted.

"Let's get out of here," I murmur against her neck, making her shiver.

"But I want to dance," she protests, giggling when I nip at the sensitive skin just below her ear. "Come on, let's stay here for a little while."

I pull away so I can stare into her pretty blue eyes. I can't believe she's mine. I can't believe she loves me like I love her.

"Thirty minutes."

Eden mock pouts. "An hour."

"Forty-five minutes," I compromise.

"Deal." She smiles triumphantly. "Where do you want to go after this?"

I steer her through the double front doors, my hand pressed against her lower back. I know she doesn't have a bra on with this dress. Is she wearing panties? A thong? I can't wait to find out. "I was thinking my house?"

"Is your mom there?" Wide, questioning eyes meet mine. The music is so damn loud inside that I have to speak up.

"No. She's gone for the night."

"So it's just the two of us."

I nod, barely able to contain the smile spreading across my face. "You okay with that?"

"More than okay." She takes my hand and leads me toward the dance floor. "Now let's go dance!"

Chapter Eighteen

JOSH

I'm buzzing around my bedroom, trying to set the mood when there's a knock on the door. Eden opens it before I can say anything, and she's peeking her head around the door, her expression hopeful, yet a little nervous, too.

"Is it okay if I come in?"

I toss the last of my dirty clothes in the hamper before I pull the closet door shut. "Yeah, come in."

She walks into the room and closes the door behind her, then glances around. My room was already pretty clean, just an old sweatshirt thrown over my chair, a pile of dirty clothes here and there on the floor, and my desk was sort of a mess, covered in papers and textbooks. I tidied everything up while she waited in the living room for me like I asked. I even managed to light the candles I found in my mom's stash earlier, when I was feeling hopeful.

Turns out my hopes and dreams came true, because the most beautiful girl I've ever known is standing in the middle of my bedroom tonight.

"I have been in this room hundreds of times," she says as she takes it all in.

"Maybe even thousands of times," I add, making her smile.

"Yeah, true." Her gaze meets mine. "But I've never been this nervous about it before."

"Well, we've never done anything like this before." I hesitate. "Well, we sort of have."

"Yeah." Her cheeks look like they're on fire. "We have."

"And it was good." I take her hand and pull her in close so we're pressed against each other. I've already ditched the jacket and tie. She kicked off her heels the moment she climbed into my truck so she's back to short Eden. The girl who I can tuck just beneath my chin where she fits perfectly.

"It was really great," she murmurs, laughing nervously. "Josh, is this weird to you?"

"Is what weird to me?" I wrap her up in my arms and press my mouth to the spot where her neck meets her shoulder. Her body goes limp when my lips make contact with her soft skin, and I hear her sigh.

"That two best friends are about to have sex for the first time? Together?" She pulls away slightly so she can look up at me. "You wanted me to help you find someone for you."

"Yeah, and you did. You found yourself. And I think it's pretty freaking awesome." I kiss her once. Twice. Three times, and then she's sighing against my lips, her tongue circling mine. I break away from her tempting mouth, and the sound of frustration she makes has me smiling.

"Are you sure you're not—disappointed?"

This girl is crazy. I cup her cheeks, our gazes locked. "I love you, Edes. How can I be disappointed? There's no one else I'd rather be with. Just you."

She smiles, her eyes sparkling. "There's no one else I'd

rather be with, either. Just you."

"Glad we agree, then." I kiss her once more and then reach down and grab at the hem of her dress, slowly pulling it up. She doesn't protest, doesn't say a word, just lets me pull the dress up, up, up, until she's shifting away from me and holding up her arms so I can take the dress completely off of her.

Aw damn, she's gorgeous. Even though her hands automatically go up to cover her chest, and she gives me this smile that's more like an apology than anything else, I still think she's the most beautiful girl I know.

"Drop your hands," I tell her, my voice quiet. "Let me see you."

"Take your shirt off," she says. "Let's be on an even playing field."

Chuckling, I quickly unbutton my shirt and yank it off, letting it drop to the floor. "There you go." Her gaze wanders hungrily over my chest, and then she slowly lets her arms fall to her sides.

"Take off your pants," she whispers, and I do that, too, kicking off my shoes, shucking the pants off so I'm standing in front of her in just my blue and white checked boxer shorts. It feels like her eyes are gobbling me up. "Oh *wow,* Josh."

It's the *oh wow* that does me in. I grab hold of her, burying my hands in her hair as I kiss her like I'm desperate for her. Which I am, by the way—I'm totally desperate for her. For Edes. She tastes so good and feels even better and when we fall onto my bed, our legs tangle, and I press her into the mattress, my entire body covering hers since she's so small. I'm careful not to crush her, but soon I forget about my worry and allow myself to get lost in her body, exploring her, touching her everywhere, peeling off those tiny little panties she's wearing until she's completely naked.

And then I'm completely naked and I have the condom,

and with shaky fingers I tear off the wrapper and roll it on. She's shaking, too, and I whisper sweet words in her ear, telling her how much she means to me, and how good she feels. How good I'm going to make her feel. We're sweaty and we're fumbling and she laughs when I somehow get it wrong and then she's guiding me where I need to go. Her touch makes my eyes cross and my blood run hot, so I think of trig problems and college essays just to slow everything down and revel in the fact that I'm actually having sex with my best friend.

With this beautiful, sweet girl who knows all my secrets.

All my faults.

Who's not afraid to tell me when I'm being a jerk.

Who says I have a dirty laugh.

Who makes fun of the way I dance.

Who appreciates all my jokes.

Who genuinely cares for me and is always there when I need her.

Who didn't make fun of my *Bachelor* references.

Who kisses me like she never wants us to stop.

Who's whispering my name right now and running her hands up and down my back, making me shiver.

I'm with the girl who loves me.

Who's in love with me.

I'm with Eden.

And there's nowhere else.

I'd rather.

Be.

· · ·

EDEN

"Are you okay?"

I nod, hardly able to catch my breath, my heart is racing

so fast. I'm shivering even though I'm not cold, and my entire body feels electrified, like I stuck my finger in a light socket and was electrocuted.

"Good." Josh kisses my sweaty forehead and tucks me in close, our legs intertwined as we lay side by side. I rest my head on his chest, and I can feel his heartbeat beneath my ear. It's going as fast as mine, and I close my eyes, savoring the feel of him lying next to me.

We just did it. And while it wasn't perfect and it was sort of awkward and it hurt a little bit, too, and he definitely finished while I definitely did not, that's okay. It was perfect because it happened with someone I love and trust. It happened with Josh.

"Are you okay?" I ask, amusement lacing my tone because I know he is beyond okay. He has to be.

"I'm fucking great," he says just before he starts to laugh. I join in, the both of us laughing like a couple of freaks, and when we finally get ourselves under control, Josh rolls over, pinning me beneath him, his hands resting on either side of my head, his knees on either side of my hips. "You're beautiful."

He kisses me before I can say anything, and when he finally pulls away, I whisper, "You're beautiful, too."

Josh is smiling. I don't think I've ever seen him look like this before. His entire face lights up, and he's looking at me like I'm the most precious thing in the world to him. And maybe I am, I don't know. It's still hard for me to wrap my head around the fact that he's in love with me.

Josh Evans.

In love.

With.

Eden Sumner.

Who knew it could happen?

"Want to do it again?" he asks, sounding hopeful.

I laugh. Press my lips together. Nod once. Then again.

He lowers himself so his hips are pressed against mine, and I can feel that he's ready. "I'll make sure it's better for you this time."

"Promise?"

Josh nods, his expression solemn. "Always. I love you, Edes."

My humor fades, replaced by the same sincerity I'm receiving from him. "I love you, too, Joshua."

He kisses me gently, his lips capturing my lower lip and giving it a tug. "Maybe we should practice a lot tonight. Make sure we're doing it right."

"That sounds"—I kiss him—"fun."

"I know, right?" He frowns. "Though, wait a minute. Where do your parents think you are? You have a curfew, right? Shit, they're going to kill me."

"Stop. Don't worry." I touch his face with my hands, rubbing his jaw with my thumb. He has the sexiest jawline. I want to kiss it. "I texted them earlier and said I was spending the night with Molly. She'll cover for me."

He's still frowning. "They'll hate me if they knew I violated their daughter."

"Joshua!" I lightly slap his shoulder. "Don't say it like that."

"It's true, though. I have to make it right with them. Tell them how I feel about you."

"You're going to tell my parents how you feel about me?" My heart is soaring, I swear. It feels like it's going to leap right out of my chest and float into the stars.

He nods. "I'm going to tell them I'm in love with their daughter, and I'm going to do everything in my power to make sure she's happy."

"Really?" I'm breathless again, this time because of his words, the sincerity in his gaze and his voice.

"Definitely." He kisses me again, his tongue doing this delicious swirly thing that makes my entire body tighten with need. "Whatever it takes to make you happy, Edes, I'm going to do it."

"This makes me happy," I say as he kisses my neck, my collarbone. "Being with you."

"Same," he whispers, and we both crack up because it's just weird to think that we like each other so much, yet we're in love, too.

But I guess that's what happens when you fall in love with your best friend. You get the best of both worlds. Josh and I, we're the lucky ones.

So yeah.

I'm with Josh.

And right now, in this very moment.

There's nowhere else.

I'd rather.

Be.

Epilogue

"I can't believe you convinced me to do this," Josh grumbles good-naturedly as we pull up to the front of Molly's house.

"Stop." I punch him lightly in the arm, which kind of hurts considering he's ripped. The boy has arms that don't quit. "It'll be fun."

The front door opens, and Molly appears, Abraham right behind her. He shuts the door and wraps his arm around her shoulders as they head toward Josh's truck.

That's right, Abraham and Molly are semi-officially a thing. They had so much fun together at the winter formal, they've been hanging out ever since. They're not boyfriend and girlfriend yet, but it's going to happen. I guarantee by Christmas, which is exactly three days away.

Josh and I open our doors and hop out of the truck, pushing back the seats so Molly and I can sit in the back bench seat. The guys are too tall, their legs too long, and all Abraham would do is whine and complain if he had to sit in the backseat. It's easier to do it like this.

Though we probably should've brought my car, but whatever.

"Aren't we too old for this crap?" Abraham says once we're back on the road.

"No freaking way," I protest, making Molly laugh. She's been extra cheerful lately, now that she and Abraham are spending so much time together. "Trust me, you're going to love it."

I direct Josh where to go, since he's never been to this particular neighborhood before, and the closer we get, the thicker the traffic is. I eventually encourage him to park about a mile out, and we all tumble out of the truck, me going to Josh's side and curling my arm around his. "You ready?" I ask, smiling up at him.

He leans down and kisses the tip of my cold nose, then my lips. "Lead the way, Edes."

The glow of the lights is obvious, and my stomach starts to do happy flips. We're going to Candy Cane Lane, the most decorated neighborhood in our small town. Josh and Molly haven't been here since they were little kids, and unbelievably, Abraham has never been before.

Mom and Dad take Travis and me here every single year. It's tradition.

"I'm glad you had us park," Josh says as he takes my hand and laces our fingers together. The streets are clogged with barely moving traffic. "Walking is much better."

"I know."

We ooh and ahh over the holiday decorations, stopping to buy hot chocolate from a family who's selling it out in front of their house. There's a guy dressed up as the most realistic Santa I've ever seen, and when he asks Josh if there's anything special he wants for Christmas, he looks over at me and grins.

"I already got everything I want."

He says a few words to me, looks at me a certain way, and I'm melting. Always.

Molly's giggling and bouncing up and down, losing it over every overly decorated house we pass. Abraham is getting totally into it thanks to Molly, and by the time we've walked the entire lit up neighborhood, Abraham is actually disappointed.

"That's it?" he asks when we stop at our starting point.

"We've been walking for over an hour," Josh tells him.

"Maybe we should walk it again," Molly suggests.

So we do. Josh starts complaining, and I kiss him every few houses to make him stop. I kiss him so much, a little kid walking behind us complains to his mom.

"That girl won't stop kissing him and giving him cooties!"

Josh and I start laughing so hard I think we freaked the parents out.

After our second lap, we load back up into the truck, and Josh drives back to Molly's house. Then we go to his house, which is empty thanks to his mom spending the night at her boyfriend's place.

"You know you wanna come in," Josh says with that sexy smirk that I find both irritating and intriguing.

"No funny business tonight," I warn him because I have to get back home. I didn't tell Mom I was spending the night at Molly's, so I have to be home before my midnight curfew.

Though Mom and Dad know Josh and I are together, and they happily approve, especially Mom. When Josh told her that we're official, she literally pumped her fist into the air and yelled, "Called it!"

So embarrassing, but Josh only laughed and agreed with her that she made the right prediction.

"Come on, at least a little bit of funny business," he pleads just before he hauls me into his arms and kisses me until I can't think straight. His lips are so soft and persuasive.

His hands wander, and the kisses escalate, until the truck's cab is steamed up and we're both panting for breath like we just ran a marathon.

"You should probably take me home," I tell him after I check the time on my phone. He shoots me a disappointed look before he starts the engine, and next thing I know, we're at my house. The tree is still lit, the curtains pulled back to reveal it in all of its Christmas glory. I smile when Josh pulls me in close to him, and we both stare at the front of my house.

"I had fun tonight," he whispers near my ear.

I snuggle closer. "I told you."

"Abraham loved it. Probably more than he'll actually admit."

"I'm so glad we took him."

"It was a good idea."

"And you thought it was going to be lame."

"I was wrong." He pauses. "At least I can admit it."

If that's a jab at me for not liking to admit when I'm wrong, I'm choosing to ignore it.

"I love you," I tell him instead, glancing up at him with my best adoring look. He chuckles under his breath and leans down, brushing my lips with his. My skin tingles, and I close my eyes when he deepens the kiss.

"I love you, too," he whispers against my mouth minutes later. "I should go. You're turning orange."

He's teasing, always saying I'm going to turn into a pumpkin like Cinderella's carriage when the clock strikes twelve, just like the movie. He knows that Cinderella is my favorite Disney princess, too.

"I am not." I shove away from him but he just tightens his grip. "You're coming over for Christmas, right?"

His family does it big on Christmas Eve, while mine throws a family party on Christmas day. Mom wants him to come—she is absolutely thrilled we're together—and I really want him there, too.

"Yeah, I'll be there on Christmas." He smiles. "Can I spend the night on Christmas Eve so we can open our stockings together?"

"I don't think so. Mom probably won't approve," I tell him with a laugh, shaking my head.

Though we'll probably end up moving in together when we start college next fall. We've applied to the same universities, and odds are we'll end up together. Maybe forever.

I know I can't imagine my life without him.

See that's the thing when you fall in love with your best friend. They know all your faults and your strengths, they know how to tease you, how to make you laugh, how to console you when you're inconsolable, how to get under your skin. They know your secrets and your fears and what brings you happiness.

It's been so easy, what Josh and I share. I thought it would be weird, to go from being best friends to actually being in a relationship. But it never felt out and out wrong—and now it feels so right, so freaking perfect, I don't know why I never realized just how great we could be together until now.

Guess it took him asking me to help him lose his virginity to figure it out.

Can't get enough Monica Murphy? Don't miss her contemporary thriller, *Pretty Dead Girls*, available online and in stores everywhere on January 2, 2018!

Beautiful. Perfect. Dead.

They're arranged in a particular way. Their faces turned at the most flattering angles, their designer clothes immaculate, as immaculate as their carefully made-up faces. Only the slash of blood across their necks mars the perfect surface. Only the vacant stare in their eyes indicates they're dead.

The most popular girls in school are going down, and Penelope Malone is terrified she's next. All the victims so far have been linked to Penelope—and to the mysterious loner boy from her physics class. The one with the lopsided smirk and intense stare that's almost...cute? Even though she's not sure she can trust him, she reluctantly agrees to work with him to figure out what's happening. All while trying to stay one step ahead of the brutal serial killer on the loose.

But this killer won't be satisfied until every beautiful, popular girl in the senior class is dead—especially Penelope. And the killer is closer than she thinks...

Read on for a sneak peak!

Chapter One

I finally get her where I want her, folks, and wouldn't you know, she starts giving me attitude within seconds.

"And why am I here again?" Gretchen snags the lit joint from my fingers and brings it to her mouth, taking a long drag. She holds the smoke in, her bright green eyes narrowed, her expression almost pained, before she blows it all out.

Straight into my face.

God, she's such a bitch sometimes. Though I envy her fearlessness. She's rude and mean, and she just doesn't give a damn.

I realize she's waiting for me to speak, and I clear my throat.

"Look, I know you're never going to believe me, since we haven't talked much in the past. But we've gone to school together for a long time and I just wanted us to...g-get to know each other better." I stumble over the words, and I am thoroughly pissed at myself.

I practiced this little speech over and over again the last few days, preparing for this moment. In the mirror, reciting the words back to my reflection. Late at night, while I lay in bed and stared up at the ceiling, mesmerized by the slow spinning ceiling fan above my head.

Yet I mess it up, falter because I'm actually in front of her, just the two of us. Gretchen Nelson, one of the most beautiful, most popular girls in school. She has *everything*.

I have nothing.

All I want is a little taste. Just a tiny sample of what she is. What she has. What I could possibly be.

"So what? You tricked me to go out with you?"

"It's nothing like that," I reassure her.

"What do you mean by getting to know me better, then? What exactly are you talking about?" She takes another drag off the joint, this one short and fast, and she coughs out the smoke, hacking a little. The glamorous, perfect Gretchen Nelson mask falls for the briefest moment, and it's like I've just been treated to a sneak peek of the real Gretchen. She's just a girl who likes to get high, who's aggressive, and who treats other people like shit. I mean, I already knew she was like this but... "Please don't tell me this is your idea of a *date*."

The contempt in her voice is obvious.

"No, not at all!" I sound too defensive, and I clamp my lips shut. "That wasn't my intention. Can't we just be...friends?"

She shoots me a sardonic look, her lips curled, her delicate eyebrows raised. She's still wearing her shorts and T-shirt from volleyball practice, and she has to be cold, since both car windows are rolled down, and once the sun disappears, the temperature drops rapidly.

My gaze falls to her legs. They're sturdy, her thighs are thick, and I can't help but stare at them. They're thicker than the other cheerleaders', which made her a great base. Gretchen was known for tossing the flyers into the air higher than anyone else. I remember watching her. Watching all of them...

Not that Gretchen's a cheerleader any longer. She quit at the end of her sophomore year, wanting to focus on volleyball instead. She's a strong player. Fearless. Downright mean on the court. Yet she's also beautiful and poised and smart.

"*You* really want to be *friends* with *me?*" She makes it sound like an impossible feat.

I nod.

"We have nothing in common."

"We have a lot of things in common."

"Name ten."

I frown. "You really want me to name *ten?*"

She nods slowly, places the joint between her lips. It dangles from her mouth, giving her this tough, rebellious air, and I can't help but admire her all over again. At school, she's absolute perfection. Right now, in the passenger seat of my car with a joint hanging from her lips, her dark-red hair a wild tangle about her head, eyeliner smudged, and her cheeks still ruddy from the chilly nighttime air, she's not quite as perfect.

But she's a lot more real.

"That's stupid," I tell her, and she sits up straight, yanking the joint out of her mouth so she can gape at me.

"Did you just call me stupid?"

The venom in her voice makes me recoil away from her. "N-no. I mean, I just took a hit off that joint. My head is spinning. How do you expect me to come up with ten things we have in common, just like that?" I snap my fingers for emphasis.

"*God.* You're just like everyone else. Always thinking you can buy me off with sex or booze or weed." She tosses the joint at my head, and I dodge left, so it sails out the driver's side window and lands on the ground outside. "Bringing me to a church parking lot, too. Real classy."

With those last words, Gretchen climbs out of my car and slams the door behind her, so hard she makes the vehicle rock.

Panicked, I bolt out and follow after her. Her long legs take her far across the parking lot as she heads straight toward Our Lady of Mount Carmel Church. But I can run fast when I need to, and I catch up to her quick. I grab hold of her arm, and she snags it out of my grip, whirling on me with wild eyes.

"Get away from me!" I grab her again, and she shakes me off, her expression full of disgust. "God, you're so freaking *weird!* Just leave me alone!"

It's the *weird* comment that gets me. It always gets me. They all single me out. They all point their fingers and laugh. With every step forward I make, something like this happens, and I'm pushed four steps back.

She turns away, breathing heavily, but she's not going anywhere. Odd. She's usually dying to get away from me.

That's when I realize she has her phone in her hand. And she's tapping away on the screen, like maybe she's texting someone.

Hell.

"Gretchen, come on." I keep my voice even, like this is no big deal. Like I'm not hunting her down in the church parking lot on a Tuesday night. The wind whips through the giant pine trees that surround the lot. I can hear the branches swing and sway, the hoot of a lonely owl in the near distance. It's dark up here. Quiet. No one drives by. The street is abandoned, and the nearest house is a quarter mile away.

Feels like it's just the two of us out here.

All alone.

"Fuck you, you fucking weirdo!" She turns to face me and starts to laugh. No doubt when she catches sight of the stricken look on my face. "I can't wait to tell everyone about this. Wait until I spread this story around—I will *ruin* you."

A roar leaves me, unlike any sound I've ever made before in my life, and it makes my lungs ache. I run up on her and shove her hard, so she tumbles to the ground. She's distracted, in shock that I shoved her, and I take my chance and sock her in the face. I meant to hit her mouth, but my knuckles only glance off her jaw and my entire hand throbs from the impact.

I can't believe I hit her.

"What the hell?" She touches her face gingerly, working her jaw to the side, and she winces. "You punched me!"

"You deserved it." My voice is eerily calm as I stand over her, both of my hands clutched into fists.

She tilts her head back, all that glorious red hair spilling past her shoulders. Even after I hit her, she still challenges me. I don't know whether she's brave or just stupid. "What are you going to do to me now? Beat me up?"

I say nothing.

I don't need to.

Instead, I smile. Laugh.

Actions speak louder than words, after all.

Acknowledgments

I had so much fun writing this book and now when I go back and re-read it, I feel nostalgic and even a little...sad. This book is so incredibly personal. Many of the tiny details in this book are based on real people in our lives, sweet teens who both live with me and those who are friends with my children. I name no names. I don't point any accusatory fingers and I'm not trying to call anybody out, but I want to thank these anonymous teens from the bottom of my heart for being so open and real and honest with me. I seriously love them all.

Now for a few quick thank yous:
— Thanks to K & H for the middle name
— To A for the "go elf yourself" underwear
— To J for his love of Dr Pepper
— To B for all that fierce loyalty
— To S for *The Bachelor* love

About the Author

New York Times, *USA Today*, and number one international best-selling author Monica Murphy is a native Californian who lives in the foothills below Yosemite with her husband and children. A workaholic who loves her job, when she's not busy writing, she also loves to read and travel with her family. She writes new adult and young adult romance and is a firm believer in happily ever after. She also writes contemporary romance as *USA Today* best-selling author Karen Erickson. Visit her online at www.monicamurphyauthor.com.

Discover more of Entangled Teen Crush's books...

The First Kiss Hypothesis
a novel by Christina Mandelski

Eli Costas is an injury-prone lacrosse star with a problem—the one chance he had at winning over the girl next door resulted in the most epically sucktastic first kiss ever. And now she's... trying to get rid of him? Hell no. It's time to disprove her theory and show her *exactly* what she's missing.

Offsetting Penalties
a *Brinson Renegades* novel by Ally Matthews

Isabelle Oster is devastated when the only male dancer backs out of the fall production. Without a partner, she has no hope of earning a spot with a prestigious ballet company. All-state tight end Garret Mitchell will do anything to get a college football scholarship. Even taking ballet, because he gets to be up close and personal with the gorgeous Goth girl Izzy. But she needs him to perform with her, and he draws the line at getting on stage. *Especially* wearing tights.

Approximately Yours
a *North Pole, Minnesota* novel by Julie Hammerle

Danny Garland asked out Holly's cousin. Elda is a mess at flirting and has no idea he's Holly's long-time crush, so when she begs Holly to intervene, she does. Holly helps her flirt with him over text. And then again. Now she's stuck texting him as her cousin, and Elda is the one going on the date. Holly thought she could settle for just conversation, but talking with Danny is some kind of magic. He's got the perfect comebacks, she makes him laugh, they text until everyone else is asleep. She just can't ever tell him it's her he's really texting.

Boomerang Boyfriend
a *Boyfriend Chronicles* novel by Chris Cannon

Free-spirited Delia is starting to see her BFF's brother in a new light. When did Jack-the-Jerk turn into a hottie? Seeing Delia in her retro waitress uniform throws Jack's world out of whack. But she's always been just another pain in the butt little sister... not a datable female. Delia and Jack's sparks could combust into a fabulous relationship, or they could crash and burn into oblivion.

CPSIA information can be obtained
at www.ICGtesting.com
Printed in the USA
LVOW12s1519151117
556396LV00001B/29/P